The Pharaoh's Sacrifice

Cameron Brett

This book is dedicated to all the writers that have unknowingly shaped and influenced this one. There are too many to list.

Chapter 1

Rebuild Thebes—or be buried beneath the sweeping sands of time.

Merkhet could never forgive himself if he only survived banishment and captivity to oversee his family's legacy crumble into the abyss. For the tales told around evening campfires and those painted on temple walls would not even blink twice before forgetting Pharaoh Merkhet and the proud lineage that preceded him.

He had returned—even after all the pain and humiliation of his exile—but Egypt didn't owe him anything and never would.

So, as the sun beamed down on his bare back, Merkhet pressed another mudbrick into place. Even though his face stung from the hot grains of sand deposited by the winds, he didn't brush them away. He couldn't. Another mudbrick landed in his palms. Taharva and a whole horde of laborers were right there beside him, spurring him on.

The pharaoh matched the builders' pace, but not without cost. Sweat streamed down his chest cavity, soaking in his loincloth. Though the Double Crown protected Merkhet's shaved scalp from the brunt of the sun, he wore it as a symbol for all Egyptians to see.

Ra, renewed once more, shone with fury on the lands. The river was alive again, too. Citizens just had to grace the Nile's banks to know that much was true.

Merkhet scanned the dwellings around him. Order may be restored, but Thebes bore a vague semblance of its former glory. Scorch marks marred what little remained of upright walls. The villages of craftspeople and laborers alike, decimated by sandstorm and flame.

As he lumped another mudbrick onto the wall, Merkhet paused. The repairs for this hovel were almost complete, the fifth such dwelling he and the workers had restored that morning. No matter how laborious—brick by brick, stone by stone, citizen by citizen—rebuilding was not a difficult decision, even for the least experienced pharaoh of the Eighteenth Dynasty. But it meant a return to the diplomatic way of his grandfather would have to wait. The wilting trade relations and their associated peace treaties could not come before the restoration of Thebes, or Egypt as a whole. Nothing could.

'Scrollworm,' Taharva said from beside him. 'The job is not yet done. Do your feeble muscles grow weary?'

He turned towards his most loyal friend, not the least bit irritated by the insult. The Nubian warrior had near enough saved Egypt by himself in the ravine of Aladaglar and to hear his gruff voice in the flesh was comforting. A red strip of cotton was bound tight around Taharva's wrist, concealing the engraved hunter's bow of

Pharaoh Nekhet. 'One week as a free man,' Merkhet said, 'yet you still torment me.'

'Would you change it?'

'Never,' Merkhet said, unable to contain a smile.

'Then why are you here, Your Grace? Your insistent involvement is bordering on foolish.'

'We need every able hand. There's so much to rectify. This is more than just a rebuild.'

'Go rectify, then. Your people will support you.'

'Protection amulets for the citizens. Ushabti to support them in the Afterlife.'

'That's what holds your concern, Scrollworm, mere amulets and ushabti?'

'Yes,' Merkhet said. 'Why should our most vulnerable be denied the simple safety provided by the gods?'

'No amount of amulets could have ever stopped the chaos that happened here.'

'It all helps, Captain, as do the Hittite spoils. Enough food was secured to sustain us until next harvest.'

Taharva grunted an acknowledgment. 'The army?'

'They must recover. Their role will come when—' Merkhet cut himself short. Should he discuss such plans in front of the workers? Perhaps he shouldn't, but shrouding matters in secrecy had not served their country well in the recent past. 'A main contingent will head north, recruit more hands from the neglected delta regions along the way, and then begin constructing Father's dream of a great fortress.'

'What else bothers you? Your eyes speak of a terrible sadness.'

Merkhet glanced a dozen huts down the way. Llora's home. Portions of wall were missing, the roof collapsed. But the state of her hut didn't hurt nearly as much as her betrayal. One week back atop the Golden Throne, and his rage had waxed and waned with each passing of the moon.

Of all the people …

Peronikh.

Once Merkhet's brother, always his competitor. Hunting, charioteering, their studies, Pharaoh Nekhet's affection, and then for the same throne and the same girl. What chance did Merkhet ever really have when Peronikh exuded such assured confidence?

The truth of that made him ready to lay down and weep. All the unnecessary pain and anguish because he was too ignorant to realize the signs. Or even worse, just didn't want to heed them.

Taharva could read him better than most. It was astounding how easily he could understand a situation and provide sage advice. 'Talk to her. Make your peace, whatever that may be. Egypt needs your complete focus.'

The Nubian was right, as always. 'I will,' Merkhet said. 'As soon as we are done here today.'

Was a week long enough for all the raw emotion to spew out of him, so that he and Llora could pardon each other's insensitivity?

It might be. He hoped it would because other matters were certain to arise, pleading and demanding for the pharaoh's attention. He had come to accept that part of the role. What choice did he have? If the people of Egypt were to truly forgive him and honor his family's legacy eternally in the temples and stelae, Merkhet could not afford the luxury of rest.

An older worker, shifting mudbricks at a steady pace, handed him another. Merkhet lifted it into place and pressed it down into the holding resin with as much pressure as he could muster. Almost at the peak of its daily journey across the sky, the sun would set the bricks quick now.

The rhythm of their labor carried the workers right through the afternoon. Merkhet was sure they acted out of Theban pride more so than indebtedness to him or the gods. A day's labor was worth more to their pharaoh than they could ever know, but many more were required to restore their city.

When the sun began to dip on another productive day, the men and women packed away their tools and stored them along with the unused mudbricks in an adjacent hut. As they did, Merkhet was already drifting.

Llora. Always her.

He wanted to hate her. The bump in her stomach and the treachery it represented …

The pharaoh, fresh from his Heb-Sed rejuvenation, should despise her for so easily giving up on him. Yet the old Merkhet would seek to atone and redeem himself for smashing her pregnancy amulet. Conflicted, he understood one thing to be true.

He would at least visit her and listen to the concerns she held for the welfare of her brother, Wuntu.

Taharva must have retreated to the palace because a pair of royal guards trailed him now. Passing by the next four dismantled hovels may as well have been four hundred. Was there any end to the destruction wrought upon their homeland? Merkhet failed to fathom how he would ever earn back the trust of the people.

The children didn't seem to notice, though, as they crept about in a fierce contest of *Don't Wake The Mummy*. A girl lay on her back in the center of a circle, the sand crudely marked by dragged feet. While her eyes were shut, all the other children had to try and sneak closer to her. Whoever was farthest away when the mummy woke up would take her place in the sand.

This was a tense game, as two boys were daring each other to rouse the girl playing mummy. She was patient, though, perhaps even aware of their antics. Merkhet slowed himself, interested to see how it would unfold. If either of the boys laid so much as a fingernail on her, she would retain her role for another round, but if she could return the favor to either of them before opening her eyes, they would become the mummy.

Both boys reached in to secure her fate, devious grins on their faces. Side by side, inches from her arm, one of them was about to win. Then the girl's arm flung through the air like a cranky cobra, striking the taller of the boys. He stood there, motionless. With mouth agape in disbelief, he was unable to form the usual protest cries of cheating.

All the children around the outer edges cheered her victory. Their elation was at such odds with the trepidation smothering Merkhet's heart, which tightened with every step. He never enjoyed confrontations, or the awkwardness that followed them.

As he approached Llora's hut, pure dread overcame him. Lingering outside, a shrill cry emanated from within. Unsure of the source, it became increasingly frantic, and Merkhet abandoned his reservations.

Leaping through the hut's entrance—no sign of anyone. Not Llora, nor her mother. The wail reverberated all around him as he slipped in the entrance of Llora's room. Dazed from the fall, Merkhet lay sprawled in a puddle of water. What had happened here?

As his blurred vision eased, comprehension seized a frightening hold of him. The puddle was more of a pool, and the liquid was not water. Red and thick, Merkhet tried to scramble out of the blood and get himself upright.

The cry started again, louder than ever. Where were the guards? Could they not hear the clamoring whelp over the play of the children outside?

The whelp didn't stop, and then the pharaoh understood the blood and the commotion.

A baby—Llora's baby. She had given birth. But where was she?

He hoisted himself up to his feet, needing to know where Llora was. His hands, stomach, and loincloth were drenched in blood.

Then he spotted the baby, squirming in the corner, also smeared in the bright red liquid. Despite the disturbing fluids covering it, the baby's face was sweet and gentle. Just like her mother's.

Llora must have gone to the village well, or maybe even to the river, to rinse herself clean of the terrible mess. But would she have really left her newborn girl behind, alone and distressed? Merkhet couldn't even begin to understand how she might.

As he lifted the baby up, he saw Llora. Not her resemblance, but in the flesh. The truth floored the pharaoh, again. The infant still in his clutches—her shrieking reached a terrifying new pitch, but it was dull compared to all else.

The girl he once adored was lying on her reed mat. Still. A bloodied knife alongside her naked body, and the broken Aten necklace that she once gifted him, clasped in her crimson hands. A deep cut ran up the length of her inner thigh. Beside her body, a toy lion.

Merkhet reached for the toy and the pendant. Covered in the congealing blood of his first love, helpless and weeping, he swayed back and forth. With Llora's baby in his arms, he slumped against one of the hut's crumbling walls.

Had his fury and neglect pushed Llora to take her own life? How could they resolve their differences if she were no longer alive?

As Merkhet cradled the restless baby, he wished he could wake from the cruel nightmare of the past year.

Chapter 2

The newborn girl slept in Merkhet's arms, her wails of distress having ceased sometime earlier. Her peaceful, innocent breaths couldn't shake the symbolism or truth of what had happened.

Llora was beside him, dead and bloody, and he was carrying her daughter. Peronikh's daughter.

Merkhet's wrists ached, burned. She might be tiny, but like most things, the weight over time could be deceiving. He balanced her along one forearm, so that he could shake the numbness free in the other. She didn't stir, not even as he swapped arms.

When his royal guards did finally come to check on him, Merkhet insisted that they wait outside the hut. He did not want to speak with anyone. He just wanted to be. Hours later, bright stars now shone through the gaps in the decimated ceiling, and Merkhet expected that the guards would resurface at any moment when Llora's voice cut through the darkness, so full of vibrant energy and promise. He rubbed along his temple, but the sound didn't disappear. Denial had not waited long to greet him.

'Llora! Llora!'

Her sweet, familiar voice echoed through the hut. 'How?' Merkhet asked, scarce more than a whisper.

'Llora, where are you? My sweet, sweet daughter, we are finally back.'

Tiaa. Llora's mother. She sounded so similar to her daughter that it could only be her, but how did she slip past the guards? Was she just returning now, after escaping Thebes at the height of its chaos and destruction?

Somehow, Merkhet needed to shelter Tiaa from stumbling upon her still daughter. The hapless woman was already missing her son. If she were to witness these harrowing images, even under the gleam of moonlight, no amount of consolation may be enough to heal her heartache. He had to try and spare her.

'Do not enter. Your pharaoh commands you.'

'Wuntu! When did your voice become so deep? When did you get home? I've missed you both so much.'

'I'm not your son. Do not come in,' Merkhet stated again, firmer on this occasion.

His grumbles disturbed the baby girl, and she awoke with an ear-splitting cry.

He curled the baby up against his chest with one hand and hopped to his feet—anything to prevent Tiaa from uncovering Llora's limp body—but she swiveled under his outstretched arm and brushed him aside.

Tiaa sidled through the blood, resting on her knees next to Llora. At once, her maternal instincts knew something was amiss. 'Llora,' she said, grabbing and shaking her daughter by the wrists. 'You need to wake up now,' she sobbed.

Merkhet didn't dare tell Tiaa that her efforts were futile, that Llora wouldn't wake. What could he say to a mother kneeling beside her dead daughter? Nothing would —*nothing could*—comfort her.

'What has happened here?' Tiaa pleaded, before her sobs escalated to screams, overshadowing even her granddaughter's.

Two royal guards came rushing into the hovel, their spears drawn and braziers guiding them. 'Your Grace, what is it?'

'Secure the area and prepare the chariot,' Merkhet commanded them over the clamor. 'Get us to the palace.' He shuffled outside, loincloth soaked and dripping as he still nursed the babe.

The guards spoke hurriedly between themselves. Soon after, they emerged, escorting Tiaa from her home. She whimpered between them but was vacant of defiance. Merkhet would need to speak with her, offer her every comfort he could, but tonight would not serve.

He was relieved of the whelping baby, but Merkhet couldn't follow what the guards were saying to him. Their faces moved without sound, and their blurry hands grabbed for him.

Llora …

After bathing and exchanging his ruined garments, Merkhet placed the Aten necklace and toy lion on the war table. He collapsed on the Golden Throne, and as soon as he graced the smooth surface, Lufu arrived.

'Horus preserve me! Not now, Lufu.' Merkhet's

hands contracted like claws around the throne's lion head fixtures. 'Is a private moment too much to ask?'

'I'm sorry for your loss, Your Grace. Given what has happened, it may be best to delay our plans.'

'We must not deviate.'

'Stalling momentum for two or three of Ra's solar journeys will make little difference in the end.'

Merkhet met the gaze of his adviser, his voice deteriorating to a rasp. 'When I stop, she's everywhere.' Before all the messiness, Llora had been as fond and as constant in his life as the rising sun. Then his exile changed everything. 'I get lost between what I know and what I want to believe. We forge ahead now. I fear it is the only way for me.'

'Will you reconsider?'

'No,' Merkhet said.

The vizier conceded with a *humph* and curt nod. 'What now, then?'

'Return to Memphis, friend. A full cycle of seasons has passed since you were there.'

Lufu considered the statement. 'I suppose that's true. What of Upper Egypt, though?'

'What of it?'

'Your Grace, who will advise you here? You need guidance in the south, too.'

'Do I?'

'It has been so for thousands of years. The unification of Egypt is the way of solidarity and prosperity.'

'Where was all that when I was rotting in a Hittite cell?'

'We failed you. We did. But you have a chance to appoint your own vizier now. Someone you trust.'

That was the problem. The very reason the pharaoh could no longer slip into a restful sleep. Who could he trust?

'I'll consider it,' Merkhet said.

'Is your mother still to accompany me?'

'Yes,' Merkhet said, the vision of a grand city, a military fort once again flooding his mind. 'She will bring Father's dream to life.'

Lufu smiled. 'I guess even your conflict-starved father wanted an end to the incessant clashes with the Hyksos and Hittites. He just didn't realize it.'

Merkhet was drawn to Thekla. Leaning against the war table, the war hammer rested on its large golden face. Whether it was reburied in the Valley of the Kings or commemorated in the mortuary temple once it was constructed, Thekla had to be returned to his father.

'Horus knows it,' Merkhet said, acknowledging his adviser. 'If the fort doesn't deter them, it will at least stop them.'

At last, the vizier dismissed himself, accepting the pharaoh's judgment as fact. The mood between them had shifted somewhat after Merkhet's Pharaonic Trial conquest. No longer did Lufu press and press and press him, like he had with the incompetent and indecisive young boy that first inherited the throne.

Merkhet released the lion heads. His palms may be blotchy and stinging but focusing on that pain had prevented the roiling emotion from bursting out of him.

The Eye of Horus, etched into Horakhty, demanded his attention as it hung on the wall. Splintered and fractured, the conquest of the river demon at his Pharaonic Trial came with a hefty price. Could his cherished bow ever be restored to its prime?

He moved for it, carrying Horakhty back to the throne. Once he learned to master his own inefficiencies, his bow had never failed him. As the frame was now held together by the thinnest strand of wood, that might no longer be true. Then there was the minor detail of the bowstring that was also snapped in half.

Merkhet sighed, pulling the separated bowstring together and tying a messy knot near the upper end.

Few names of pure dependability came to him as he began to pluck away some of the bow's many splinters.

Besides his mother, Taharva was the only person he trusted without question. Without even being summoned, the reliable Nubian appeared.

'How are the mother and daughter?' the rugged yet soothing voice asked.

'Tiaa is beside herself, and the baby hasn't stopped crying. Even in the first few hours of her life, she has had to face mortality. Barely out of the womb and already stripped of her innocence. The gods try so hard to shield us ...'

'What will you do for them?'

'They are being cared for here in the palace. After that, the harem village, I guess.'

Taharva gave him a quizzical look.

'No! Not like that,' Merkhet said. 'I don't know if I will continue the harem tradition. Besides, I'm not sure Haliya would tolerate other women.'

Bemusement, and a hint of confusion stretched across Taharva's brows. 'What of Llora, then?'

'Physicians are examining her body.'

'Sahra?' Taharva asked.

'Yes. I begged her to oversee this for me.'

'Have you said goodbye yet?'

'No. How can I ...'

'Forgive her? Forgiveness is in your *ba*. You've been learning it since birth,' Taharva said, moving closer and tapping him on the chest. 'It's in there, just trust it.'

'I'm not sure it is. Everything hurts so much. Just knowing about her and …' Merkhet didn't want to utter the name, but he swallowed his pride. 'Pe-Peronikh. How can I show Llora earnest remorse if he doesn't receive the same courtesy? Wolves have probably dragged him into the forest by now.'

'Worry not, my friend. What will be, will be,' the Nubian said over his shoulder as he left. 'The gods are on your side.'

Merkhet shuddered, remembering a recent period when they were not. Sandstorms and priesthood revolts. Flood waters so paltry they could scarce deposit nutrients into the soil. Misery followed the early part of his reign like some sort of sticky shadow.

With some privacy at last, the pharaoh should have used it. But he was restless, unable to sit still, and understood sleep was out of the question tonight.

Sahra was conducting her examination in a small room adjoining the palace's entry hall. It was the coolest place to preserve the body until the embalmers could get to work.

The physician was busy when he eased his way in to join her. A low table supported Llora, and Sahra was hunched over the body. Merkhet had never even seen some of the tools on the bench by the physician's side, but he concentrated on those because …

Closer and closer to Llora, the same horrible giddiness enveloped him as when he had said goodbye to his father. This farewell was not any easier. Sahra spotted him, went to speak, but instead vacated the room.

When Merkhet looked down at Llora, all the unresolved tension and fury faded. A cloth covered between her neck and privates, but her face and legs were exposed. Llora's eyes were shut, peace set upon her face. An oil salve was spread thick along the expansive cut on her thigh.

He could not begrudge someone no longer in the land of the living, no matter how much he wanted—or deserved—to. It wasn't right, so he just took her frosty hands in his own and kept quiet. Their boundless hours, once spent in harmony on the terrace, warmed him where her presence no longer could.

Merkhet had desperately wanted to make peace when he ventured to her hovel. He was cheated, and Llora even worse so. How could it have come to this ...

Had she taken her own life when the birth became too painful? Had she given up all hope, or was it more to do with Peronikh's absence?

Peronikh.

Merkhet had willingly denied him a chance at the Afterlife. Even at a juncture when he still believed them to be brothers. How could he, as Pharaoh of Egypt, atone for that?

He wasn't sure he could, but the regret of not visiting Llora sooner convinced him to at least try. Merkhet needed to retrieve Peronikh's body and give him a just burial.

Above the rule of pharaoh, the gods reserved the right to decide Peronikh's fate.

As he readied himself to pull away from Llora, a tear threatened to cascade down his cheek. Life had changed irrevocably. The simple years of his royal classes and leisure were lost to him. Responsibility and duty were his life now. Despite the enduring bitterness, he would gift his first love a queen's burial.

'Farewell, Llora. May the Fields of Paradise welcome your soul.'

The gurgle of an infant caught his attention. Merkhet whirled around to find Tiaa holding the baby. She didn't even speak, but the swirls of agony enveloping her confirmed what must be done.

'I will look after you,' he said, 'and ensure the baby is cared for.'

She rushed over to embrace him, the baby girl resting between them. 'Thank you,' she said between sobs. 'You are a kind pharaoh.'

He was kind, but Egypt needed more of him than that. Llora was gone—was he to blame himself for that? Could this have been avoided if he were more understanding and receptive to her appeals?

'Thank you,' Tiaa said again. A brief smile appeared.

Fleeting though it may have been, her strength was empowering. With her daughter departing this world for the next and the whereabouts of her son still unknown, Merkhet would set right what he could.

He placed a reassuring hand on Tiaa's shoulder. 'I will leave you be.' Merkhet stepped back from her, saying, 'Everything she did, she did for you and Wuntu.'

'Her reckless need to provide for her family held us together. I should never have left her on that path alone.'

'You did the best you could, Tiaa. My father was insensitive to the plights of the villagers. I've not been much better, but I am learning.'

She didn't vindicate him, and he didn't wish that of her. Sometimes, the best lessons involved pain and suffering. 'He once cared for us,' Tiaa said, 'but out of sight, free from responsibility.'

Merkhet didn't understand her remark so said nothing. Then, while cradling the baby with one arm, she reached into her robe and retrieved a wad of papyri folded inward. The outer sheaf almost had a vibrant glow, far more recent than the faded and tattered scrolls that it enclosed. A tinge of red streaked the edges.

'What is that?' he asked.

She obliged him, holding out the sheaves of papyrus for him to take. 'Found them in Llora's dress.' Tiaa strained against a sob. 'Journal maybe.' She handed the wad to him. 'Will you tell me what it says?'

'Of course,' Merkhet said, a wash of curiosity and nervousness coursing through him. Llora's hieratic scrawl was only just developing before his exile, but he suspected what information might be recorded on the sheafs. Did he really want to know how little she cared for him and how much she desired Peronikh?

'The last one is different to the rest. Not her writing, much neater.'

He walked from the room, the papyri clutched against his chest, but stopped and spun back around. 'You should call her Llora.'

Tiaa gave him a questioning stare.

'The baby,' he said, clarifying his intention.

She nodded, water swelling in the corners of her eyes. 'Pharaoh Merkhet,' Tiaa said. 'My Llora did not take her own life. She could never. Wuntu did not abandon us of his own accord. I beg you, Your Grace, you must investigate these tragedies.'

Merkhet left the distraught mother, unsure of what words might comfort her, console her. He paced through the palace. When would everything slow down? When would he get a chance to breathe and relax?

Inside his chambers, Haliya greeted him with an exotic stare, a longing.

The mysteries of the papyri could wait.

Chapter 3

Llora's papyrus sheafs lay on the war table, next to the snapped chain of the Aten necklace and Wuntu's toy lion. A collection of hurtful reminders. Merkhet crossed the room and reached for the papyri when sudden brightness startled him. His eyelids fluttered to adjust to the light flooding into the throne room. It was unusual, as Haliya was always determined to keep the veil within their private chamber drawn for as long as possible. Something to do with the long, dark winters of the north.

She was already edging into the hallway. 'Come,' she said.

Merkhet trailed Haliya as she led him through the palace to the courtyard, where she hovered at the edge of the dune's descent. He studied her, desperate to understand how she had come to be with him in Thebes. There were moments spent in his frost-bitten prison cell in Hattusha when he wasn't sure he would ever leave, let alone return to his homeland after a great military conquest and with a foreign beauty at his side.

Of all the inexplicable occurrences on the ravines of Aladaglar, that was by far the strangest turn of events.

'Embellishment is weakness,' she said in Hittite.

'Sorry?' he asked, matching her mountain tongue.

Haliya pulled away from him, a torrent of frustration around her as she pointed down the slope at a band of artists swarming around one of the few undecorated hieroglyphic walls. After constructing the palace, Nekhet was no stranger to boasting of his achievements.

Merkhet approached the artists, Haliya still insistently pointing. In truth, he had not noticed the dedication before now. Whenever he plotted up and down the dune, he was often too distracted with any of a hundred competing matters. How did Lufu find a spare moment to have this mystery work commissioned?

'Excuse me,' Merkhet said. 'I wish to see the relief.'

A group of four artists turned to look at him and stopped mid-stroke once they recognized him. They parted as one, revealing the relief. Merkhet doubted if Haliya could read the hieroglyphs for their true meaning, but the dedication gave meaning enough. A gallant pharaoh conquering the retreating Hittites. The gods and Egyptians were beside him, part of him. The Hittites—a third of Merkhet's scale on the relief—never had a chance.

The wall was still incomplete, though it was not the most truthful retelling of what happened. Taharva was the real savior on that day, but surely Haliya wasn't taking issue with that.

'Where is the knife?' she asked, changing to an alluring inflection of rough Egyptian. Somehow, her coarse voice added a rich flavor to her words and dispelled the world around him.

He had almost forgotten about the knife she had left

for him. The very knife that allowed him to escape his binds during the battle of Aladaglar. At the time, it seemed to be too good to be true. Still did.

Merkhet needed to ask her again. Why had she slipped him that blade? He had tried from the back of the chariot when it happened, and she just smiled at him.

The outcome of the warfare might not have changed, given Taharva was a man possessed by the will of the gods, but still …

Merkhet feared pushing her away and losing what they had—whatever that was—but he must demand the truth from her. Haliya would have an explanation, and perhaps, he could learn to understand and accept her actions.

'Why did you—' he began, catching himself for a moment. 'Why did you leave the knife and allow me to escape?'

'Tired of the cold,' she said. 'Heat is better.'

He waited for her to give him the real reason, as he was still becoming acquainted with her northern quirks and humor, but she did not say anything else. Baffled, Merkhet clamped his mouth shut, unwilling to risk offending her beyond what the relief had already achieved.

Could there be any malice to her motives? He failed to see how. She could have used the same knife to slice him from foot to ear while he was a bound captive in the Hittite chariot. Yet she didn't.

'When will you honor me?'

'Honor you?' he asked, certain his confusion was setting himself up for a whirlwind of misery. Did she mean on the hieroglyphic wall?

'As your Great Royal Wife,' she said, her black eyes as piercing as ever. They had a gleam to them, though, in much the same way the dark stone pendant that hung around her neck did. 'Is that the title that will secure your dynasty?'

Secure the dynasty …

The thought of establishing a peace treaty between Egypt and Hattusha had consumed his thoughts on every harrowing step back from Aladaglar. Unifying their countries and bringing children into the world had not, and the notion now terrified him. Haliya was right, though. Egypt could not enjoy respite without some plan for succession. The efforts to rebuild would have minimal consequence if he died and the Eighteenth Dynasty came to a crashing cessation.

Merkhet desperately wanted to rejoice and cry out his acceptance to her offer, but it was so soon, so sudden.

He'd only just said goodbye to Llora, and had he even truly grieved for her yet? And there was still so much left for him to overcome.

'Well, Pharaoh Merkhet, what is your command?'

Of everything to consider, he could not deny her beauty. For mystifying reasons, she had chosen a new life here in the desert sands, and who was he to question such a majestic goddess?

'Of course,' he started.

Haliya looked at him expectantly.

'But not yet.'

She made to challenge him, and though part of him enjoyed that smoldering fire within her, he tempered the passion. 'The rebuild takes priority. The unity of the people must come before our union.'

The Hittite queen gave the slimmest of nods, acknowledging his terms. She ascended the dune back to the comforts of the palace.

Merkhet summoned one of the nearby artists,

whispering the required revisions into her ear. She bowed before him, and the artists recommenced their work. Merkhet sighed inwardly. It was quite the relief to solve a problem before it escalated helplessly out of his—and everyone else's—control.

The stone terrace soothed Merkhet where most else failed.

The light breeze softened the harsh sun and carried with it the smell of the river. A scent he would not misplace, as it reminded him of hunting expeditions with his father and Peronikh.

The frenzy of the wildlife on the distant Nile's banks, a relieving distraction. Difficult conversations were on the way, and his newfound instinct did not delay in disappointing him. Lufu appeared, somehow blathering a season's worth of reports in one breath.

'What do you mean our galleys are in short supply?' Merkhet asked him. 'What happened to them?'

'Sunk, mostly. I have secured just enough galleys to transport the military—'

'Sunk?'

'Yes, Your Grace,' the vizier said, regret in his tone. 'When Peronikh commanded the fleet north to try and retrieves you, a band of Hittites ambushed them in the delta.'

'Anything else from my absence still yet to arise? These daily surprises are wearisome.'

'No,' Lufu said, dropping his gaze to the stone floor.

'I hope not. This constant uncertainty is too draining.

Not to mention the irony.'

'The irony?' Lufu asked.

'Peronikh is the reason I have need of galleys, but also why we have so few of them left.'

'Excuse me, Your Grace, but I do not follow. Fatigue addles my mind.'

'I was wrong to leave Peronikh in the frosts of Aladaglar. It is for the gods alone to judge those who should dwell in the Afterlife. Even a pharaoh has no such right.'

'The odds of finding him …'

'Are less than Isis materializing to join us for supper at the palace, I know, but with everything else going on, I cannot just willingly leave this unresolved. It's too painful, too distracting.'

'I understand. The soldiers for that mission can join Merep and I. After Memphis, they can let the galley carry them all the way to the sea if they dare.'

'Should they return with Peronikh, can you begin the embalming straight away?'

The vizier nodded. 'Whatever the outcome, I'll handle it, and when the soldiers come back, I'll enlist them to bolster the construction efforts.'

'Thank you, Lufu. How are the other preparations progressing?'

'The military should be ready to depart later today.'

'*Will* depart today. We have delayed too long already.'

'Of course, Your Grace. Today. I will leave to brief them now.'

'I'll escort Mother to the river at dusk, and you can sail through the night.'

The vizier nodded, then disappeared.

Merkhet went back inside, through the royal

chambers and into the throne room. As he sat, he bumped his foot against Beebee. The feline didn't stir as such, just emitted an irritated bird-like chirp. Something about Beebee's lack of concern and tendency for slumber made the pharaoh want to curl up on the throne and forget about everything, too.

But forgetting was not possible. Cruel reminders surrounded him. Merkhet leaned forward to stroke Beebee but found himself hovering over the cat, unwilling to commit. Llora was one of a select few people that could wake Beebee without suffering a clawed consequence.

As Merkhet relaxed back into the throne with a sigh, the hieroglyphs appeared to swirl around the walls, swallowing each other in a brutal struggle for dominance. He blinked, and the momentary haze faded. Horakhty, hanging on the wall, stared him down. There was still time before he would escort his mother to the galley …

Had the pharaoh not earned a reprieve from the constant toils of labor and wallowing?

Inside his chambers, Merkhet collected an aged linen vest and tucked his long hair underneath it. He also removed the royal loincloth and replaced it with one a commoner might wear, then ditched the crown on the throne—anything to protect his identity. Stringing Horakhty across his back, he escaped the palace in record haste.

A pair of guards tried to follow him as he left the palace complex. Merkhet could not bear to suffer the burden of carers. He didn't want company, so he turned on them with an expression of unyielding conviction. The royal guards exchanged a shrug between themselves and returned to their posts.

Through the markets and administration precinct without any hassle, Merkhet stalked the Nile's eastern banks. A single measly ibis entered his peripherals, the only noise around him was the bird skimming across the Nile's surface in outstretched flight. It didn't stop. He was alone.

No Llora. No Peronikh. Just him, his full quiver, mangled bow, and pervading misery until a hippopotamus floated downstream in the river currents. It was maybe half the size of the one he killed to fulfill his Pharaonic Trial, but on that day, he had channeled the energy of the citizens supporting him.

He lifted Horakhty from where he had it slung across his back and inspected every inch of its once wooden perfection. After entering the maw of the river beast, the bow was one splinter short of being retired. Somehow, by the graces of the gods themselves, the frame was still intact. Though, as Merkhet tugged on the knotted bowstring, its tautness was underwhelming.

Horakhty may no longer be fit for the rigors of hunting, but he was determined to experience some success. Merkhet padded for his knife. It wasn't there. How could he be so careless, to head out on a solitary hunt and not even check for his full complement of weapons?

He sighed. More than anything, the pharaoh needed a good rest. Why hadn't he afforded himself that luxury?

The hippopotamus moved past him, letting the strong currents carry it, but not before a crane settled on the tail end of its back. Merkhet trailed the creatures, ambling alongside the river. Not daring to get too close to the soggy mud, he struggled to find an opportunity to loose an arrow.

With a bow in perfect condition, he could strike through the smallest bird from over a hundred yards. Yet with a mangled one ...

Merkhet groaned, forgetting the unenthusiastic chase for the crane. He should just give up the hunt altogether. Besides, the sun was high overhead and would soon begin its descent. The army was due to depart—his mother and Lufu along with them.

Merkhet spotted a small, abandoned raft. They were often neglected by their owners, more concerned with completing their trade deals than securing their property. A portion of its hull was wedged into the soft bank.

He didn't have enough time to cross the river in search of better game. Not even close, yet Merkhet found himself wading through the mud to hop into the raft. He grabbed the worn wooden paddle that lay inside and pushed off with it.

The raft caught in the rapid, churning Nile, and he struggled, paddle in hand, to prevent being swept away. The hippopotamus was almost a distant speck, and maybe the crane wasn't even on it anymore. But it didn't matter, because at last, there was some distance between himself and the mounting duties of pharaohship.

Standing on the bow of the vessel, he lurched forward with one leg. The western bank supported him, though his sandals sunk an inch into the soft silt. He whirled around his other leg and dropped quickly to grab hold of the raft before it could drift back to the middle of the river.

Merkhet hoisted the vessel from the brown-green slosh, securing it. Other than to visit the Valley of the

Kings, people had little reason to venture over this side of the river. Away from the city's bustle, it was a haven for the wildlife and for the pharaoh. Over here, Merkhet was nobody. He was free.

Striding north, he followed the course of the river. The limestone cliffs rose on his left. They offered him no shade yet, but the sun would sink behind them within moments. He needed to be quick.

A lone hawk circled above the Valley of the Kings, but the incarnation of Horus never drifted down to greet him, and the magnificent bird certainly never glided into the range of his weathered bow.

Could Horakhty be restored? The city was being granted another lease on life, so surely a craftsman could breathe some into his treasured bow. Scanning ahead, Merkhet searched for a jackal, hyena, gazelle—any of those creatures would do.

The cliffs opened up, but the shift from the continuous rock face was so subtle that unless you knew it was there, you would miss it. Merkhet almost stumbled over himself when he saw someone appear between the gap. The man's face was familiar, but not one he had seen in some time. He couldn't place it.

The pharaoh moved closer, but the man was gone. Had he been there at all? If so, who was he? Not knowing would irritate Merkhet more than a futile hunt ever could. Much, much more. He shook the confusion away. The sun was setting now, just about to disappear behind the peaks of the cliffs.

Merkhet was due, verging on overdue, to collect his mother from the palace, so he increased the tempo on the return to the raft. He had roamed farther than intended.

Merkhet could see the raft, but he also spotted an unsuspecting jackal. It had its head down, sniffing a scarce patch of vegetation at the cliff's base. Even with its ears standing tall to detect inbound threats, the jackal had not heard him approach. He could sneak up on it and celebrate a successful hunt after all.

Forty feet away, the beast was none the wiser. Merkhet reached for an arrow and nocked it. Drawing on the lax bowstring, Horakhty was in worse shape than he realized.

Even if the arrow reached its target, chances of a kill were slim. The force wouldn't be enough. His arrow was just as likely to reflect off the beast's gray mottled fur as it was to dig into flesh. Yet, still, he persisted to line up the jackal.

When Merkhet loosed the arrow, it wobbled through the air, missing by the grandest of measures. As the arrow skimmed across the dry ground, the beast turned to face him. Its dark eyes studied him, deciding whether to flee. But the jackal made no such move, for the beast had judged him as its next meal.

Release another arrow as it bounded for him, or dash for the raft?

Merkhet didn't do either of those things. He didn't do anything. His old companion, faithful battle nerves, flashed their unwanted fangs. The jackal did the same. Its rotten teeth invoked a swift and stern reminder of the time when he had almost lost his face to a ravenous hyena. That day—the last his father had spent in the living world—tore at him like no other. Just like this marauding jackal was about to.

The pharaoh rallied himself to loose another arrow. He fumbled with the fletching over his shoulder, and then the beast was about to leap. He could not nock the arrow quick enough. If he did get hold of it, Merkhet would need to use it as a blade.

The jackal was gliding through the air, a blur of snapping jaw and spittle spraying everywhere. A meager arrowhead stood between him and a gruesome mauling. He raised it in front of his face, more in hope than an act of conviction. The beast rammed into his chest, and they both went tumbling backwards.

Dust puffed all around them. Everything ached but nothing screamed. A warm substance lathered his hands, but Merkhet didn't think he had been bitten. He was far from sure, though.

The dust settled. Still holding the arrow, the sharpened head had pierced through the jackal's maw, pinning it shut. The beast's eyes pleaded with him, begging him to end its suffering. He was already covered in its blood but didn't have a knife to end its life quickly. The encroaching darkness was setting, the sun now fully behind the cliffs.

Merkhet let go of the arrow's shaft and slid the jackal's eyelids closed. It would not survive the night, but he could not expedite its departure into the darkness. He looked down at the sad state of Horakhty, a symbol of what he knew to be true.

Everything—and everyone—Merkhet once trusted and relied upon …

Horakhty. Llora. Peronikh. The viziers. His father. Where were they now? Gone, broken, or just as good as. Some of it his own doing, yet the cruelty of it all weighed him down mercilessly.

Would his mother even still be waiting at the palace for him? He may have pushed his luck too far this time. Not wishing for the final moments with her to be strained or rushed, Merkhet scrambled to his feet and back to the raft.

As he paddled with vigor, the army's preparations

came into view. The remnants of Egypt's naval fleet were docked adjacent to the temple district of Luxor. Braziers were staked in the mud, lighting the area, as hordes of soldiers hauled supplies aboard the galleys.

Back on the eastern bank once again, the pharaoh attempted to maintain his frantic pace, but Lufu cut him off. 'Where is your mother? Why are you so filthy?' he asked, deep curiosity in his tone.

Merkhet wanted to bury himself in the soft, dark silt. 'Long story,' he said, waving away the questions. 'I have one last task before you leave.'

'Of course, Your Grace. What do you require?'

'Find the original bowyer.' Merkhet passed Horakhty to his adviser. 'Have them repair it.'

Lufu's open mouth formed the shape of speech, but words never escaped.

'Dead?' Merkhet hung his head in disappointment. 'How emblematic of my life.'

'No, no. Nothing like that. He lives in Memphis. The man is a meticulous creature of the craft. Maybe a little too meticulous. You'll be wanting another weapon in the interim.'

'Please,' the pharaoh said.

'I will see to it.' Lufu looked at him, a curious grin on his face. 'And what of your mother?'

Merkhet grimaced before speaking. 'Right. I'll be back soon. With her,' he added, legs already in motion as he hurried for the allure of the royal palace atop Ptah's Point.

Chapter 4

When Merkhet arrived at the palace, his mother was waiting for him in the dining hall. If Merep was aggrieved by his delay, she declined to announce it.

Two young servants, a boy and girl, were behind her, carrying the bulk of her belongings in flax bags.

'Ready, Mother?'

'Are you sure you want me to oversee this project? I could be gone for months, years.'

'I will visit as often as I can, but no one else can bring this city to life. Father spoke of it often with you.'

Her eyes glistened with the sheen of tears that were yet to slide down her cheek. 'He did,' Merep said. Her gaze drifted, and for a brief moment she appeared to reunite with her beloved. 'I will build the city. But what will we call it?'

'Did Father have a name for it?'

She shook her head. 'Not that he mentioned.'

'The gods will reveal it in time, then.'

Merep smiled. Even in the week since he returned, she was beginning to resemble the radiant and endearing woman from his childhood. If anything could spur him on, to continue fighting for everything they held dear, it was that. Given time, things would improve. His mother was all the testament to that he needed.

The chariot waited for them at the bottom of the dune. The servants handed Merep's bags to the guards, who stored them on the baseboard. Merkhet and his mother boarded for the short journey to the river and the galley that awaited her.

With hands clasped together, words were not necessary. Except for the soldiers on their civic duties, the city's alleys and lanes were lifeless under the pervading nightfall. They rolled through the administration precinct, braziers blazing around its perimeter. Some of the buildings around the open square were too damaged to restore and suffered from all sorts of ailments. Toppled pylons had barricaded entrances. Walls were cracking and threatening to collapse.

His mother must have seen him studying the destruction because she spoke in a low tone. 'It wasn't just the gods. The citizens were angry and scared, too.'

'They did this?' he asked.

'Some, yes.'

Merkhet wanted to curse. The toil ahead of them was endless. Maybe now wasn't the time to be starting an ambitious construction project. But then again, the busier Egypt was, the safer it was. When he inherited the throne, there were far too many influential voices competing to shout the loudest.

Another row of braziers illuminated the Nile's banks, where the galleys were docked. The chariot halted beside the flowing currents. Hundreds of soldiers were already clambered atop the vessels.

Merkhet helped his mother down to the ground.

Lufu, in his sweeping white robe, came over to them. 'All is ready, Your Grace.'

'Excellent. I want letters sent at every moment of stillness. Remember, Memphis will assume responsibility for the restoration of our naval fleet and weapon reserves.'

The vizier bowed before him and Merep.

Merkhet wrapped his mother in a firm embrace. 'Together, we'll secure his legacy and worship.'

She squeezed him tighter until his face was lost in the fabric of her dress. 'Bye for now, my sweet, sweet boy. I love you.'

'Love you too, Mother,' he said, pressing her away.

Lufu and Merep cleared the gap between land and vessel. The various captains barked orders from their respective sterns, and the ropes holding the galleys in place were set free. Immediately, the boats were caught by the strong currents and soft winds, sailing away.

On the bough, his mother waved to him and blew him kisses. He farewelled her with everything he had left to give for the day.

When the galleys disappeared from sight, the chariot was ready to take him back to the palace.

Atop the dune's ascent, Taharva was waiting for him. Slumped against the acacia, as Merkhet often did himself, the Nubian was deep in thought.

'Are the gods listening, Captain?'

'Never. They don't care for the musings of a haggard Nubian.'

Merkhet grinned, almost succumbing to a chuckle. Taharva was a man in his physical prime, no matter how many seasons had come and gone.

'Did you enjoy your hunt, Scrollworm?'

'How do you—'

'I know everything, mostly.'

The pharaoh considered arguing for his privacy but settled against it.

'Not your finest moment. Leaving the palace without so much as an intact weapon.'

'I managed.'

'Looks a different story from here,' Taharva said. 'You're a muddied, bloodied mess.'

Merkhet didn't know what to say because the captain was right.

'Hey,' Taharva said, adding some seriousness to his voice. 'You can have your freedom, but don't even think for a second that you aren't vulnerable. My guards are watching, always.'

Merkhet nodded. 'Thanks, Turn-Tide.'

'Did the army set off, then?'

'Farewelled them just now.'

'Your mother?'

'Aboard one of the galleys with Lufu.'

'What is next?' Taharva asked.

'We continue to rebuild, friend.' Merkhet sighed, unsure how to find the words. 'Will you consider it this time?'

'Consider what?' the Nubian pressed.

'I still wish to appoint you as Vizier of Upper Egypt.'

'No, my place is at the head of the Royal Guard. I don't need a prestigious title to impart wisdom.'

'But you are the only person I can trust.'

'Not true,' Taharva said, nodding towards the entrance of the inner palace.

'Raina?!' Merkhet inquired with a hoarse whisper, though he doubted his voice was soft enough to avoid her keen senses. The scribe was never too far away from official and *unofficial* gatherings, reed pen always ready.

'Why not?' Taharva asked, but it didn't feel much like a question at all. 'I must complete my rounds. You should rest, Scrollworm.'

His body wanted nothing more than to heed the advice of his loyal friend, but the pharaoh was not sure he would find much joy.

The captain had given him something rather unexpected to deliberate.

Merkhet tossed and turned all night, but not from troubled thoughts. The potential for Taharva's suggestion was staggering. This was what the pharaoh had been waiting for—and what Egypt needed to ensure an expedited rebuild.

Eventually, he gave up on sleep, slipping around the heavy veil and into the throne room. Staring at the hieroglyphs where Horakhty was usually hung, the empty space commanded his attention. The thrill of the hunt distracted Merkhet from his duties unlike anything else, and sometimes he needed that.

How long would pass before the bowyer could restore his hunting companion? Merkhet had no way of knowing. Lufu was handling the repair, and the pharaoh would have to settle for that.

The vizier was denied the pleasure of a simple vacation to Thebes. He had arrived for a short visit to witness Merkhet's Pharaonic Trial but was instead greeted with the death of Pharaoh Nekhet and all the turmoil that followed.

So much had happened during the course of a single seasonal cycle. Merkhet flattened himself against the throne because if it weren't for the bone-numbing chill on his backside, he wasn't sure he would have the wits to differentiate between the actual events and the fabrications that threatened to crowd his mind.

Yet there was no rebuffing the interference from the gods in the throne's succession. Resting his father's sarcophagus in the Valley of the Kings. The inconsequential inundation, among other signs of distress from the gods. Merkhet's own unjust exile and eventual return. The subsequent loss of what he considered his brother, then that of a false lover.

Though, courtesy of Ra, new horizons were looming. Brighter horizons that promised a flourishing land and empire. Not even farewelling the palace for another grueling day of rebuilding hovels could prevent him from exuding such optimism. Nor could the lingering uneasiness of a sleepless night.

The sheer possibility of Taharva's counsel intrigued him all through the day. So much so, that when Merkhet returned to the palace, tired and dirty in the afternoon, he readied himself to speak with Raina. Then he summoned her.

The mute scribe's keen eyes gleamed at him through the gloom of the throne room. The flickering braziers brought her in and out of focus, and in the silence, the pharaoh found it most unnerving.

How this could ever work …

Was Taharva's proposal offered more in jest than something that should be taken for serious contemplation?

Yet the lack of critical voice in his ear could be

liberating. Of that, the pharaoh was certain, for in the prelude to the underwhelming floods, he was let down by the viziers on many occasions. After Merkhet passed his trial and restored some semblance of normality, the citizens were more inclined to accept something that would differ from tradition.

A woman presiding in the crucial role of vizier.

Merkhet wasn't sure if it had happened before—or what the reaction to such an appointment would be. Not only would the critics flock to him as quick as flies to fruit but would also condemn him to a life beyond as Osiris' servant. Change invited fear, tradition affirmed safety.

As Raina smiled at him, her lips never once threatened to part and spill twisted truths. The promise of what she could offer outweighed the probable backlash and resentment.

'Thank you for coming to see me so quick,' the pharaoh said. 'Documenting the rebuild is a delicate and important matter.'

Raina nodded, compact and efficient, yet wildly compelling. Just like her writing. As her eyes pierced through him, they implored Merkhet to arrive at his point, for a thousand other things demanded her attention. So much honesty without a single word, and not at the cost of respect.

She must be the Vizier of Upper Egypt.

But how could he present his desire in such a way that she couldn't dare refuse it?

Unsure, he mumbled some more. 'Which of our scribes did you assign to accompany the army?'

She looked at him blankly, and Merkhet was swift to correct his style of question.

'Sorry,' he said, 'did you send accomplished scribes

north to the delta?'

Another nod, and her gaze penetrated him even fiercer this time.

Of course she did, you utter fool. 'Raina,' Merkhet said, his voice steady despite the nerves. Why wouldn't the words come naturally? It wasn't as if he was asking her to join him for a sensual sunset on the stone terrace. 'Will you do whatever Egypt requires?'

Raina didn't blink, confirming her unwavering loyalty. At least that was how the pharaoh interpreted it. 'Excellent,' he said, relief coursing through his clammy tips. 'That will be all for now.'

She delivered a quizzical expression from beneath her knotty fringe, bowed, and then departed. Had Raina even spoken in the throne room after his Heb-Sed festival?

Maybe Merkhet had imagined it all this time. He would need to confirm with Haliya, but the Hittite queen would probably not hear of anything unrelated to plans for their immediate union.

He summoned a passing servant to him. 'Have Lady Raina fitted for a vizier's robe.'

The young girl bowed, then scurried away. Left to dwell on the distant memory of his own robe fitting for the Walking of the Walls ceremony, an unseemly thought came to him.

Merkhet would need to visit someone so vile he had hoped he would never have the displeasure of doing so again. If Raina's appointment were to proceed, the pharaoh did not have a choice.

How could he have been so careless at Prahmun's Judgment to make such a gross oversight?

Thankful for a reprieve from the strains of laboring, Merkhet climbed aboard the royal chariot. Two days had passed, and Raina's freshly woven robe was ready to be worn.

As the horses eased into a trot, Merkhet could no longer avoid Prahmun, his disgraced former vizier. Even though the detainment pits were so close to where the Judgments were held, it would be the pharaoh's first visit to them. Of the numerous excavations before him, only one was actively guarded: Prahmun's.

A pair of spear-wielding soldiers were on duty and Merkhet gave them a quick hand signal from the back of the chariot. They dispersed from around the pit's edge, allowing him to sink his feet into the sand and approach.

Dug in the sand and more than double the height of its filthy captive, the cramped hole was where Prahmun was held between punishments. The recent trials of stoning and baking in the sun had him looking more haggard than ever, yet somehow, he still managed to show a grin as he looked up at the pharaoh.

Merkhet resisted the temptation to descend into the pit and launch a flurry of fists upon that wretched smile. He only had one purpose for coming here, and it was not to wreak havoc on the face of a man who deserved much worse.

'Where is it?' Merkhet asked.

'To what do I owe the pleasure, Your Grace?' Prahmun stooped low in false deference, holding a tattered robe tight around him.

'Why do you have a robe?' Merkhet asked, suddenly

curious. 'You were sentenced to face Ra for your crimes.'

'Executioner gave it to me.'

'Why?'

'He fears I will perish from severe burns and that he will lose his new pet.'

Merkhet stared into Prahmun's cold, empty pupils. If possible, his shriveled cheeks made them appear more withdrawn. 'The feather. Where is it?'

'I knew you would come here, False Pharaoh. You want help finding Peronikh, don't you?'

'Retire your novel games,' Merkhet said. 'Hand over the amulet.'

The former vizier stayed quiet, and the clamor of pummeling him grew louder in Merkhet's head. Then Prahmun cackled, shrill and distasteful. 'The same day you had me hauled down here, I had a visit from someone special. You'll be back, Your Grace.'

Merkhet turned to speak with the soldiers. 'No one is to talk with this vile man.'

One of the men had a twitch in his arm, like he was desperate to say something.

Prahmun interrupted, raising his voice to ensure he was heard. 'I'm glad this robe will serve me a little longer. I couldn't bear to miss such fun.'

'What is it?' Merkhet asked the restless guard.

'What about the executioner, can he—'

'He's fine. No one else.'

The soldiers nodded.

'Don't worry,' Prahmun called out, once again abandoning his manners. 'My friend won't be back here again. You will, though.'

'I'm here for the amulet, nothing else,' the pharaoh said, 'and as soon as you—'

'Care to stake my freedom on it?'

Merkhet ignored the question. How did he—how did his father—ever tolerate such a man as an adviser? 'The amulet.'

'I lost it,' Prahmun said, smirking.

Merkhet did not have any more energy to waste on this despicable human. As soon as he had the Amulet of Ma'at, Raina's appointment ceremony could commence. 'Retrieve it,' he told the soldiers, facing them once more.

They obeyed the command without delay, lowering themselves into the snug pit. Prahmun wailed as they landed beside him. One threatening wave of a spear and the silver feather surfaced above frayed robes. A feigned jab and the prisoner lifted it from around his neck. Once he had given the amulet to a soldier, Merkhet dropped a wooden ladder into the pit for them. Sadly, Prahmun wasn't silly enough to try and use it for himself.

With the Amulet of Ma'at returned to him, the pharaoh was more than satisfied to leave the desert demon in his hole.

Prahmun's searing taunts followed him all the way to the administration precinct, where a crowd gathered. Arriving in the royal chariot, Merkhet's appearance cast a temporary silence over those gathered. The bulk of the precinct's stone buildings around him were charred and crumbling, still recovering from the gods' vengeance.

Merkhet couldn't blame the people for deserting him and their homes but was glad to see that they were back living in Thebes and cramming into the open square. Their presence warmed the pharaoh more than the sun ever could. His decree to restore private dwellings first, no doubt eased any reservations about returning to the capital. Each daybreak brought Egypt another step closer to forgetting their recent trials. Order was in his firm grasp and prosperity was once again within reach.

The throng of Thebans gave him the hope and energy to keep rebuilding, every bit as much as appointing Raina to Vizier of Upper Egypt did. If she was shocked by her elevation to the pharaoh's adviser, she did not say as much. Then again, when did she ever?

Certain they would form a formidable partnership, Merkhet climbed the stairs onto the wooden platform, and as he did, the excitable chatter resumed.

On the ceremonial dais, he was reminded of the recent Heb-Sed celebration, where Taharva's slavery status was abolished. The pharaoh was confident in his decision to host the rejuvenation festival, as he was with acknowledging Raina at these proceedings. Both events were much unlike the Walking of the Walls, where Merkhet was petrified the sands would part and Osiris would claim him.

Much had changed since then, but nothing hurt more than the absences of Peronikh and Llora. Their faces were not present and never would be again. Sadness threatened to overtake him, but the crowd's buzz was fading. They were expecting the ceremony to begin.

Merkhet glanced all around him. The High Priest was not present. None of the priests or priesthoods were. He would need to follow that up, but after all the uncertainty endured, the pharaoh would not keep the citizens waiting.

The words came easy, flowing from him as soon as he opened his mouth. 'From the time of unification, viziers have been appointed to give counsel to the pharaoh. In light of unfortunate recent events—'

Murmurs begun around the crowd again. Merkhet could see the disdain with which they muttered *Prahmun*, a sentiment he was more than capable of echoing.

'—an opportunity has arisen.'

The pharaoh gestured for Raina to join him on the platform. Her new white robe clung tightly to her figure. A perfect fit. A curious expression dominated any nerves she might have as she gracefully made her way up the stairs. Merkhet never informed her of his plan, at least not directly. Her ceremonial robe fitting may have given it away.

When she was beside him, he spoke again. 'Raina, a diligent scribe of unrivaled prowess, will join rank alongside Lufu. I present her—the new Vizier of Upper Egypt—with the Amulet of Ma'at.'

Raina stepped forward and bent slightly before him. He slipped the feather over her head, and the crowd erupted in applause.

No discord from those gathered. The pharaoh accepted this remarkable woman as his adviser, and they did, too.

No interruptions to the proceedings—the priesthood didn't even have the decency to show their presence, let alone support the occasion.

No immediate vengeance from the gods.

Raina would be his silent adviser, and Merkhet was certain the rebuild could only gather a rush of momentum from here.

Chapter 5

If taking a risk on Raina was what he did, Merkhet was at complete ease within a matter of days.

He didn't see much of her. The vizier tended to rise even earlier than he did. Each morning she prepared a scroll, summarizing key events from the day before and outlining the plan for the day ahead.

No longer did the pharaoh need to guess what the viziers were up to, or how they could next undermine him. Everything had a written record, and everything was progressing as it should.

Minimal sunlight crept into the throne room. Its main source came from within his chambers when the veil was not drawn, but with Haliya still sleeping, it was pulled over.

Still, Merkhet made no mistake in finding the papyrus note Raina had left for him on the war table. Servants skittered about in the adjacent hall as he sat down to read.

A standard report—all about the rebuild and channeling the Nile's waters, ready for planting the crops and grain, and somehow, she convinced a southern village to part with seventy pairs of hands to assist with the pressing matters in Thebes. All further justification of his decision to appoint her.

Then something surprised him, right at the very bottom of the scroll.

I have received correspondence from the viceroy.

It couldn't be. Not so soon. The Nubians couldn't be mounting an uprising. Their tribal chieftains were renowned for their love of war and hostility, but most commonly it was among themselves, within their own lands.

We must meet with Taharva.

The report concluded with that, leaving Merkhet baffled. What could be happening, and how did it involve Taharva? Why didn't Raina leave whatever was sent from the southern-most Egyptian official for him to read?

Perhaps a threat to himself, or the palace. By no means a rare occurrence, and Raina probably just wanted to ensure that the Captain of the Royal Guard received a timely and accurate brief of the threat. Or could it be something else?

The viceroy was expected to send a general report on life in the Nubian lands twice a year, or at any time if an urgent matter arose. The most likely cause of such correspondence would be a looming assault on the mines near Abu Simbel. But not a single raid had occurred since the reign of his grandfather, further piquing the pharaoh's interest.

Whatever the news may be, it would have to wait. Neither Raina nor Taharva were presently at the palace.

Merkhet almost tripped over Beebee, napping on the cool stone floor. A reed pen awaited him at the table, and he scratched a directive of his own into the papyrus.

Knowing his vizier would receive it later, Merkhet placed the pen atop the scroll, and a huge weight lifted from him. With volunteer reinforcements on the way, some of his attention could be directed elsewhere. The unresolved matter of his father's eternal worship. Pharaoh Nekhet, not perfect by any means, but the land and people flourished under his rule. No one disputed it, and the Egyptians were in the midst of reclaiming those ways.

Slower than Merkhet would have liked, but it was happening all the same, and there was no better way to commemorate this than by honoring his father with a mortuary temple. When life went according to plan, pharaohs built their own tombs and temples. But when did it ever? Now that things were becoming less strained, Merkhet could finish what he should have done long ago.

In Pharaoh Nekhet's short and painful absence, inexplicably, his tomb had been compromised. The same fate would not befall his mortuary temple.

Only the most despicable of individuals could ever perform such an act, and Merkhet had every intention of seeking them out and learning from them.

Maybe he already had stumbled upon one …

Merkhet recalled the face that emerged between the cliffs. It was so familiar—yet he could not make the connection—then or now.

He read his simple message one last time. *Enlist the*

services of a tomb robber. Be discreet.

Satisfied, he poked his head inside the royal chambers. Haliya was still sound asleep. He doubted she had stirred from the moment he escaped the sheets. The Hittite queen could slumber as well as any weary soul.

He tried to steal away unnoticed, but not before he regretted it.

'It is rude to spy,' she said, her mountain accent and language sending chills all over him.

'I didn't know you were awake,' he replied in Hittite.

'And that makes it fine?'

'I guess not.'

'What of our union?' she asked, her cheekiness unrivaled.

Merkhet laughed, careful of unintended condescension. 'Patience, my goddess, patience.'

He didn't mean to make such a reverent remark but had no intention of taking it back. If anything, it seemed to appease her.

As Merkhet first graced the courtyard, Taharva and Raina stepped forward to join him.

The pharaoh glanced at his vizier, but she was silent, unmoving. Was this how it would always be in her presence? He went to take a seat beneath the acacia tree but almost collapsed to the ground before he could.

Raina spoke. She actually spoke. At long last, he could put to rest his unease. Merkhet had not imagined their brief conversation in the throne room after the Heb-Sed festival.

'Read,' she said, handing him a scroll.

He struggled to accept the papyrus, still trying to recover from the shock of her gentle voice. Merkhet gave the scroll a quick, cursory glance. He could see that it was signed by the viceroy and had come from Egypt's southern border. That did not help him understand the relevance of why they were meeting about it.

Raina just glared at him. She was not about to reveal the scroll's secrets to him. He would need to read it for himself, and he did.

At first it just seemed like some sort of sorry preamble, and he could sense Taharva's impatience growing, festering as the captain paced around the courtyard.

Merkhet's hands grew clammy and tight as he read on. A cooperative Nubian family were looking for their long-lost son. Taharva.

'Horus in the bluest of skies, I do not believe it,' the pharaoh muttered.

'What is it, Scrollworm?'

'One moment,' he said, holding up his hand to pacify Taharva while he finished reading.

The message went on to say that while it was against tradition to grant recourse to slaves, or even dare present such a request, that a special exemption should be considered. The Nubians in question were selfless and gave much to satisfying all Egyptian interests. They deserved to be reunited with their son.

The viceroy was yet to receive word of recent developments. Taharva was no longer a slave. He was a free man and searching for his family would not defy any established tradition.

'Scrollworm, you're dragging my entrails through the sand here. What is it?'

For the swiftest of moments, Merkhet wanted to suppress the contents of the letter. Cast it aside, forget about it entirely. Taharva was his friend, protector, and the person he trusted most. He was no different to the cliffs in the Valley of Kings that fortified the burial tombs for the pharaoh. The royal guard couldn't just leave on the whim of an unverified note, not after Merep and Lufu were already elsewhere. But the temptation to intervene faded. 'It's your family,' Merkhet said at last. 'They are looking for you.'

'Sorry?' the Nubian asked, his mouth agape.

Merkhet pointed at the scroll. 'The viceroy says so right here.'

Taharva kept pacing, spinning on his heels every few steps. 'What do we know of him?'

'Not much. An appointment before my pharaohship, but he has maintained order at the border for many seasons.'

The captain grumbled something, then they all sat in silence. If Merkhet understood anything, Raina would be the least likely to break it.

'My family wants to reunite,' Taharva said. 'After all these years, I thought my parents must have passed on. Surely, they could not still … What am I to do?'

After that glimmer of selfishness receded within him, Merkhet didn't need to deliberate on this through the night or discuss it with anyone else, like he might with a new policy or military matter.

Of all the people in his life, Taharva deserved this opportunity without question.

Merkhet could sense Raina examining him. No doubt, under her veil of silence, she would be judging his decision. Maybe that's why she made herself present at this meeting, to subtly influence it. But thoughts such as those were not helpful. If he could not yet trust his new vizier, Merkhet could at least grant her a chance to perform the arduous role entrusted to her.

'It's obvious, friend,' Merkhet said.

Taharva raised his head, awaiting the pharaoh's verdict.

'You are going to find your family.'

The captain could not find the words to form a protest. He bowed, which he had not done in many seasons, other than as a form of mock flattery. Then he left the courtyard in a hurry.

Merkhet turned to Raina. 'Did you see my addition to your morning report?'

She nodded, relieving him of the viceroy's request and also departing with haste.

Chapter 6

Raina descended from the heights of the palace, walking through the open gates for the distant glow of the worker villages.

Things were quite a bit different now, after being presented with the Amulet of Ma'at and sworn in as the Vizier of Upper Egypt. Of all the madness to unfold since Pharaoh Nekhet's death, this upswing in fortune was possibly the most inexplicable.

Trudging through the sands, Raina wasn't heading back home to her hovel for rest. She was no longer an invisible scribe, writing in the shadows. She was an agent of change. As strange as the pharaoh's latest directive was, Raina was eager to impress.

Merkhet left no justification, and nor did she expect him to. Her duty was to fulfill his desires, not question or undermine them. Of all the Egyptian citizens, she couldn't help but think that was part of the reason he selected her.

She would face challenges, sure. No longer could

Raina hide behind her reed pen and papyri every waking moment. Sometimes, she would need to interact with the world around her and the people in it. The expectations of the role aside, she was the first woman vizier in hundreds of years and that would come with its own complications. So, Raina was not the least bit surprised when her steps began to flounder as she neared her destination.

Drinking hovels, common in the villages, were not her ideal place to linger of an evening. She much preferred being curled up on a sleeping mat with a lit brazier beside her, sifting through accounts of past pharaohs from all the distinguished scribes that came before her. The intricate details of the Great Sphinx's construction would have to wait for another night.

Raina sidled inside the first riotous hovel she came across, settling in a shadowy spot just by the entrance. She tucked her silver feather amulet under her robes. Despite her elevation in responsibilities and status, she was a committed pupil to the art of remaining unseen.

For every person huddled in the hovel, maybe thirty in all, there were four or five empty mugs and flagons in front of each of them. The patrons spoke with such slurred gusto, and then that compounded by the rabble of so many concurrent conversations, she could not decipher much of anything.

How would she find a tomb robber among all these incoherent gluttons? Her heart thumped within her as she tried to pluck up the courage to speak. Even if she did manage to mumble something, there was only a slim possibility that Raina would understand their drunken responses. The evening appeared destined to yield nothing.

Despite this, she edged inside a little farther. If a

conversation idled, perhaps she could thrust herself into it. More likely, Raina would just stare at them awkwardly and not open her mouth. Her vow of silence could not be shaken, or forgotten so easy. That harrowing day of unconscionable weakness would remain with her, eternal.

Moving deeper into the hovel? Mistake. An intoxicated man grabbed her by the wrist and pulled her so close that she began to choke on the rotten stench emanating from the cavities in his mouth. Despite his impaired speech, she had no trouble understanding this vile creature. 'Lon' brown hair and all'er teeth. The perfec' woman.'

Raina tried to writhe herself free, but his grip was too strong. A laborer, or maybe a sailor. She gave him a frustrated, pointed look.

He understood her meaning. 'Well, honey, what you think I'm af'er?' The man laughed at that.

Even worse, others were starting to take notice. His unrelenting handle on her made her stomach churn. Stuck in that filthy hovel, attached to that filthy man— she may as well have been sharing her sleeping mat with a legion of scarabs, their spindly legs skittering and crawling all over her.

Taharva sprang to action. In his urgency, the full beer in front of him was knocked all over the surrounding patrons. They cried out in dismay, but what choice did he have. No person should ever be held against their will.

Witnessing such a cowardly and dishonorable act from the far side of the hovel, the rage formed quick. Taharva passed by the irritated men in soaked linens too quick for them to dare challenge him over their misfortune.

Two determined strides and the Captain of the Royal Guard was standing behind the pathetic man, who had no intention of releasing the young lady of his own accord. Raina struggled to remove herself from his uncompromising grip.

Taharva set about enforcing justice, quelling his burning intrigue. The reason for the vizier's presence in a dreary hovel could be uncovered later. He growled, long and fierce, drowning out all other noise.

Every patron snapped their heads to face him, including the gutless drunk. He gave one frightened up-and-down glance at the Nubian, before unhanding Raina with an unbecoming quiver. Taharva resisted the urge to wallop the man for his indecency. Even if it were justified, such a violent act would only stir unnecessary trouble for Merkhet.

'Enjoy those fingers, you filthy rat?' Taharva asked him.

The drunk stayed quiet. Even though his eyes swayed all round their sockets, the Nubian could tell he was listening.

'Ever think about trying force like that again and you'll lose 'em. All of 'em.'

This time, the slimy desert rat nodded. Taharva reached forward and picked up the drunk's mug, pouring out the frothy contents all over his head. If not the fear inflicted, the shame of the evening would have the man think twice in future. Even better if he curtailed his habit of mindless consumption.

Raina, wide-eyed, hurried from the hovel. Taharva gave a final grunt of disgust and followed her out. She did not get far in the dim of night before he caught up with her.

Her eyes were wet and glistening, but no tears escaped them. 'Thank you,' she said, a strange swirl of embarrassment and determination embodied in her voice. Though it was raspy from disuse, the gentle and soft way in which she spoke left him craving more.

'What were you doing in there?' he begged of her. 'It is madness to enter such a place on your own.'

She was already withdrawing from him, her eyes and face sinking beneath that signature brown fringe of hers. To think that she might open up to him, it was too good to be true. In a way, he was thankful. If Raina did talk to him, she might be inclined to ask why he was staring at a beer whilst dressed in his royal guard uniform—or why his lips never tasted the hops.

Taharva wouldn't have a firm answer for either question, but it didn't matter. As much as he, the vizier was entitled to her silence, so long as the safety of their pharaoh and Egypt were not risked or compromised in doing so.

She started searching her robe pockets, but before Taharva could ask what she was doing, it became obvious. Papyrus and reed pen in hand, Raina scribbled away.

'I cannot rea—' he tried to tell her, but the vizier, clearly annoyed at the interruption, raised her writing hand to stop him.

Curious, he let her be. The new Vizier of Upper Egypt deserved at least that much. A few fleeting moments and she was done. With the pen tucked away in her robes, she was dragging him closer to the same hovel they had just exited in unceremonious fashion.

'What are you—' he tried to ask in protest, but once again she quieted him.

Her formidable scowl was just yet another surprise from this fascinating woman. If she could avoid the worst of Thebes, Taharva was sure that Raina would fast prove her capabilities beside Merkhet. Having suggested the appointment, he was grateful that she was rising to the task. Or was he allowing his judgment of the vizier to be mired by his admiration of her?

There was a still a big unanswered question: what was she doing out in the villages by herself at this late hour?

Outside the hovel but back in its warm glow, she beckoned him to lean in. She held the scroll out steady for him. Taharva was immediately thankful to be taking in a sketch. Forget hieratic scrawl. Even hieroglyphs he struggled to interpret, always confused about whether a symbol represented a sound or something literal. Drawings were much simpler.

A man covered in jewels. Beside him was some sort of opening, with lots of shapes and objects contained within. Beneath these, the detail sharpened. Raina had obviously spent most of the short time working on the perfect depiction of Merkhet upon the Golden Throne, lion head grips on the side and all. The Double Crown atop his head. Full features of his face—the bump in his chin, and even his luscious length of ponytail.

'Merkhet sent you out here?'

Raina nodded.

'Not by yourself, he hasn't.'

She remained still, and he was unable to take meaning. Taharva returned his focus to the scroll. A rich man next to a hole. What could that signify?

He looked to her, hoping that it might be one of those rare moments when she was willing to break her silence. It was not, and he found himself wondering how she had come to be mute. Had something traumatic happened? A matter of confidence or self-preservation? Her bright eyes drew him in but leaked no hints.

Men with unimaginable riches—the pharaohs—are placed in sealed chambers to enjoy the Afterlife. Is that what Raina meant?

Taharva didn't think that was right. Who else could acquire wealth? Reflecting a moment, he joined his ideas together. 'You're looking for a tomb robber?'

The vizier showed him a wide grin, her teeth glinting in the borrowed light.

'Why didn't you say so?' he asked, then laughed at the irony of his question. 'Let's go find one. A different hovel might be best. By order of the pharaoh or not, this one would be glad to see the back of us.'

Taharva ushered Raina away from the hovel. Another would not be hard to find—Egyptian laborers loved a drink in the evening.

Raina followed the captain's lead. His strides were so massive that she had to lift the hem of her robes just to keep from falling too far behind.

She was curious to know why Taharva happened to be in the very same hovel as the one she first visited.

Ungrateful, she wasn't. If he had not intervened when he did, she would be …

Refusing to dwell on her unfortunate encounter with the darkest side of Thebes, she closed the gap. Taharva turned sidewards, nodding approvingly as she matched his pace. Most hovels were void of sound and light by this late hour, but Raina could see one glowing in the distance.

The captain bounded toward it. Did he approach all facets of life with such ferocity, or was it because he would head south to find his family when the sun rose?

Raina didn't even really know Taharva. Yet somehow, should he leave, she knew she would miss him. She wasn't even sure that all the papyrus in the world could help her explain it. His presence just set her at ease and gave her notions of safety she had never known the like of. Given the night she had already endured, that was something to be admired.

At the hovel's open entrance, Taharva didn't even hesitate. He gave her a quick smile as he headed inside, and with nothing to do but follow him, Raina did.

The empty mugs and flagons were piled even higher in here than the last place. Lighting was dimmer, too, but that didn't stop all the patrons noticing her and Taharva's arrival. Their conversations stopped so abruptly that Raina wondered if a question or two would be tossed their way.

However, after a good stare—probably where they realized the true size of Taharva, or maybe even some of them recognized him—they returned to their drinks. Raina eased in behind the captain, where they squeezed on to the end of a stone bench.

Two mugs appeared in front of them, courtesy of the hovel's owner. The overbearing hops jumped out of the mug and gave her caution. She had never tried beer before, preferring the sweeter, fruitier taste of wine. Taharva seemed no more inclined to sip the beer than she, looking at it for a long time.

In the end, he set it aside, and another patron swigged from it straight away. Raina could tell the stranger thought he was clever sneaking a beer, but Taharva allowed it to happen. She was sure of that.

The captain hadn't spoken yet, so Raina had a nervous sip. Fear of embarrassment was all that stopped her from spitting the bitter drink from her lips. She swallowed with great difficulty.

Was Taharva lost for words? Was that even possible for a man with such a striking shape? The same bulging muscles that left her mouth a tad ajar were no doubt what stopped the drunks from questioning their late and uninvited presence.

Raina desperately wanted to say something. The silence was never awkward. Never. Not for her.

Yet tonight it was, and she hated the way it made her want to escape his company. She was not worthy to be around such an honorable man. As she was panicking over which few words she might blurt out, Raina became aware of Taharva watching the man beside them.

The Nubian did not attempt to conceal his actions, and the greedy drunk did eventually notice, shifting uncomfortably.

The pen and papyrus buried in the lining of her robe seemed to call for her, bouncing against her side and demanding attention. The instruments didn't want to miss marking the occasion where a man soiled his loincloth in a crowded hovel. Raina could not oblige her tools, despite every part of her wanting nothing more. If her compulsive scribbling compromised the pharaoh's mission in any way, she could never forgive herself.

The young drunk could not help himself. 'You pushed it towards me. What was I supposed to do?'

Taharva resisted a reply, waiting.

'What's your deal, big man? Plenty more beer.'

'I don't need beer,' the captain responded at last.

The crude man squirmed a little, and the air reeked with tension. None of the other patrons were any the wiser for the sudden shift. 'W-w-what do you need, then?'

Was that a feigned stammer in some helpless scheme for them to take pity on him? Raina suspected so.

Taharva grunted, already disapproving of the drinker and his attitude. 'A tomb robber.'

'None of those here. Sorry, can't help.'

'Now, now, friend,' Taharva said, putting a firm grip on the man's shoulder. 'Can't or won't?'

'What is this? I've seen your face before. Aren't you the Captain of the Royal Guard?' The drunk's eyes welled with wetness as Taharva squeezed even harder. 'All right, all right. What's your deal? I might know a couple.'

'Much better,' the captain said, releasing the young man.

'Will cost you, though.'

'Everything always does.' Taharva flashed an amber jewel. 'How will this do?'

'Very nicely.'

'Are you the tomb robber?'

For once the young man stayed quiet, and the silence confirmed his appetite for the surreptitious trade of thievery.

'You'll meet the lady and a friend of ours here tomorrow,' the captain barked at the man.

If the drunk noticed the change in Taharva's tone, he did not show it. 'Tomorrow? Should be fine.'

'*Will* be fine,' Taharva corrected him, a sudden weariness overtaking his demeanor, and the tomb robber noticed it that time, shrinking back at once. 'If you show and prove yourself useful, you'll get your jewel.'

'Tomorrow,' the young man agreed.

The captain rose from the bench and motioned for Raina to leave ahead of him. She stalled, unsure whether to raise that they had not made the necessary trades for their drinks. Taharva did not seem concerned, though, continuing to usher her out of the hovel. Maybe he was friends with the owner, but she didn't ask him, and just allowed herself to be guided into the cool night air.

'One last problem solved for the pharaoh,' he said as he gave her the amber stone, all but confirming that he would be leaving to try and reunite with his family.

She clasped her hand around it. Was it remiss of her to ponder how long he might be gone?

Chapter 7

Strolling across the palace courtyard and past the solitary acacia, Merkhet began to descend the dune. Under the waning strength of Ra's afternoon rays, he stopped to study the most recent hieroglyphic addition on the walled slope. The artists had completed their work, and his own depiction now included him gripping a silver knife. Would Haliya approve?

A short, sharp whistle carried up the hill. Taharva was already waiting outside the palace gates. He had traded his royal guard red for a faded commoners' robe. Once black, the outfit was now more of a dull gray. Given the captain's prominent physical stature and scarring on his bald scalp, the change of clothes only gave him a slight hint of anonymity.

The captain was rummaging through a pack straddled against Tendrence. Surprisingly, Raina was beside the steed, too. They weren't talking but seemed at ease in each other's company. Merkhet had not requested her presence for this farewell, and for once, Raina did not have a pen in her hand.

Taharva had reported to Merkhet just after first light, and according to Taharva's flattering account of Raina's work ethic from the night before, she was warming to her duties. The pharaoh was glad to hear it. He would need her in the coming seasons if he were to maintain Ma'at and appease the citizens. Everyone else Merkhet trusted had already vacated Thebes or was on the verge of doing so. Lufu and his mother were needed in the north, and Taharva was departing for the southern border.

Tendrence was ready for the journey, nestling up to the Nubian. Merkhet stretched out for a pat of his own. It was hard to resist the swelling fondness he had for the stallion, their inadvertent hero on the slopes at Aladaglar when he crushed the Hittite king with his thunderous hooves.

But Tendrence's black fur and shaggy mane stirred dark memories of his original owner. Would the soldiers find Peronikh's body and return it to Egypt? Merkhet doubted it. Too long had passed, and the wintry weather could only preserve a body for so long.

The real tragedy was not just in Peronikh's loss but in all those that had departed this world. His father. Llora. All the soldiers at the hands of the Hittites. So much unnecessary loss.

At least Merkhet would soon have a tomb robber at his disposal to safeguard his father's Afterlife. A meeting, taking place at nightfall, would reveal how that could be achieved.

Taharva stood before him, ready to leave. 'Are you sure, Scrollworm? Twenty-something harvests. Will they—' He stopped himself. 'Will my sister even remember me?'

'Say no such thing, friend. You know you have my blessing and that of the entire pharaohship.'

Taharva gave a slight nod, deep appreciation in his restrained expression.

'Raina has sketched a map to guide you.' Merkhet handed him the scroll, which Taharva tucked away in his plain robe. 'Any sense of how long you will be leaving us for, Captain?'

'Three or four days of furious pace to Abu Simbel. From there, hard to say. Nubia is a vast land. Might be that the administration precinct and villages are restored before my return.'

Raina gasped beside them, but she quickly muffled it with a palm.

'That is a conservative measure of my faith in you,' Taharva said. 'Both of you,' he added, gesturing towards Raina. 'My cover is primed for duty. Inebni will not let you down.'

'Any man you care to endorse will always be accepted. Ride well, my friend,' Merkhet said, holding out his hand.

The Nubian declined the pharaoh's outstretched arm, instead dragging him in.

'I'll be back soon, Scrollworm. Trust yourself, always,' Taharva murmured quietly.

Merkhet did not say anything at first. Out of the embrace, he said, 'The gods are with you. Egyptian and Nubian. See you soon, Turn-Tide.'

Taharva turned to Raina. She bent forward in an awkward curtsy, instant sunburn flushing across her cheeks. The Nubian lifted her up and wrapped her in a hug even tighter than the one he gave the pharaoh.

He also muttered something in her ear, but Merkhet didn't catch it and found himself grinning. Neither of them were aware of his amusement, and that made it all the more interesting.

Taharva hauled himself atop the steed with a single hand while the other secured his treasured bronze spear in place. The Nubian showed no sign of slowing down. He was still as impressive as Merkhet's first memories of him, when he would stalk the palace grounds and interrogate any unfamiliar faces trying to gain access to the royal residence.

The Captain of the Royal Guard smiled at them as he grabbed a firm hold of Tendrence's reins, who responded at once, trotting south to the city walls.

After farewelling his dearest friend in the late afternoon, Merkhet held a brief meeting with Inebni. The man was of a similar build to the loyal Nubian he was replacing and also spoke with a measured calmness that set the pharaoh at ease. The differences were stark, though. Inebni's skin was fair for an Egyptians, and he had a full head of hair that could rival the sheen of desert sand. He was not Taharva.

Merkhet declared an end to royal matters for the day, and Inebni heeded without delay. The pharaoh was just about to slip behind the veil and retire to his chambers when Tiaa entered the throne room.

A pang of guilt rippled through him. He had forgotten to check in on Llora's ongoing mummification and didn't even know which stage of the delicate process the embalmers were up to. He had neglected to read the papyri Tiaa entrusted him to read and could not say what messages were contained within Llora's scrawls.

Aside from Taharva's sudden expedition, everything else was progressing as planned. Merkhet had consumed himself in the steady rebuild of their capital; the preliminary construction of a new fortress in the north; rejuvenating their tired military operations; maintaining the gods' satisfaction after the recent inundation promised grain aplenty for all; nurturing Raina's development as vizier; and celebrating the deafening silence of the Amun Priesthood.

None of the things that Tiaa cared for and not anything that she expected of him. Half-melded in the shadows, she shuffled through the open space and hunched over beside the war table. The small of her back leaned against it for support, and her distraught, weary eyes said that she needed every bit of the assistance.

Merkhet motioned for the guards to reignite the wall-mounted braziers. One of them departed to retrieve a live flame, the other holding steady in his position.

'Good evening,' the pharaoh said, somehow startling her, even as the guard returned and moved through the room to light the braziers.

'My gracious pharaoh,' she said, not rising from her crouch.

'How can I help you, Tiaa? Are the village servants meeting yours and the baby's needs?'

'The service is fine. Everything is … fine.' Her face told a different tale.

'Sorry, I've not been able to attend you. The demands of pharaohship are endless.'

Tiaa nodded, absent from the present.

Merkhet sighed. How could he help heal her pain when he could not even carve out a moment to address his own? Reminders of Llora were everywhere. Every time he hopped into the royal chariot, sat on the stone terrace, gazed up at the constellations, or locked hands with Haliya.

Llora was there. Every time.

'Told you before,' Tiaa croaked, 'my Llora would never …' She couldn't finish that thought, not again. 'You must think I'm mad.'

'How could I think that? I believe you, Tiaa. But who would want to hurt Llora in such a way?'

'She was so fearful when the gods were at their most enraged. More than anyone else, and she wouldn't explain it. What did her scrolls tell?'

More guilt. Merkhet had not yet read the papyri sheafs that Tiaa gave him. Avoided them, more accurate. He feared the harsh truths they might reveal about their relationship. Not ready to admit his own failure with the scrolls, he deflected as best he could. 'Your daughter was pregnant. She had a better reason than any to be frightened.'

Tiaa shook her head this time. 'Didn't seem like that at all,' she said, but did not add any reason to her argument.

When she broke the silence, sadness crept into her voice. 'I'm sorry, truly am.'

Merkhet wandered closer to her. 'For what?'

'Should have told Llora.'

'Told her what?' he asked, a slither of impatience growing with the grieving mother for the first time. The half-thoughts, posed as riddles, reminded him of how Peronikh and Llora would skirt around a difficult subject with similar infuriating reluctance.

'About her father,' she said.

'She never mentioned her father.'

'Llora never knew who he was,' Tiaa said. She looked up at him, eyes wide with strain.

'Well?' Merkhet insisted.

'Pharaoh Nekhet.'

He scoffed. 'Impossible. I have no time for such

whimsical delusions. You need some rest, Tiaa. A chance to accept your loss.'

'It's true,' she said. 'Around the time he met Merep, maybe just before. He loved her above all others and did not want me to join his precious harem.'

Merkhet squirmed under the urge to shout and roar until the feeble ceiling came crashing in, and then resisted the temptation to lash out at the hieroglyphic walls that retold his father's conquests.

What Tiaa said couldn't be true. Couldn't be …

He sat on the throne, head buried in his lap and knuckles digging into his temples. Anything to silence the torment, but nothing availed.

Llora couldn't be his sister. They had kissed, held hands, and intended to marry. Did his father even love his mother, or was she just the luckiest of the ladies he courted?

Merkhet lifted his neck, just enough to speak. 'What about Wuntu?'

Tiaa wailed at the sound of her son's name. 'Yes,' she cried. 'Your brother is missing. Your sister, murdered.'

Merkhet didn't want to believe her familial revelation. Llora had concealed secrets, had deceived him. Why would her mother be different? 'Please, Tiaa, you must leave now.'

She was already on her feet as the guards came in to escort her. 'You know what must be done,' she said.

Merkhet needed answers. That's what he needed. Parting the veil, he strode through his chambers. Haliya was not there, but he couldn't be concerned about her. Not right now. He collected the great wad of papyri in his arms and stalked back into the throne room.

Dumping the folded scrolls onto the war table, his fingers reached for the freshest one. Tiaa had said that the writing was different, so that's where he would start.

Merkhet separated it from the others. The message had a few short lines, which he read holding his breath.

He retreated to the Golden Throne, collapsing on it. The foundations of the palace, of his life, seemed to shatter around him.

Merkhet let go of the scroll, and it drifted to the ground. Everything was far from coming together. Maybe it never was.

Chapter 8

Thinking he might actually savor the prospect of enlisting a tomb robber to his service? Merkhet couldn't have been more mistaken.

He tried to hide from that bitter truth out on the royal terrace, but he couldn't. Even there, where the harmony of nature and order flirted with a mesmerizing potency, the scroll and its devastating implications still haunted him, carrying the power to unravel all the momentum he'd been building since his return.

Though Merkhet held the scroll open in his palms, he couldn't read it under starlight alone. That didn't matter. The words were part of him now, seeping into his consciousness. Each time he revisited them, the fury and disbelief raged anew, further souring his mood.

Dismantle the pharaohship before the commencement of the Opet. Fail to heed this directive at your own peril, for the Hidden One is rising. He is as impatient as his reach is powerful—the peasant girl knows the truth of it. His time has come. Egypt is ready to soak in his glory.

Merkhet was shaking, itching to tear the scroll apart. He was angrier with himself than the threat. How had he ignored that great wad of papyri given to him by Tiaa for as long as he did? All to protect his own feelings.

Llora was murdered. Her life taken by the fanatical Amun Priesthood, the very same priesthood his father had warned him about. Whether she was his sister was as irrelevant as whether the High Priest committed the fatal slice himself. For mere association, Merkhet would end the withered man's ignominy.

Staring at the constellations scattered across the night sky, he was transported back to the desert hunt, where Llora saved him from a certain mauling. Just before the Hittites arrived and slaughtered his father. Or was it their father?

If Tiaa's account were true, did Nekhet know the girl they stumbled upon in the desert was his daughter? He must have. Her eyes were the exact same shimmering blue as Tiaa's.

Worse still—Ra shone his light on all these developments, not even a half a day after Taharva left Thebes on horseback. Merkhet was tempted to mount Abacca and give chase to the captain. He could beg him to return at once.

The High Priest's letter was a threat to Egypt's traditions and existence. Just as everything was getting back on track, how would Merkhet overcome this treasonous act, and without the guidance of his most loyal friend?

Was he the unluckiest—or the most incompetent— pharaoh to ever grace the Golden Throne? How could the gods be so cruel, again …

Merkhet had to crush that last thought, vanquish it,

before the grips of indignation took a firm hold. This was not the work of the gods. This had nothing to do with their primordial protectors. The glowing moon and the peaceful serenity of the lands below confirmed as much.

This was the High Priest's meddling. Him and his score of initiates were acting with complete discord for their country's sacred ways. Merkhet could not ignore this plight any longer. The priesthood needed to be dealt with.

Another thought struck him hard. If Tiaa was right about Llora's passing, what else was she right about? At the very least, he would investigate the disappearance of other children around Thebes.

As soon as Merkhet saw Raina, it became obvious. He was not ready to share these revelations in their entirety. Not yet. Maybe soon, he hoped. Even though his vizier may be the only person currently in Thebes he could rely on, it was still too soon to be involving her in his personal drama.

The pharaoh didn't want any distractions from the task required of him in the drinking hovel. His father had already suffered enough setbacks on his journey to the Afterlife. Every day he suffered—without certainty and security in the Fields of Paradise—was an insult to his memory.

Merkhet considered showing the vizier a few of his favorite constellations but didn't know how to begin the conversation. He sighed, and she looked at him, a twinkle of support in her eyes as she emerged from the peripheries. They were due to leave for their arranged meeting with the tomb robber, and he doubted that those in the profession were a pleasant or punctual bunch.

At this point, he would welcome just about anything to divert his attention from the promise of looming chaos.

Raina stepped out onto the terrace. Immediately, concern spread right through her, fanning across all her limbs.

Something was not right with the pharaoh. He did not notice her presence—or reverent curtsy—until she was within easy reach of him. Distracted and somber, his eyes didn't show much recognition of her. Of anything, really.

Should she delay the meeting at the hovel? Not knowing the true purpose of why they were engaging with the tomb robber made it difficult to form an enlightened judgment. What had happened for Merkhet to be so withdrawn?

The worry sat in her throat, unspoken. The rare occasions when Raina talked, it always surprised her just as much as it did the people in front of her. She had become so accustomed to clamping her mouth shut, that when she did have a chance to wonder what she might say, it was easier to say nothing at all.

The pain of the day when she vowed to be silent, all them years back, was no less vivid now than it was then. It crippled her, more than anyone realized.

Besides the strange quiet that enveloped him, Merkhet gave her no stronger indication that they should diverge from the plan. Raina began to suspect he was just coming to terms with the departure of his loyal friend and protector, or finally grieving for the loss of the village girl.

She edged closer to Merkhet. Her insistence to leave, and that it was time to do so, came when she swayed and leaned with a heavy bias for the chambers back inside. The pharaoh heeded her silent directive, following her through the throne room and beyond.

The royal chariot, complete with canopy and spacious seating, was waiting for them at the base of the palace grounds. Beside its golden gleam, an open chariot of inferior design. Accompanying the transport were four royal guards, all dressed in pristine red robes.

The escort was a parting gift organized by the Captain of the Royal Guard. He was probably approaching the island of Elephantine by now. Not that Raina had ever visited the island herself, but she had it on good account from various records that the locals there worshiped Khnum with the same vigor accorded to Amun in Thebes.

A tinge of envy stole through Raina. Taharva was embarking upon a grand adventure, and she was left ruminating in Thebes, conducting mysterious errands. Though she wasn't enamored by the prospect of successive stints on horseback, getting to know the captain better did hold some appeal. Enough to abate all her concerns of raw and cracked skin? Maybe. Such was his calming influence, everything around him happened so effortlessly.

Merkhet sidled past her into the rear of the golden chariot. The pharaoh's mare and another horse from the royal stables were tethered to the reins. Joining Merkhet, the chariots rolled forward under the constellations.

Despite her awareness of it, Raina couldn't help but fidget. The acting captain turned around to speak to them, and she couldn't be more thankful. Anything to distract her. Not knowing what the evening would hold for them made relaxation unachievable.

'We are almost there, Your Grace,' Inebni said.

She would not be surprised if Merkhet had not heard the new captain, but the horses suffered no such problem, shifting to a canter. When the chariots finally stopped, the guards jumped off the baseboard and restrained the gentle beasts.

Raina was about to leap from the chariot, but a hand held her back. She looked to Merkhet; graveness stretched deep into the furrow above his brow.

'I have an important duty for you,' the pharaoh said. 'A delicate matter.' He must have sensed that she was not in the talking mood because he continued. 'I need to know if there are any missing children around Thebes, particularly from the villages.'

She accepted her charge with a protracted blink, and Merkhet must have expected as much because he was already halfway out of the chariot. He held out his hand, and she accepted that too.

Unlike on the previous evening, her nerves vanished when she hit the ground. Raina strode with purpose to their destination, a drinking hovel situated among the mudbrick huts. She had no idea what any possible meeting might entail, but inside, she spotted the young man from the night before.

She had held up her end of the bargain and delivered a tomb robber to the pharaoh.

Merkhet was so deep in thought, he was barely aware of

assisting Raina out of the chariot.

How could he have predicted such an ambush? What a message to receive after all the trials they'd already endured under the gods' wrath …

But he could not afford to dwell on it right now, for Raina was powering her way towards the glowing and noisy hovel before them. Inebni and the other guards pressed around him, carrying him forward. His vizier disappeared through the entrance, and as soon as Merkhet followed her, it was obvious he had misjudged this situation.

Two dozen faces looked up from their beers, gaping at him. No doubt the crown on his head and the red wall of royal guard fortification behind him did little to put the patrons at ease.

Perhaps a more discreet arrival would have been favorable. Or even a different setting, for one man rushed to escape.

'Son of a scorpion's stinger,' Merkhet said, remembering the familiar face he had glimpsed near the Valley of Kings on his recent hunt. 'What's the matter, Snef? No time for an old friend?'

Snefrey hesitated as Raina reached for his arm to hold him still. The guards hemmed his lean figure inside and then forced him in front of the pharaoh.

Merkhet turned to Raina. 'Is this the man you arranged to meet?'

She nodded. If she was surprised that he was already well acquainted with the tomb robber standing before them, it could only pale against his own disbelief. What a difference a full cycle of the seasons could make. Once competitors and peers of near equal status, and now …

'Please, Snefrey,' Merkhet said, waving to a bench. 'Relax and have a seat. I just want some advice.'

With a dainty flick of her wrist, Raina signaled to the many curious faces in the hovel that they should carry on with their own conversations. Somehow that gesture even carried an air of scolding to it, informing the patrons that they were being rude by eavesdropping. Only she could convey so much in such a simple action.

With the Amulet of Ma'at proudly worn over her robe, not a single patron was unwise enough to ignore her. Having the weight of the Double Crown and four royal guards behind her didn't leave them with much choice in the matter.

Snefrey was the slowest to accept defeat, but he did, eventually. He headed back to a bench, which soon cleared for Merkhet and Raina to join him. The pharaoh and his vizier did just that. The guards loitered by the entrance.

The tomb robber—if that's what he even was now—did not look as calm and confident as he did during their formative years spent charioteering. Even though they were familiar with each other, Snefrey's discomfort was evident. The perspiration began just beneath his neat hair and streaked its way down through patchy clumps of black beard. A complete mismatch of grooming standards if the pharaoh had ever seen one.

Merkhet stiffened, though. This would not be as simple as jovially reminiscing over which charioteering duo was the superior. Why was Snefrey so nervous? What crimes had he committed …

Could this nobleman, turned robber, have been one of the treacherous thieves that breached Pharaoh Nekhet's tomb? It defied all expectation of decency that someone could interfere with the journey to the Afterlife in such a calculated manner.

Guilt swarmed around Merkhet. He, himself, was

not innocent. Far from it. He denied Peronikh the opportunity of eternal life, abandoning him at the frost-capped ravine at Aladaglar. Outside the borders of Egypt with no way for the gods to weigh his heart in the Hall of Two Truths.

The soldiers he had sent to the Anatolian lands would be there soon, but would they be able to return Peronikh to Egypt? Doubt seeped in around him, the deep regret swallowing him whole.

Justifications formed clear in his mind, but he wasn't sure that the gods would honor the differences. He had no more right to meddle in traditions than any priest, tomb robber, or commoner.

Then there was ignoring Llora's pleas to find her brother. After everything Tiaa revealed, Llora and Wuntu could even be his royal siblings. Irrespective of whether there was truth in those claims, could Merkhet return Wuntu to Tiaa? A polite nudge came from beside him. Raina.

'How can I help?' Snefrey asked, a look of bemusement on his face, which he buried behind a massive gulp of beer.

'I need your wisdom,' Merkhet said, 'and it would be very much in your interest to provide it.'

'How so?'

'My father's tomb was compromised—'

'Horrible stuff, that. Some people have no respect.'

Merkhet glared at him. 'Interrupt me again.'

The young man waited a moment. 'Sorry, Your Grace. What can I help you with?'

Merkhet dropped his voice to a whisper, even though the clamor of the hovel had renewed. 'I want my father's tomb relocated. His eternity in the Fields of Paradise deserves to be peaceful, undisturbed. I need to know everything about your trade to ensure that is so.'

'What kind of payment did you have in—' He must have seen the flash of rage across the pharaoh's face because he stopped talking at once.

'How you decide on which tomb to target. How you learn of the tomb's interior. Everything.'

Snefrey nodded. 'Your Grace, I can think of no man better suited to fulfilling your task. I would also like it put on the record,' he said, glancing at Raina as she scribbled notes, 'that I had nothing to do with the abhorrent acts committed in your father's tomb. I raid only the tombs of the wretched and greedy priests from the Fifth Dynasty, and those are hidden in the hills of Saqqara.'

'Care to explain your presence in the Valley of Kings, then?'

'So,' the tomb robber said, 'you did see me.' He swirled his beer around in its mug. 'Sometimes, the soldiers posted there become a little too complacent, so I go over there to make sure there aren't any indecent people lurking about.'

Merkhet couldn't help but smile at that, trying hard to ignore the strong sense of Ma'at's justice that had compelled him for most of his life.

'When can we get started?' Snefrey asked.

Raina tossed him an amber jewel, which he snatched from the air with viper-like reflexes.

'Cease all your current exploits,' Merkhet said.

'All of them? You can't be serious.'

Merkhet hesitated. Maybe this was a terrible idea. Their history would complicate matters to no end. 'Yes, you serve your pharaoh and country now.'

Chapter 9

Tendrence's reins bore the brunt of Taharva's senseless optimism. He gripped them as fiercely as he clung to the hope that his parents and sister were still alive. That, unlike him, their wrists were never branded by the pharaoh's mark.

Though he had not been this far south in about five harvests, the slow and subtle shift from desert to dust plain was unmistakable. The Nubian border was nearby, and so were the memories of his former life. All the cherished moments spent in his village and exploring the plains with his family.

Soon dominating his thoughts—as always—the agonizing uncertainty of the day Taharva became a slave. Were his heroics in challenging and besting Pharaoh Nekhet enough? Had his eventual enslavement ensured his family's escape and survival? Until the viceroy's letter arrived, no opportunity had ever presented itself for him to find out.

He urged Tendrence to gallop faster along the winding trail south. They stopped only for quick respites from the heat and the occasional meal. The Nile's many fishing villages were generous, providing them with adequate succor and making certain that their pace was not encumbered by an over-abundance of supplies. All they required was a full water skin and some grains so that Tendrence could graze between villages.

The breaks were more for the steed than himself and never lasted long. They tended to ride through the night, spurred on by grit and a near lifetime of unabated concern. The possibility of wrapping his mother and father in a hug, of ruffling Ebara's head. Just imagining his sister's exaggerated protests and all the moments stolen from them was enough to sour his mood.

On the eastern bank of the Nile, the desert was no longer visible. Great sandstone cliffs climbed around him and Tendrence, wedging them between those and the river. The morning sun was yet to reach full strength and exact all their energy.

Soon they would arrive at Abu Simbel—the gateway into Nubia—and where the viceroy had requested that Taharva present himself. He could not know whether he would be successful in reconnecting with his family after such a passage of time, but the mere promise of their existence kept him surging toward the outpost at the border.

If anything were to happen to Merkhet in the captain's absence, Taharva wasn't sure he would be able to forgive himself. He needed to locate his family quick. So, when a pair of massive stone statues came into view, satisfaction swept through him.

Patting Tendrence, the captain gently tugged on the reins. The steed was happy to obey, easing to a canter as they approached the imposing figures of Pharaoh Turkhet. Where were the military units? Taharva could not see anyone in the immediate vicinity. If they weren't here, how could they nullify the advance of a bold Nubian chieftain into Egyptian territory?

Standing under the shadows of Merkhet's grandfather, it was eerily quiet. A mountain of regret, almost as big as the ones in central Nubia, rose inside him. Where was the viceroy? How could Taharva discover the whereabouts of his family if the border official never came back?

This was a terrible mistake. He should never have left Thebes. Yet he couldn't even consider turning around. Not now.

Taharva consulted the map he was given. A prominent gold mine lay to the south-east, maybe a half day's ride. Perhaps, he could get answers there because the mystery of the abandoned border only added to his determination. After all these seasons, the call of a possible reunion was just too compelling for him to ignore.

The captain wasn't certain he could believe the viceroy's letter. Nothing would satisfy his lingering doubt except holding his family and breaking honey bread with them.

His sweet sister, Ebara, must have a husband and several children by now. Could it even be possible that his father and mother were still alive? They were struggling to move even at the time when the Egyptians terrorized their remote village.

Apparently, Tendrence agreed that the mine was their best chance because the horse started back up at a tenacious trot. Not even the sun at its harshest could deter the steed, but they didn't get far.

A group of men, all on horseback, were galloping at them. As Taharva gripped his spear, the leather almost worn right through to the metal shaft, he could only hope that it was the viceroy and the soldiers under his command.

'Captain,' the man at the center of them said, his voice full of energy. 'It is good to see you. A little later than we expected, but a delight all the same. We have much to discuss.'

The soldiers thumped their swords against their shields in unison, a greeting of respect.

Taharva acknowledged their reverence with a curt nod. 'I'm ready to talk, Viceroy.'

Taharva didn't say much as the relief of dismounting Tendrence set in. While waiting for the Guardian of the South to take charge and deliver news of his family, the captain's thoughts turned to them. After all these years separated, what would they think? Would they be open to joining him in Egypt?

'You must excuse our leave of absence at the border,' the viceroy said. 'We were required elsewhere for a short while.'

Taharva sensed the man was expecting him to seek explanation, but there was only thing the Nubian was curious about. His family.

'Please tell, Pharaoh's Heb-Sed, was it a joyous affair?'

'The rejuvenation festival?' Taharva asked him.

'Yes, the Heb-Sed.'

Taharva brushed away a swarm of flies that were congregating on his barren scalp. 'Joyous enough. What word do you have for me?'

'Your family, of course. They are nestled in a village far to the south.'

'*They?*' Taharva pressed him. 'Figured my parents were long gone, but Ebara?'

The viceroy shrugged. 'The message we received came on your sister's behalf. That is all I know.'

'How far to the village?'

'Hard to say,' the man said, 'but it would be best if you head on your way soon. The jungle can be dense and maddening after the rainy season.'

'A bit of jungle growth will never stop me from reaching my family,' Taharva said, his mind and heart racing. 'Are they expecting me?'

'Chieftain Chaka is, yes.'

Was the man perspiring, or was Taharva just in dire need of a rest?

An undisturbed sleep would be most welcome, and Tendrence would offer little resistance to the idea. Despite being left behind in Thebes, the captain's luxurious reed mat taunted him. The way it comforted his skin, sheltering him from the demands of his duties.

Taharva blinked once, then again. Somehow, Nubia was even hotter than he remembered, and he was struggling to focus.

'You look like you could use a nap, Captain. How about we escort you to our outpost and you can head off once you've recovered a little?'

Taharva didn't object. Rest appealed greatly to him. The emotional torture of chasing after his family was more draining than the physical nature of it.

The viceroy held open his arm in welcome. 'Come

now. We'll mark your map and prepare some supplies for you.'

Unable to argue with the generous offer, Taharva allowed himself to be led by the soldiers, back to the outpost that he and Tendrence had just come from.

The sun's afternoon gleam illuminated the dwellings. They were not made of mudbricks, as they were in the Theban villages. Set just away from the statues of Pharaoh Turkhet, the rock caverns were not visible from the main thoroughfare. Much like the tombs of the royals, these caverns must have taken an age to carve. Painstaking—more work than what could be carried out across a single pharaohship.

Taharva tied Tendrence to a tree, where other horses were likewise restrained, then he followed the viceroy into one of the shallow caverns. Inside, a mat was rolled out, ready for him to sleep on it.

'Please,' the viceroy said, gesturing at the mat. 'You are our guest now.'

Taharva nodded and laid down, welcoming rest for his aching muscles and mind.

'Just one thing before you drift off.'

Taharva looked up at the Guardian of the South, a weary irritation soon to overcome his manners.

'Your map, please. We will mark the location of the tribe for you.'

Hesitating a moment, Taharva's fingers wrapped around the bound scroll. He did not want to part with a gift from Merkhet, even less so, given that Raina sketched it herself.

It was his physical connection to his friends, as much as his guide to the world. The course of the rivers. The extent of the deserts and seas. The locations of villages and settlements.

The viceroy insisted, holding his hand out to receive the map.

Taharva gave it to him. 'Thank you,' he said, then lowered his head to sleep.

The cavern was dark, cool without being cold, but rest did not come. Guilt reared. Sighing, he stared into the dimness.

Inebni was more than capable of maintaining the peace. If Taharva hoped to reconnect with his family, he had to trust in that. He just needed to be hasty about it because a personal endeavor should never be undertaken at the expense of his critical duties, whether it came with the pharaoh's blessing or not.

After a time, the quiet of his surrounds passed through his mind, and he was able to get some sleep.

Later, sunlight beamed into the cavern, and Taharva tried to shield his eyes. But it was no good. The light was too bright, too invasive. It had to be early. His eyelids drooped with heaviness. Had he rested at all?

The viceroy approached him, the rolled up and bound scroll wedged underneath his arm pit. He stood at the lip of the cavern, waiting for Taharva, who rose and ambled out to meet him.

The map was held up, and the captain was thrilled to relieve the viceroy of it. With the knowledge of his family's whereabouts, Taharva could finally get on with what he left Egypt for.

'Thank you for your assistance. It comes with great appreciation from myself and Pharaoh Merkhet.'

The viceroy bowed in reverence. 'Honor is all mine. We don't get many visitors down here, but they are always welcome.'

Taharva nodded. 'I'll be on my way.'

'Safe travels, Captain.' The Guardian of the South

left, a host of soldiers following him. They rounded up their horses, and once atop them, trotted beyond the outpost's perimeter.

Taharva went about preparing his belongings for the next part of his own journey. He would check in with Tendrence and study the map.

Tethered to a nearby tree, the stallion jostled about within a restricted range. He was no doubt thankful for the break from the rapid pace his human companion had set, but Tendrence definitely carried an air of impatience, maybe even one of boredom. It was time to leave.

The steed enjoyed his greeting of pats and a cuddle. While the horse nestled against him, Taharva unfurled the map. His jaw stretched open and stayed that way.

It couldn't be that far …

The viceroy had marked the map for the location of his family—a place called Nurita—and it just so happened to be in the very southern reaches of Nubian jungle.

His home country was vast. Boundless plains were just the beginning. A journey of that distance could take weeks if the terrain proved unkind or unfavorable, and that was without considering what would happen if he were to lose his way in the misery of the verdant jungle.

He would need to check the accuracy with the viceroy at once. Taharva looked around, but the man and all his subordinates were already out of sight.

Should the captain track them down for confirmation, or wait here for their return?

Or should he just forge ahead? A wild chase would only cost him valuable time.

Tendrence nudged him again, and Taharva mounted his companion. Nurita awaited them.

Chapter 10

How could the Amun Priesthood's wickedness be overcome? Merkhet retreated within himself, pondering how he would deal with their ever-present threat, as he oversaw his daily duties. Four days of Judgments passed by in a blur. All trivial matters when stacked against what Egypt now faced, and still a sound solution had not materialized.

The scroll was exactly where he left it, prior to the meeting with Snefrey. On the stone floor beside the throne, taunting him. Merkhet had not even summoned the courage to read the rest of the papyri. From the briefest of glances, they were Llora's personal scrawls, and they remained on the war table, untouched.

How long before Tiaa came back to demand action from him?

A wounded mother would not just abandon the memory of her children without resolution. Never in a million inundations could she just let it go, and he respected that, but what could he do or say to set a grieving woman at ease?

Starting with an apology wouldn't lead him astray. Tiaa never doubted that her daughter was murdered. The pharaoh—the god living among his people—had.

Frustratingly, Taharva was probably just out of the country, and from almost the moment he left, Merkhet needed his wisdom more than ever.

His mother and Lufu, whom he also often conferred with, were far north in the delta regions, overseeing important matters.

Raina entered the throne room. *What's that scroll?* her quizzical brows demanded of him.

Her nose wrinkled when he didn't speak. *Today would be nice. You may be pharaoh, but don't you dare waste my time. No one is entitled to that.*

Was he seeing things? Maybe, he mused. Otherwise, Raina was finally comfortable enough in his presence to grant him some access to her inner thoughts and feelings. 'This, here,' Merkhet said, holding it up for her, 'is your next duty.'

I'm listening, she seemed to say, her hazel hawk-like eyes pressuring him to get on with it.

Somehow—and without an exchange of words—they were able to communicate. Merkhet couldn't explain what had changed, but by the glorious graces of Horus, he found himself able to interpret her expressions now.

Merkhet dropped his gaze back to the scroll and struggled through it one last time.

Dismantle the pharaohship before the commencement of the Opet. Fail to heed this directive at your own peril, for the Hidden One is rising. He is as impatient as his reach is powerful—the peasant girl knows the truth of it.

His time has come. Egypt is ready to soak in his glory.

Its text was every bit infuriating as the last dozen reads. A looming threat with no clear consequence. The Opet could not be far away now. This could be ignored no longer.

Merkhet handed the scroll to Raina, and within three flickers of the brazier, her free hand clamped over her mouth. Was she shocked by the treachery of the demand, or did she do so to prevent herself from speaking?

The vizier looked up at him. Her body was still, but her face rippled like waves, an endless sea of emotion. *What do we do? We can't let this stand.*

'Why do you think I was so distracted before our meeting with Snefrey the other night? I'm torn on what to do. The priesthood has always been difficult and greedy, but never so …'

At once, she turned to support him. *We will figure this out. They cannot get away with this. They will not get away with this.*

Even though challenging times lay ahead, Merkhet's shoulders loosened a touch. The stubborn knot in his stomach eased too. Just another testament to his decision to raise Raina from scribe to vizier. She was motivated by little else than the wellbeing of Egypt. If there was anyone he could trust in the absence of all others, it was someone acting as a selfless custodian for the Amulet of Ma'at.

Yet discord still lingered in his mind. Peronikh and Llora were once trustworthy, too. Until they weren't.

Would this relationship end in the same way? Was this the natural course of life—as envisioned by the gods—you bring people in, so even when they aren't around anymore, they can tear you down?

Merkhet didn't want to believe that as he studied Raina's face. Nothing alarmed him. Her features were gentle, radiating with care and compassion.

'I need more time to deliberate. Keep this to yourself for now. Find out what is happening with the Opet preparations.'

She nodded, and there was nothing to be gleaned from her neutral expression.

'Oh,' he added before Raina could leave. 'What has the investigation into missing children yielded?'

She reached into her robe, pulling out a tightly bound length of papyrus. Unraveled, it could very well stretch to the Nile's delta, or so he suspected. Carefully rolling it out, the vizier tore off a small portion from the top.

Raina scrawled across the scroll, then gave it to him. The contents were staggering.

Eleven children missing, having disappeared at various stages in the time since he inherited the throne.

'Thank you,' Merkhet said, and Raina took her leave.

As many as eleven families ripped asunder, now hollow and incomplete. Could he blame the priesthood for that, too?

Merkhet dispelled those thoughts as he heard Haliya rustling about in the adjacent chambers. Could a couple of lazy hours replenish him with enough energy to stride through the temple district and resolve the problem of the Amun Priesthood?

The pharaoh stepped through to his chambers. He dragged the heavy veil behind him, closing off the rest of the palace. It certainly couldn't hurt.

Merkhet left his chambers, a calming aura accompanying him, though the clarity he sought still evaded him.

He waited for Raina in the throne room. Her report on the state of the Opet would be of great insight. Merkhet could use it to plot their course away from tragedy.

One thing he did know: the Feast of Opet was well overdue. Usually, the initiates would parade around the market alleys, chanting of its arrival. They even ventured as far as one hundred miles up and down the Nile to deliver the news to the abundance of fishing villages. Not this year. Not so much as a single whisper of its preparations.

Always held in celebration of the life-giving floods, Merkhet wasn't sure why the Amun Priesthood had not begun the Opet's festivities. In the calamity of the weak inundation early in his reign, the festival was overlooked, but now in a period of stability …

If the priesthood could not perform their duties, Raina would. But that wouldn't help Merkhet with their biggest problem—how would he bring the High Priest to order? He couldn't just relinquish his pharaohship to satisfy the delusions of such a wretched and immoral man, no matter what he threatened.

If Merkhet could uncover what the priesthood were planning, all the uncertainty would disappear, and he would have sufficient recourse to recall the army from their northern construction project.

As it stood, the pharaoh needed to exhibit patience like never before. Rashness would not serve, not when it was so critical that the country was rebuilt and that the citizens had faith in his rule.

Raina returned.

'The feast,' Merkhet said, standing to greet her. 'When will it start? What plans have been made?'

The vizier whipped out fresh papyrus and started scrawling. The reed pen seldom left her hand.

A message too difficult to convey through expressions, perhaps. Or maybe she hadn't enjoyed their new means of communication, and Merkhet couldn't blame her if that was the truth. In a strange way, it was like he had been speaking directly with her ka, and her soul was kind enough to lay out her thoughts bare.

Raina scratched away, pausing on a few occasions. Usually, the words flowed out of her in one big smooth motion, where her hand was the current of the Nile at the height of the inundation, ceaseless and mesmeric.

'What is it?' he asked her.

She regarded him thoughtfully, adding a few more strokes to her small length of scroll. When she handed it to him, she shrank away and gave him a chance to read it.

The message was not nearly as detailed or complex as Merkhet was expecting.

The Temple of Amun is empty. Feast of Opet preparations have yet to commence.

Her delay in crafting the words must have stemmed from her disappointment and worry. He could see that on her face now. Profound creases of concern streaked from the corners of her eyes as she pondered their best course of action.

'You went to Luxor, and all the way through to

Karnak?'

Raina nodded.

'Just now?'

The dread, etched deep in the graveness of her expression, confirmed as much.

'We go again in the morning,' Merkhet said. 'Organize the royal guards for our escort. Inform Snefrey that our meeting will need to be adjourned. We have more urgent affairs to address.'

Merkhet was relieved to treat himself to a full night's rest, but rather than calming him, the linen sheets were suffocating.

He did not doubt Raina's report, and despite being accompanied by verification from at least six royal guards, something inexplicable compelled him to see the temple district for himself. Bearing witness to the treachery might stir him to action. Restore his wits. Something, he hoped.

It was one thing for the priesthood to make obscene demands and take the life of an innocent woman—their unfounded greed was nothing new—but another entirely for them to abandon their crucial civic duties.

They had already protested outside the Temple of Aten during Merkhet's short reign. Was this latest act more of the same, or the start of something much worse?

Passing from his chambers into the throne room, a twinkle caught his gaze. A shiny curved sword and wooden shield, embossed with the Eye of Horus. A note from Lufu accompanied them—Horakhty was in safe hands, those of the master craftsman that first breathed life into the bow.

Merkhet collected the Khopesh-style sword and accompanying shield, striding through the palace. He held no intention of naming either of them, wishing Horakhty would be back with him soon.

The chariot gleamed as it waited for him. It was early, the sun not yet halfway to its peak. The horses were tethered, the guards with a firm grip on the reins. Merkhet clambered into the back, and Raina fell in beside him.

Abacca rolled her head to the side, whinnying. The gentle sound reverberated off the dunes around them as they started to move. On the outskirts of the markets, Merkhet swelled with pride. Hundreds of people were there, bartering and making trades with a frenzy not witnessed since the immediate days after his father had died. Merkhet would never forget the citizens' contributions—gathering incense and performing offerings for the gods—to aid Nekhet's journey to the Afterlife.

The temples of Luxor loomed large. Inside the walls of the complex, Merkhet was disbelieving of how quiet the district was. It had none of its characteristic bustle. Did the issues extend far beyond that of the Amun Priesthood?

Maybe not. A smattering of priests still wandered about the district. They paused at reliefs of Mut and Khonsu, offering prayers and gifts, but there was a definite lack of enthusiasm in their conduct.

The chariot steered its way onto the Avenue of the Sphinxes, towards Karnak and the Temple of Amun. A short journey when compared with the walk. Raina wriggled beside him in anticipation of their arrival, eager to hop out and explore the temples. Her desire would soon be met, as they were greeted by massive statues of Pharaoh Turkhet, either side of a gateway.

As he studied his grandfather's smooth features, Merkhet wished he could speak with him, tell him of his plans to unite Egypt with their foreign neighbors.

Abacca and her equine companion dragged them into Karnak, where they were hemmed in by the prayers and stories that lined the hieroglyphic stone walls.

Merkhet shuddered, dread rising. Not a soul in sight, and an eerie silence, save for the shuffling of hooves. He jumped down from the chariot and paced towards the Temple of Amun. Raina followed him, not half a step behind, with the guards in tow behind her.

None of them could keep up as he brandished his new set of weapons in front of him. The sword and shield already felt comfortable in his grasp.

The shadowy entrance, a long hallway, led to many prayer chambers, and eventually, the inner sanctum.

No candles were lit. The darkness swallowed him whole as he started down the hallway. Voices echoed from deeper inside. Merkhet slowed his approach, desperately trying to listen to the low murmurs.

He couldn't make sense of the words, but there were two males. The pharaoh was certain of that. Part of him wished it would be the High Priest, so that everything could be settled with the Khopesh sword in his hand.

Merkhet wanted to crawl into a sarcophagus forever contemplating that Llora could have harmed herself. He was an utter fool. She was murdered. The letter found in her dress made no effort to conceal that fact. Whether she was his sister was irrelevant. The Amun Priesthood could expect the pharaoh's vengeance.

Beyond several more chambers and annexes,

Merkhet entered the inner sanctum. A faint light came from within, but it was not lit by any priest.

Snefrey and Akuteb—a pair of his royal class companions—stopped mid-stride when they saw their pharaoh.

Chapter 11

Nails dug deep into soft palm as Merkhet clenched his fists tight around the hilt of his Khopesh sword. He was such a fool to trust the likes of a tomb robber, even if they did share some history.

'Your Grace,' Snefrey mumbled, a couple of ornaments slipping from the bag slung over his shoulder as he bowed down. The ceramic shattered as soon as it struck the ground, shards scattering everywhere.

Akuteb did not move at all. So strong was the paralysis binding him, he didn't even blink. Nor did the torch brazier tremble in his hands, its steady flicker cast a faint glow across the inner sanctum.

Merkhet swiveled to meet the faint slither of metal. The royal guards shuffled in behind him, drawing their weapons as he relaxed his own. Snefrey, still at the base of his stoop, made a clumsy effort to pick up the biggest pottery shard in front of him.

'Don't,' Merkhet growled at him. 'Didn't I make

myself clear?'

'You did, Your Grace. This rare opportunity got the better of me,' the tomb robber said, disappointment ripe in his voice.

Whether it was feigned, Merkhet could not tell. Either way, he found he didn't much care as the sudden rage subsided and an unusual rebellious streak took hold of him.

The Amun Priesthood deserved worse than smashed ornaments. The High Priest and his army of initiates were placing the very essence of Egypt at risk again, so soon after ...

The balance of order was delicate. Ma'at had to prevail, above all else, and as pharaoh, he was critical to ensuring that could happen. 'No more. We have work to do,' Merkhet said.

Without even being asked, Snefrey placed his spoils on the altar behind him. Akuteb followed his companion's lead, knowing there was no way to appease the pharaoh and keep the goods. Raina, perhaps curious as to what the young men valued, approached the altar. When had she slipped in?

'What now, Your Grace?' Snefrey asked in what was most definitely forced deference.

Merkhet studied the tomb robbers. Could he extend his faith after this violation? Maybe it was a trick of the feeble light, but they appeared contrite with a slight downward curl to their bottom lips. 'As discussed, we scout.'

Both Akuteb and Snefrey nodded, proving that they could conduct themselves in an appropriate manner when it suited them. Beyond the tomb robbers, Raina sifted through the reclaimed spoils.

Merkhet directed his voice to her. 'In the

priesthood's absence, you will prepare the Feast of Opet. After what happened last year, it cannot be delayed a moment longer.' The vizier showed no recognition of his command. 'Gods to Raina. Will you be able to manage that?'

She snapped to the present, but it was obvious by her blank stare that she had not heard him. Now that he was pharaoh, Merkhet would repeat himself for few people. She was one of them.

'The Feast of Opet. It must go ahead.'

Raina nodded, departing the inner sanctum straight away.

'Where to now, then, Scrollworm?' Snefrey asked.

'You'll know better than I. Let's discuss it from the comfort of the chariot. This place creeps me out. And don't think, even on Ra's dullest day, that you can get away with calling me that.'

The tomb robbers delivered a peculiar salute, where they clasped their hands together and raised them to their chests. Merkhet had never seen such a gesture before but didn't sense any malice or condescension in it.

He allowed it to pass, then the guards led the way out of the dank den of Amun.

Raina couldn't recall much of the exchange between Merkhet and his tomb robber acquaintances. Wherever she was as he scolded them, it wasn't within the dreariness of Amun's inner sanctum.

How was Taharva faring? Had he tracked down his family yet? Maybe. If the gods were kind, he could even be on his way back to Thebes. Raina relished the prospect of calling upon the formidable Nubian to assist with royal business again. He commanded the unfortunate situation in the drinking hovel when her own flaws had threatened to expose her. He may even have enjoyed himself. She had.

After finally hearing what Merkhet was saying, Raina heeded his directive. She left him, the royal guards, and the thieves behind, though the audacity of those scoundrels followed her. For a brief moment she considered the pharaoh's safety, but Snefrey and Akuteb were unarmed. Aside from the four guards accompanying Merkhet, he carried his new sword with him.

Outside the temple, Raina derived great satisfaction from pounding her feet along the Avenue of Sphinxes. The simplicity of putting one foot in front of the other gave her clarity. It reminded her of what must be done and what was at stake.

Thebans expected order and routine, and the annual Feast of Opet was no exception. After the harrowing events of losing their way with the gods, a timely celebration was the least citizens deserved.

Oh, how they'd all suffered when Ma'at fell out of alignment. Hapi delayed the inundation, and then when it did arrive, the annual flood was one of the feeblest ever recorded. But the other gods were not to be outdone. Set released sandstorms and plagues upon the city, Geb rumbled beneath the desert, and Ra's refusal to shine.

Thebes had endured so much chaos, so much hurt. The temples were spared the worst of it, though, the gods careful not to desecrate their own dedications.

Raina needed to find some priests to aid in the procession. She would search whatever temples she had to and enlist whatever help she could find in the absence of the Amun Priesthood. How typical of their greed that they abandon one of their most critical duties.

The royal chariot and its accompaniment overtook her before she made it back to Luxor. Unlike earlier when passing through, the priests of Mut and Khonsu were there and almost fervent in the manner they conducted themselves. Scurrying every which way, they paid no heed to her or the silver Ma'at feather around her neck.

Busy in preparation. But for what, and how could she rally them to her cause unless she could speak to them?

She waved at a nearby priest and flicked stray curls off her shoulders. Nothing. The man was so intent upon the incense that he carried, that short of barreling him over, she wasn't sure how she could get his attention.

Thankfully, Raina was saved from any further acts of embarrassment. The initiate stopped to ruffle his robes, a crescent moon stitched across his chest, and just started talking to her. She was not going to protest the change in fortunes.

'Preparations,' the man said.

Raina pressed her stern gaze upon him.

Whether he noticed her amulet or not, he accepted that as a command and offered more. 'Opet is to begin next week. High Priest's orders.'

How interesting—the enigmatic priest was still overseeing matters despite not being visible.

She bowed before the initiate, thankful for his assistance. He scampered off, seemingly happy for the painless dismissal, so that he could fulfill his duty of shifting the incense.

From past celebrations, Raina suspected that bundles of scents would be set beneath each of the sphinx statues. Great clouds of the near-invisible perfume would hover over the avenue as the festivities took place between Luxor and Karnak.

Raina rushed back the way of the palace. Merkhet would be thrilled to hear of this development.

Merkhet was growing accustomed to the movements of his new vizier. Raina appeared—and disappeared—as the role demanded.

She was rising to the arduous task with aplomb. He expected no less.

The grin she arrived with told him she came bearing good tidings, but he almost fell off the throne when she spoke to him … aloud.

Not a passing word, actual direct speech, and without hesitation. 'The Opet preparations are progressing,' she said. 'The festivities can begin next week.'

The intrigue of what had just happened was too much. Raina could speak perfectly well!

He had long wondered if some impediment deterred her, but it could not be. Her words were crisp and melodic. An expert intonation and pronunciation for someone who did not partake in the practice often. Well, seldom, that he had knowledge of, which led him to settle on a matter of confidence.

Eager not to draw attention to their verbal

communication, he responded in kind. 'Excellent. What has sparked this?'

'Did you not see the hustling and bustling of priests on your ...' she said, then trailed off. Raina shut her mouth, then clamped both hands over it. Her eyes screamed at him, like she had offended the gods with some wicked slur.

'Raina, please, take away your hands. This has been a most pleasant surprise. Whatever ails you, I'm certain it is not as bad as what you have convinced yourself.'

She did not accept his invitation to speak again, nor did Merkhet insist. 'The Opet celebration is an important milestone in our recovery,' he said. 'Given all we have suffered throughout my pharaohship, it cannot be delayed further.'

The vizier nodded, still wide-eyed, and still refusing to reveal her mouth.

'What of the High Priest?' he asked, more as a wish than anything else, already knowing the answer.

Raina shook her head. Once.

'The scheming murderer will surface, and we will apprehend him as soon as he does. While we wait, the rebuild has to continue and the investigation into the missing children must proceed.'

Merkhet dismissed her, unwilling to linger on the rare occurrence of her talking. It wasn't until she was two steps out of the throne room that she lowered her hands. By that point, he could no longer see her face to have any clue about what she was thinking.

His vizier chose not to speak when she was more than capable—a bemusing curiosity. Hopefully, as their partnership blossomed, her confidence would grow and more direct interactions could occur.

Yawning, Merkhet drew back the veil to the inner

chambers and was greeted by a pair of enchanting eyes. Haliya was waiting for him. What was the Hittite queen to him? He wasn't sure. Given time, she would become his Great Royal Wife. That was already decided as a matter for after the Opet, but before the pharaoh could indulge in personal celebrations, a few matters required his attention.

Bringing the Amun Priesthood to order. Locating a safe place for the construction of his father's mortuary temple. Ensuring his mother and Lufu had everything they needed to complete Egypt's northern fortification.

Haliya clicked her tongue, and Merkhet was lured back to her eyes. *Don't you dare ignore me,* they said. *You've strayed too long.*

Chapter 12

The early morning rays were gentle and forgiving. Abacca whinnied as Merkhet flung himself atop her. Rarely would he descend the palace dune without pausing to indulge in a sweet tea, but the fear of Snefrey barging through the palace at full voice was too distressing to risk.

Besides, this important task required immediate action and subtlety. As Merkhet had passed through the throne room, he slid into a pair of tattered black linens, pinned his burgeoning ponytail at the base of his neck, and declined to collect the crown from where it lay on the war table. No one would recognize him unless they were familiar with Abacca, and thankfully, a brown-furred mare would seldom attract as much as a second glance.

Snefrey was already astride another horse, courtesy of the royal stable. Looking into the steed's bulbous eyes, Merkhet was stung with longing. Before he was pharaoh—when his life was simple—he would always spend his leisure time at the stables.

He missed his escapes there, always between classes and never for long enough. The horses were thankful for the company just as much as Merkhet was of theirs. People were exhausting in ways that animals weren't. Especially when everyone held such lofty expectations of you. Expectations, even now, he was struggling to fulfill.

'Osiris lands a sloppy kiss on the pharaoh's cheek,' Snefrey said, waving his arms all over the place. 'I can see you, but are you *here*?'

Merkhet smiled wanly at him. 'I'm here. Where are you taking me first?'

'You'll just have to wait and see, Your Grace,' the tomb robber said, scampering ahead on his steed.

Merkhet spurred Abacca on, following his old charioteering friend out of the city walls and into the desert expanse.

'What happened to Ak?' he asked the tomb robber, not wanting a single moment of silence. A free and empty mind would soon be burdened by Egypt's enduring threats. 'He could have joined us, you know, just like old times.'

'He was mortally embarrassed after you sprung us in the inner chamber. In our defense—'

'Say no more,' the pharaoh said. 'All I ask is that you give your all to this task and ...'

'And?' Snefrey pressed him.

'You do not defile our resting kings and queens.'

'How about greedy priests?'

Merkhet chuckled, his belly aching from the unexpected laughter. 'Resting—or alive—your pharaoh does not need to know.'

'Miss our classes sometimes,' Snefrey said, a touch of sadness overcoming his bravado.

'Compared to what I deal with each day now? Bring

on the chariot races, the hunts, and the freedom.'

The tomb robber quieted for a moment, then a devious grin spread across his face. 'Your tenderness for sentiment is astonishing. Did you learn it from all the readings you devoured, Scrollworm?' he asked, mocking.

Merkhet huffed, tugging hard on the reins. He urged Abacca forward, away from their unfortunate present company.

Whirling around to take in his surroundings, it was obvious why Snefrey had brought him to this location. The desert valley, some seven or eight miles north of Thebes, was completely encased by high-forming dunes, which formed a near perfect circle about the flat plain they now stood.

Unless someone stood at the very rim of the dunes, they would not know of the valley that lay below them. The landscape was a natural protection, which could be supplemented by armed forces. But …

'Too close to the path the traders take,' Merkhet said, after deliberating for some time.

'They would never see it, would never even know it was here.'

'You knew it was here,' the pharaoh said, before hopping off his mare.

He kicked at the sand, a bunch of it sticking between his foot and sandal. Removing the footwear, to shake it out and wipe the bottom of his foot, he said, 'Sand does not make for a great construction base. It's why most temples and huts are built within sight of the Nile. Not so close that they are subject to the flood season but close enough to use the hardened mud ground.'

'Maybe the builders need a new challenge.' Snefrey shrugged, then sighed a little as he accepted his first defeat. Having never dismounted, the tomb robber suddenly charged ahead on his steed.

Merkhet had to scramble back on Abacca and hurry her into a gallop, or risk losing sight of Snefrey as he dashed up the lip of the dune. The royal mare, his companion beyond many changes of seasons, did not let him down. She relished the chase and made quick work of it.

'Just my luck,' Snefrey said as the horses drew level. 'Thought I could lose you and head to my favorite hovel for an early beer.'

'Not that you could—' Merkhet started, his gaze dropping to his Khopesh sword, '—but do so at your own risk.'

The tomb robber laughed, rollicking back on the steed. 'You've at least changed a little, Merk. You were always so scared of your own shadow around Peron.'

Merkhet was the one to shrug this time. 'Maybe I was. The gods left me little choice but to emerge from boyhood.'

'Aye, s'pose that's true. That Raina's a bit different, isn't she?'

Surprised, the pharaoh gave Snefrey a sideways glance. 'Different is exactly what Egypt needs.'

'What, someone who doesn't talk?'

'More than you know, Snef. Besides, she's made significant progress already.'

'Progress?' the tomb robber asked.

'We had a conversation yesterday.'

'An actual discussion, with words? Did she have an alluring voice? You know the kind that makes you—'

'You're not her type, Snef. She appreciates a man with a full beard, so forget it.'

The tomb robber tried to protest, but Merkhet turned his back on him.

Abacca and the other horse, a stubborn gray beast, steadied their pace on the downslope of the dune. They were heading back the way of Thebes.

Merkhet did not know where the next potential site might be but began to relish the uncertainty. The pharaohship left him weary, even on the simplest of days, and sharing this moment with an old friend was the furthest thing from that strain.

'You are allowed to smile, you know. Your father won't think less of you.'

Snefrey was right, for once. Their search was in honor of the Great Pharaoh, and Merkhet couldn't settle on a single reason why he shouldn't enjoy the occasion. Even if just for a little while.

Chapter 13

Raina read the scroll again, as she did most nights before succumbing to her reed mat. Now, beneath the acacia tree in the palace courtyard, she was revisiting the message under the light of day.

This was her favorite spot to complete her administrative duties. Her disgraced predecessor, Prahmun, had always operated from the secrecy of the dank central administration building. After a couple of genuine efforts to establish herself there, she harbored no joy for the space, and couldn't do it.

Maybe the remnants of the gods' destruction were too distracting. Maybe it was the evil scheming that had taken place there.

Whatever the reason, it didn't matter. The courtyard's gentle breeze always invigorated her with the energy to surge through the piles of documents awaiting her attention. She also had the benefit of being close to Merkhet if she required his guidance.

Raina traced the words on the scroll as she read

them. Even though it wasn't the captain's handwriting, the mere connection to him comforted her.

How after one night together, performing a simple duty for their pharaoh, did she have such an affinity for the man? His face was gentle, yet his body rugged. His demeanor calm, voice commanding.

A pair of royal guards approached her. They came from within the palace, Inebni speaking first.

'Lady Justice, do you know where Pharaoh Merkhet is? We cannot find him anywhere. Even the Hittite queen does not know his whereabouts.'

Raina found the formality of the greeting strange. She didn't object to the title, shaking her head as a response to the query.

Merkhet had pleaded with her for a day free from the rigors of rule. Begrudgingly, she granted it to him, and he dashed at first light beyond the city walls.

'There has been a development in the temple district,' the other guard added.

She did not know this man's name but insisted he continue with an impatient wave. Raina also placed an empty water flagon on the pile of scrolls to keep a stray gust from taking them.

'The Feast of Opet has commenced,' he said.

Raina's jaw slid open. Already?! The preparations were barely gaining momentum on last check.

She needed to inform the pharaoh at once. But how? She didn't even know where that wretched tomb robber was taking him, just that Merkhet was armed. No harm would befall him.

Chariot, she mouthed, no noise escaping her. Time was precious, and they could not waste any. What if the Amun Priesthood intended to put their threat into effect? Neither her nor Merkhet could figure out what the High

Priest was planning, but she couldn't shake the sense that it was somehow connected to the missing children.

Eleven of them had vanished from Thebes over the preceding months and not a single soul could shine Ra's rays upon the mystery of their disappearance.

The guards rushed down the slope. Raina trailed them at a measured pace. The chariot was drawn in its usual position but only one horse was tethered to it. Abacca was with the pharaoh, so the guards sprinted around to the stables to fetch a replacement.

She waited, leaning on the palace gates as they readied the chariot. Where she would lead them, the vizier still did not know. Straight to the festivities, or should they locate Merkhet first?

Returning with a black mare, Inebni linked the majestic beast to the reins. Raina clambered into the back of the chariot as the royal guards climbed onto the baseboard at the front.

Hands on the reins and ready to depart, they turned around to her. 'Where are we going?'

The solution eluded her, and not from lack of effort in attempting to summon it. Panic seized her. She needed to think … needed to … keep it simple.

Roaming the desert in a desperate search for the pharaoh would not serve. The festivities were taking place in the temple district, and that was where Raina would place herself.

Questions flitted about her mind. What would she actually do if the High Priest was there and prepared for a confrontation? And where had the Amun Priesthood disappeared to—innocent explanation or nefarious schemes?

Merkhet was not shy in his bleak predictions of the latter. He did not trust the priests, and if the High Priest could not provide Raina with just cause to believe differently, then she would not either.

'Well?' the senior guard asked her, his tone insistent on an immediate response.

She pointed in the direction of the Nile.

'Luxor?'

Raina nodded, and the horses were stirred to motion. Their trotting was disjointed to begin with, no obvious rhythm to their stride. A new pairing, and quite possibly their first occasion leading the royal chariot together, so they were slow to strike an accord. Thankfully, it was a short journey, and the stuttering nature of it could only cause her limited distress.

Wafts of incense filled the air. Cinnamon, lavender, the faint scent of citrus and spices. They cloyed together and made it hard to breathe—or concentrate on the flutter of activity that spanned the length of the sphinx avenue.

Amun initiates, cloaked in their dark robes and wearing ram-horned headdresses to mark the occasion, roamed in clusters as they prepared gigantic statues for the Opet procession. The priests of all the other patron gods were dressed in white. Depending on the festival or celebration, sometimes the only way to differentiate the priesthoods was by the ornaments and jewelry they adorned.

At the start of the sphinxes, over a dozen statues of Amun were already lined up. An assortment of his various animal-headed depictions were included and more were being hoisted into position. The principal god of Thebes received disproportionate favor in comparison to his wife and son. Mut and Khonsu only boasted one statue each, and they were hidden way behind all those dedicated to Amun. It was clear that the High Priest did not care for the other patron deities of Thebes. To him, Amun was the supreme god and his only priority.

Looking beyond the sphinxes, Raina could see a tall mast rising from the Nile. The priests would often use the river as a vessel for celebration, but at this present juncture, it just appeared that they were transporting supplies to Karnak.

'What now, Lady Justice?' Inebni asked her.

Raina slid across the seat, disembarking the chariot. A hooded figure streaked towards her. She was about to scream, but then the hood was removed and Merkhet stood before her. Snefrey, just a few feet behind the pharaoh, joined them.

She eyed the tomb robber warily, but maybe it was time she gave him some credit. Alone with Merkhet all day, and they didn't have a scratch or blemish between them.

The pharaoh appeared giddy, almost jovial. 'Wasn't expecting this, Raina,' he said. 'Were you?'

She shook her head. Not even in the slightest. In the priesthood's absence, she had started planning to host the festival herself, but it was obvious now that she could abandon those notions.

'Scrollworm, I thought you told me she was speaking?'

Raina glared at the tomb robber first, then Merkhet. They both cowered a little under her furious gaze, and so they should. How dare they speak of her when she was not present to hear what was discussed.

Then calmness replaced her burst of anger. The pharaoh had every right to review her—his vizier. She hoped in future that it might be among more distinguished company, though.

Merkhet brushed aside her indignant stare. 'Curious,

isn't it?' he said, not speaking to anyone in particular. 'The priesthood disappears for however long. No one hears so much as a ritualistic blessing from them. No one knows their whereabouts or activities. Then, as if the Feast of Opet was never in danger and threats to the pharaohship were never made, they show up to take all the glory and praise.'

'How long does this feast go for anyway?' Snefrey asked.

Raina showed them two full hands, then put all her fingers away except for one.

'Eleven whole days?' he groaned, gesturing to the crowds gathering on the Nile's banks. 'Will be almost impossible to enjoy a peaceful drink with all these rural fishermen and their children stinking up Thebes.'

'Don't be so grim,' Merkhet said. 'Some pharaohs have been known to extend the festivities for as many as twenty-seven days after a vigorous inundation.'

'Please, no. You can't do it, Scrollworm. Please, I'll do anything. These priests and their festivities are the worst! Their fervent conduct creeps me out more than any mummy I've ever had the misfortune of looting.'

Raina couldn't disagree with the tomb robber. The way the priests were all covered up as they queued along the Avenue of Sphinxes irked her.

As soon as she realized her head was bobbing along to Snefrey's words, she stopped at once. The disgust in herself seemed to infect the strong incense around her, souring the scents. Lavender turned to rotting fish, cinnamon became pungent and unkempt man. Raina smothered her nose with a hand but that didn't offer her any reprieve.

'Which mummies would those be?' the pharaoh asked him.

'Best you don't know, Your Grace. The gods may never look upon you the same,' Snefrey said, a wry smile smeared across his smug face.

The jest was obvious, but Raina was not so sure that it was a lie. The annoying tomb robber may very well have breached the sarcophagi of past nobility. Just recently, Pharaoh Nekhet's journey to the Fields of Paradise had suffered unimaginable interruption.

As much as the Egyptians hoped their hearts were pure and serving the gods' wishes, there were people among them, those such as Snefrey, that had no such qualms in defying traditions. She was surprised that the response did not elicit a reaction from Merkhet.

Perhaps, the pharaoh had already made peace with what happened to his father's tomb. 'Let's retire to the palace,' he said. 'We have days of these festivities to attend. Raina, organize whatever remains of our military in Thebes and spare however many royal guards we can afford. Whenever the High Priest shows, we must have forces ready.'

Chapter 14

Perched on the Golden Throne, the grand swirl of prayers, offerings, and processions were a distant roar. The Thebans and their constant chorus of cheers were at complete contrast with the dread that sat heavy in Merkhet's core. As he waited for some sign of the High Priest to surface, he could barely manage more than a slither of bread each morning.

The citizens knew nothing of Merkhet's torment, and nor did he wish for them to carry the burden alongside him. They had earned a reprieve from their tireless service to country and deserved a chance to celebrate the Feast of Opet, which stretched between Luxor and Karnak.

Merkhet was drawn to the rest of the papyri Tiaa gave him. What horrible truths were awaiting him among those sheafs? He shifted uncomfortably, succumbing to the temptation. He needed to know what details they contained, no matter how tough they might be to read.

Standing over the war table, he laid them out. There were dozens of scrolls, the writing a little messy, especially when compared against Raina's immaculate strokes. Merkhet reached for the freshest papyrus. It was more than likely Llora's last ever recording.

He devoured the contents. Word by word, line by line. By the beauty and grace of Isis, what had transpired in his exile? Llora wandering through the abandoned ruins of Thebes as she nursed a blossoming womb. Scorched and toppled buildings. Piles of corpses down every alley. Unending darkness.

Merkhet understood the sweeping fury imposed by the gods and that the civilians' subsequent descent into madness was rapid, but never could he have imagined the true extent of what occurred in his absence ...

He kept reading. A confrontation with the High Priest when Llora was already pregnant. Why had she put herself in such a situation?

The writing was disjointed and sporadic. Her frantic mind drove his curiosity further. She mentioned the presence of Prahmun but then diverted to the sorrow she harbored for her brother. But what of Wuntu? Where was he?

Merkhet reached the end of the papyrus: *The High Priest refuses to honor his word. Wuntu will remain his captive.*

How could Merkhet have given such little credibility to Llora's desperate pleas to assist her brother? He was errant and incompetent, for allowing his own hurt to jeopardize his duty to country. Llora was acting in the best interests of her family, and Merkhet had condemned her for it. Now she was dead, all because of his poor handling of the Amun Priesthood.

But the High Priest could not elevate himself among

the gods and expect the pharaoh to just sit by and applaud. The sheer arrogance of the man, confessing to murder and not even bothering to remove any of the other scrolls incriminating him. Merkhet would not—could not—rest until he and the rest of the priesthood were brought to justice.

Sliding the papyrus away in disgust, the next was revealed. His eyes were drawn to a mention of Thekla. What concern was his father's legendary golden war hammer to Llora? Why had she—how had she—wielded it?

Rapt in silence, Merkhet recalled what Lufu had told him about the weapon's creation.

The strongest man in the world could not lift it by himself unless he had your grandfather's blood coursing through his veins.

What about a slender woman, could she command the weapon? Merkhet slammed his fist on the pile of scrolls. The truth had been right in front of him all along, and he ignored it.

Tiaa was right.

Llora was his sister.

Merkhet stood on the eastern bank of the Nile, quiet and brooding. One hand clutched the hilt of his Khopesh sword, ready to unsheathe it from his leather girdle.

'Are the soldiers briefed and in position?' he asked Raina, his voice scarce more than a murmur.

She delivered a swift nod beside him, a brief interruption to her incessant hand rubbing. Just outside the Luxor temples, their vantage was better than anyone else's, and it needed to be.

The military and royal guards were ready to storm the Temple of Amun as soon as the Opet concluded. Whether the High Priest made a personal appearance didn't matter anymore. The Amun priests were present, wearing their black robes, and they would know the full wrath of the pharaohship.

The vizier knew from the High Priest's letter that he had murdered Llora, but Merkhet had not divulged the latest revelation to her yet.

Llora was his sister.

Still trying to grapple with what that meant, one thing held true above all else. He needed to apologize to Tiaa for being such a stubborn fool.

The Opet, after all the doubt and uncertainty around its commencement, had proceeded in accordance with all the others he ever experienced. As memorable as any on record—surely in conjunction with the architectural restoration of capital and country—the Egyptians' courageous efforts were enough to repair their image in the eyes of the gods.

Whispers of a new addition to the celebrations spread along the Nile. Wagers were taking place between the citizens on what it would be. The large crowd expressed many possibilities for the mysterious final event, but the most common hunch that reached the pharaoh's ears: a re-enactment of the gods' creation.

Whatever it might be, Merkhet did not want to create a scene and stress the citizens, but if the High Priest appeared, all considerations for sheltering the innocent Thebans were precluded.

The sun was setting over the Valley of the Kings, and Merkhet was ready for the procession to begin. He shuffled from foot to foot, not quite able to stay still. Raina coped much the same beside him, her ceaseless swaying at complete odds with the hushed tones of the crowd.

A large square raft, at least thirty feet in length on each of its sides, floated on the river. It bobbed on the downstream currents but did not get swept away. Ropes of flax fettered it to the banks.

A fleet of simple galleys, carrying Amun initiates, drifted towards the main raft. Dozens and dozens of priests traded their cozy galleys for the much larger raft. They did not seem to carry anything with them as they clambered onto the raft's flat wooden beams, or if they did, it was hidden beneath their black robes.

The deserted galleys were swept away by the currents. Where were all these vessels when the military needed them to travel north? The priesthood had much to answer for. They would be held accountable.

The initiates formed rows, assembling themselves for some sort of performance. Merkhet counted forty priests in total, arranged in a perfect square around a central figure in a white robe. How many priests belonged within the ranks of the Amun Priesthood? Those before him had to be a purposeful allocation of them.

Was the High Priest among them? Was that him in the center, even though he had not been spotted since before the inundation?

Merkhet studied each face, yearning to see a glimpse of that withered and immoral man. So much frustration and uncertainty had developed in the High Priest's absence.

No ram horns were on display, but the hoods of the initiates' robes were drawn tight, restricting the view of their faces. Just then, they all bowed down on one knee.

The move, executed in unison, drew gasps from the crowd and gained their undivided attention. Merkhet found himself included in that, abandoning his hunt to identify the High Priest, settling in to enjoy whatever theatrics they would be treated to.

Raina was craning her neck so much that the pharaoh feared she might topple over into the river. He was about to tell her so when hundreds of children appeared.

On yet more galleys, two children were on each. The small vessel gathered around the outside of the large moored raft, and the children held off the river's urges with paddles. As the galleys filled the Nile, the crowd gave a raucous, continuous cheer for every one that floated into view.

The children weren't enjoying themselves as much as the spectators. Some held ornaments aloft, cobras, crocodiles, apes, rams, and geese—all representations of Amun. Others carried incense, but none of them bore smiles.

Merkhet couldn't contain his rising uneasiness any longer. 'Did you ... Did you know the children were involved?'

'No,' she croaked.

Fear and dread grew within him as the priest with a bowed head at the center stood tall. The man—if even that much were true—could be the High Priest. The height seemed about right. Yet, intriguingly, the characterizing leopard shawl was missing. Even more curious, smoke began to billow from within that central figure's robe. Merkhet could not see a flame, but a thick smog swelled all around them.

Once it also started rising from *within* the other initiates, a great gray cloud hung above the raft. The lead priest disappeared under it. As the smoke cloud continued to widen, the raft and the children were soon swallowed up by it too.

Drumming started up from a temple behind them, the smog gathering with the pace of the steady beat. Without a fire, Merkhet couldn't fathom what was causing the smoke, but was thankful for a strong gust that began to shift the enormous gray cloud downriver.

When the raft came back into view, the priest in the white robe had vanished and so had all the galleys. The rest of the initiates were still kneeling on the raft. The crowd gasped at first but then a rapturous applause took hold, reverberating off the distant cliffs.

Despite the initiates not rising, the citizens continued to clap. Merkhet gave a faint acknowledgment himself, far from whole-hearted. Where did the central priest go? What had happened?

The pharaoh had little chance to ponder before Raina nudged him. When he looked at her, she pointed back at the raft. Its restraints were cut, and now, the raft was drifting with pace. The priests lifted themselves up, swaying in a rehearsed sequence.

The crowd were clearly impressed by the performance because the pharaoh was on the move. He didn't have much choice, caught up in the throng of spectators, eager to follow the procession all the way to Karnak.

Merkhet wrestled his way free of the mob and withdrew his sword. The priest was no longer on the raft, and there wasn't even so much as a splash of the river.

'Did you see where the central priest went?' he asked Raina.

A brisk head shake. 'Nor the children.' she said.

Chapter 15

Standing at the edge of the grand jungle abyss, Taharva dangled one foot among the low green thicket, ready to find his family. The other—still entrenched in sand and dust—turned to face the screams.

Pursue his family or investigate the distress?

His hands were resting on Tendrence's back, hesitance triumphing all. The shrieks renewed, and at least a second voice joined the cacophony.

Taharva was raised better than to ignore a cry for help, especially at such a high pitch. He couldn't ignore people in need. Not now, not ever. What if their situation was dire?

He sprinted for the village, Tendrence dutifully trotting beside him. Taharva had seen it on their frantic gallop to the jungle, and in his eagerness to carry on, did not even consider stopping there. They could slurp water from the moist foliage and pick bugs from the bountiful trunks if they had to.

The huts were built alongside the fringe of the jungle, and Taharva was almost upon them. The screams—definitely multiple—scared a flock of birds as dark as midnight from inside the vast greenery. They took to the skies, beating their wings in protest and squawking in a feral contest with the people.

The captain dashed for the space between two huts, a firm grasp on the handle of his spear. Tendrence only just squeezed through the small gap, but he did, and then they were at the heart of the village ring.

A chieftain held a whip, and the threat of the coiled flax held three children in a jittering trepidation. They cowered at the feet of the man, wearing a crown of colored plumage. The rhythmic flick of his wrists promised them excruciating agony.

Crimson streams streaked across their limbs. Taharva couldn't fathom what crime any child could commit to deserve such a cruel punishment. He approached the chieftain with caution. The last thing he wanted was to end up in a fight with the man, who still hadn't become aware of the captain's presence.

The children spotted Taharva, and their sudden focus on him alerted the chieftain. He whirled around, cracking the whip on the sand.

Slowing his advance, the captain held up a bare palm. 'No need for that,' he said. 'No matter what has happened here, the whip can go away.'

The chieftain grunted and tightened his grip around the flax. He was not about to back down, not for some intruder in *his* village.

Taharva glanced over his shoulder. The jungle was just there. It wasn't too late to pass on this act of heroism and follow the map to Ebara. Perhaps the children were worthy recipients of the …

He couldn't even finish the thought. No misdemeanor could justify such treatment of a child.

'What will it be?' Taharva asked him.

Could the chieftain understand him? Had Taharva's use of Nubian language suffered from years of dormancy? The leader's eyes darted to a rack of spears outside the biggest hut—he understood Taharva well enough. The captain bounded forward, positioning himself between the chieftain and his weapons.

'This is no concern of yours,' the man finally said as heads peered out from the surrounding huts.

'I wish it weren't. Leave the children be and my concern will cease.'

The chieftain spat in the sand. 'Rich demands from a traitor. You and your fine garments are a long way from Egypt now.'

The three children were still rooted to the shadow of their village elder. Avoiding conflict became less likely with each passing moment. How could Taharva mediate with such a haughty man, and what would happen if he turned away now?

More whippings. The children would suffer most, but maybe the other villagers too.

'Enough blood has spilled today,' Taharva said, giving the man one final chance to demonstrate his worth. 'Lower your whip and allow the children to scamper.'

The chieftain spat again, drawing as much saliva as he could. 'No.'

'Right. Sorry, then,' Taharva said, lofting his spear in the air above him. It dropped on a near perfect angle, the shaft landing between thumb and finger. He hurled it with all his might.

The flying bronze spear pierced the chieftain before

he could react. It split his chest cavity and sent him stumbling backwards. The children found their feet, scuttling away quickly. When their chieftain collapsed on the ground, villagers gathered outside, clapping and cheering.

The children bolted for him, wrapping themselves around his knees. Taharva didn't enjoy their harried clutches one bit but made no effort to push them away. They retreated to their loved ones after a moment, where both children and parents sobbed alike.

One mother approached him. 'How can we thank you?' she asked.

'Your children already have.'

'There must be something?'

Taharva shook his head. 'No, I'm in search of my family and cannot delay any longer.'

'In the Green Wild?' she asked. 'Please, show me your map.'

The scroll was with Tendrence. Taharva fetched it from the steed and unfurled it for her. He pointed to Nurita. 'My sister is there.'

The woman scoffed. 'Did this map get marked in the dead of night? Nurita isn't there,' she said, beckoning with her fingers for something to write with.

A man, maybe her husband, produced a reed pen. She scratched another mark into the map. If Taharva were to guess the scale, the fresh mark could have been some two hundred miles from the viceroy's original location.

'How …?' Taharva asked.

'A question you'll need to ask your guide. The good news is that it is much closer than what was indicated.'

The captain was quiet as he strained and strained. What reason could he possibly have for not trusting the woman? 'Thank you for the correction.'

'You're very welcome,' she said, handing the map back to him. 'You just follow the stream the whole way.'

Taharva didn't move. If Nurita was marked inaccurately at the Egyptian border, what did that mean? Was his quest a fool's errand or was it just an honest mistake on the viceroy's behalf? Sadly, there was no easy answer that didn't involve covering vast stretches. One way or another, the truth would be discovered in Nurita.

Ambling back to Tendrence, the captain slipped the map inside his pack. 'Thank you,' he said, getting ready to hoist himself on the steed.

'You are owed the gratitude, not us,' the woman said, leading a village-wide bow of deference. 'But don't forget your spear.'

Many people turned away as Taharva ripped the weapon from the chest of their chieftain. He wiped it clean on the man's kilt, and then bid the villagers farewell.

The captain led Tendrence into the jungle on sunset—and somewhere in its reaches—he hoped he would find his sister. Maybe even his parents.

Chapter 16

Hundreds of children missing …

The encroaching darkness and smoke might have masked the Amun priesthood's vanishing act, but it couldn't smother the frantic yelling and panic that followed the conclusion of the festival in Karnak.

Collapsing on the Golden Throne, Merkhet lost his face in his hands. He couldn't believe. Not truly. How could the initiates have escaped on the currents—*unsighted,* with the children—when a contingent of soldiers and royal guards were waiting on the shore to apprehend the High Priest?

Those same honorable men and women were now out searching for the missing children in Karnak and beyond, with reports yet to trickle back to the throne room. All of this because he—the pharaoh—didn't heed his father's warning about the Amun Priesthood. Merkhet had allowed a sensitive situation to escalate out of his control, and now loyal Thebans and their innocent dependents were suffering.

Grabbing his mug from the edge of the throne, Merkhet cursed under his breath. Empty. He stared into its ceramic bottom, yearning for a mouthful of the sweet tea that could soothe him. He lowered it, the mug resting on his lap for all but a moment before he hurled it behind him, smashing against the hieroglyphic feature of the pharaoh's protector: Bastet. Tiny ceramic fragments dispersed all over the floor and as far as the war table. Beebee hissed at his feet.

'Better?' Raina asked him, emerging from the hallway.

'Much,' Merkhet said.

Pained concentration flitted on her face as she avoided the ceramic shards scattered across the floor. She carried a large mound of papyri in her arms.

'You've written them all?' he asked her. 'Do they include that all sightings of the Amun Priesthood are to be reported to the pharaohship at once, with no fewer than three separate messengers sent at staggered intervals?'

Raina handed him one of the letters, having furiously churned out a personalized message for every downriver village at short notice. It contained everything he requested with such concise and eloquent expression that few else could have achieved.

'And word won't reach my mother in the delta? I don't want the soldiers involved if they can be spared.'

The vizier shook her head.

'Good,' the pharaoh said. 'If we are lucky, the preliminary scouts will have tracked the children and returned them home by Ra's rising. If not, the letters are to be dispatched immediately.'

Merkhet sighed quietly. Children don't just *disappear*. He needed to confront the High Priest. A royal guard entered the throne room, shuffling in tentatively. He may have even hung at the entrance for some time, unwilling to interrupt the pondering pharaoh and the fastidious vizier. Even though the man stooped down into a bow before the throne, a slight irritability marked his face.

'Hurry,' Merkhet said. 'What is it?'

'A young man has requested an audience, Your Grace.'

'Does he have a name?'

'Snafaru, maybe? Says he has urgent tidings for the pharaoh.'

'Escort him through, please.'

'At once, Your Grace,' the guard said, giving a curt nod prior to departing.

In that small stretch, Raina gave Merkhet the most curious of looks. Oddly, he found he was able to interpret her meaning with little difficulty.

What does that preposterous tomb robber want on an evening rife with uncertainty and loss?

Perhaps Raina was right to mistrust Snefrey. Whether it was the shared experiences of ill-advised adventures with his former classmate that set Merkhet at ease, he couldn't say. Whatever it was, he was grateful that his vizier could provide him with a balanced perspective.

Snefrey walked through, arrogance enveloping his stride. The guard made to follow the tomb robber, but Merkhet dismissed him with an assuring palm. Satisfied, he waited outside the throne room.

'Not a good time, Snef. What brings you here?'

'No time like the present.'

'You've not heard, have you?' Merkhet asked him.

'Caught wind of what? Been busy myself, you know, doing the work you commissioned my expertise for.'

'Not tonight, not after what has happened.'

Snefrey studied him and Raina. 'Not sure why you're both as pale as the full moon, but thought you would want to know what I've found?' He shrugged. 'If you would prefer—'

'Out with it,' the pharaoh commanded him.

'Found the perfect spot for the mortuary temple,' the tomb robber said. 'I was out searching for undiscovered tombs and … What's happened, then? With glares as deep as those, at least one of you wish to poison me. Probably both. Or you might cry. I'm very confused.'

'Tragedy befell us at the Opet's closing.'

'What, must I pry the details out of you?' Snefrey asked. 'Whatever has happened, couldn't be as tragic as your face.'

'This is no game, friend. Over five hundred Theban children went missing tonight. We are still awaiting the final report from the villages. As stunned as ushabti, we were. Taken from right under us while we watched the smoke billowing all around the raft.'

'What are we doing here, then? Let's go rouse the culprits with the fury of a wounded hippo. Is it the Hittites? Nubians?'

Merkhet cast his head down, speaking quietly. 'This travesty was committed by Egyptians.'

'Egyptians?'

'Yes,' Raina said. 'The Amun Priesthood.' She went quiet after her solitary input, rustling the papyri in her hands.

'Still,' Snefrey said, 'what am I missing? We need to find them, don't we?'

Merkhet waited to see if his vizier would add another verbal contribution. She didn't. 'We need to tread carefully,' he said. 'Can't go charging in every hovel and

134

temple. The children will get hurt if we do that.'

'So, we do nothing?'

'Did I say that, Snef? A segment of the army and royal guards are out scouring now, and will be all night, surveying the landscape for any suspicious activity. More than anything, we are waiting to receive the demands.'

'Demands?' the tomb robber asked.

'A throng of children don't just go missing without reason,' the pharaoh said. 'High Priest wants something.'

Raina flourished the High Priest's letter around in front of her.

'Ma'at's honest truth. You're right! The demands aren't going to change, are they?'

The vizier shook her head. Irrespective, Merkhet couldn't reject the sense that they would receive further correspondence soon.

Snefrey chuckled. 'You two are an adorable team. Oh, and would you look at that,' he said through a broad smile. 'Moonglow pale to sunset orange in record speed.'

If they hadn't already, Merkhet's cheeks flushed with warmth at that remark. He couldn't help it, even in the severity of what they faced. Exchanging a guilty glance with Raina, her face was as red as his felt.

'Alright, I'll forget the mortuary for now,' Snefrey continued. 'Let's return these children home, then I can deliver the new site to you and claim my deserved riches.'

'The gurgle of the Nile to our ears, friend,' Merkhet said.

Merkhet whipped his head back against the reed mat. He twisted and turned, never able to find comfort. The morning couldn't come quick enough.

Such was Haliya's dismay at the height of the night's shadows, she walloped him firm in the chest. He didn't protest as she implored him to be still. After that, he showed great restraint but could not suppress his restlessness for the duration.

The sun's rays began to seep in from behind the veil, and Merkhet relinquished the last vestige of hope for gaining some vital rest. Haliya did not stir beside him, but he couldn't be sure she wasn't just ignoring him out of stubborn fury. He would have some serious groveling to do when he returned—whenever that might be.

Whether she was asleep or awake, Merkhet wasn't taking any chances. Heels raised high, he crept out of the chambers, not willing to even put on his sandals, lest they scuff along the cool stone surface.

Raina and some of the royal guard contingent were awaiting him in the adjacent throne room. They weren't bouncing around in a jovial mood, and that confirmed why the pharaoh had experienced no joy with sleep.

The children were not found. Likely, they were no closer to finding them.

Merkhet approached the guards, eager to listen in on what the night had held for them, but Raina intercepted his path. She was holding a papyrus scroll, much as she always was, given her affinity for scribing. Yet her face told a tale of horror and sickness. Was she bearing fresh demands from the High Priest?

Raina gave the papyrus to him, and he unfurled it with great reluctance. Taking a deep breath in, Merkhet read the scroll. Its content was short, brutal.

You have not heeded the warning.
If the children are ever to be returned to Thebes, you know what you must do.
Do not delay, much worse is sure to come ...

Merkhet wanted to scrunch up the scroll and toss it onto the nearest brazier, but he couldn't bring himself to do it. All else aside, the words might contain clues. He was adamant they would or was at least inclined to hope so.

Raina gestured for the papyrus, wanting to read it again, and he obliged her. The war table did not have any seats, crafted at the right height for standing, so the vizier drifted to the throne.

Heading right for it, Merkhet fully expected her to sit atop it. In an empty room, he would not mind—but in the company of his royal guards?

At the last moment, she looked up from the scroll and examined the throne, as if she were considering the implications of perching herself on it. Then, she bent down and sat against it.

Beebee, also at the base of the throne, opened one eye. Satisfied he was not in danger, he shut out the world again. Then, without any warning, the territorial feline rose from the ground and performed his iconic post-slumber stretch. He settled again, curling up against Raina's thigh.

The vizier did not shift her attention from the scroll, her concentration as good as unbreakable, but she did extend an arm to scratch behind Beebee's ears.

The contentedness in his *purr* carried across the room. Raina could handle the scroll's meaning, hidden or otherwise. Merkhet turned to the three guards, huddled together, discussing how sleepy they were.

'Your Grace,' they said, bowing in unison.

'What are you able to report of the night?'

'No sightings of the children, or the priesthood,' Inebni said, a glint of helplessness in his eyes.

'Is there more?'

Inebni nodded, ever so slightly, and it appeared as if words might fail him. 'We didn't have guards posted at the palace gates for a brief period last night.' Gesturing to the war table, he said, 'And that was left there.'

Revulsion welled inside the pharaoh when he saw it. A child's finger. Small and blue and severed.

Merkhet turned away, expecting to belch bile all over the throne room floor. 'Please, get it out of here,' he said. 'Anywhere that's not here.' One of the guards stepped forward, wrapped some blank papyrus around the detached finger and carried it away. The pharaoh paused to compose himself before speaking again. 'Where are our contingents posted now?'

'As you commanded,' the acting captain said. 'Some in the villages, in the event that the children wander home, but most are positioned in Karnak and Luxor.'

'Excellent.' Merkhet paused, a heavy exhale escaping him. As much as he wanted to control every aspect of this sensitive affair, it was not possible. Others would need to complete the tasks that he could not. 'Shortly, Raina will send envoys to every fishing village and trade town north of Thebes. Horus help us, we will get word to the most northern reaches of the delta if it helps us bring home the children. What of the mothers and fathers?'

Inebni scratched the side of his neck. 'Beside themselves, but they are not making our lives difficult. Could be worse, given what's …'

'Are any of your children missing?' Merkhet asked,

addressing both guards that remained.

They shook their heads. 'And bless the gods for it,' the other guard said.

'Bless them all, indeed. Stay strong, men.'

'What should we do now?' Inebni asked.

'Take a moment's rest,' the pharaoh said. 'Could be an arduous toil ahead. Bare minimum guard detail here at the palace. Everyone else is to assist in surveying the land and maintaining the peace.'

Stooped in another bow, they said, 'Thank you, Your Grace.'

The guards departed, heading back through the palace. It was just Merkhet, Raina, and Beebee.

About to inquire if the new scroll contained anything of note, she beat him to it. 'The handwriting,' she said.

'What of it?' Merkhet asked casually, as if they talked every day.

'Familiar.'

'To the first letter, you mean? Of course they are. Compare them if you're unsure.'

She shook her head. 'Somewhere else.'

'But are they both in the High Priest's style?'

Raina nodded that time, but then horror spread all over her face and a vacancy emerged in her eyes.

'What is it?' he pleaded. 'What have you uncovered?'

She still didn't say anything. Though not unexpected for the vizier to maintain her silence, when Raina offered him nothing, it caught Merkhet off guard. No suggestive glances or looks, no attempt to scrawl her thoughts. Something was dreadfully wrong, and his stomach swirled with unease.

Chapter 17

'Please, speak,' the pharaoh said, frustration coloring his tone. 'We cannot waste a single of Ra's precious rays.'

Raina wanted to talk to him—Isis the gracious goddess of rebirth knows she did.

Most people were curious about her muteness, and why shouldn't they be. It was unusual, but seldom did anyone become annoyed when she didn't speak. Merkhet was no different, both understanding and supportive. Yet now he had heard her speak and knew she was more than capable, an air of expectation hung between them.

She wasn't sure she could meet the unspoken demand. Her flippant tongue was dangerous. Nashwa might be the Vizier of Upper Egypt if Raina hadn't opened her stupid mouth after their scribe admissions test.

A vow of silence was the only way she could trust herself, live with herself. Yet now children were in trouble, serious trouble, and maybe her voice could help save them …

'Raina, please, give me something. What have you realized?'

Seated against the cool throne, she pushed herself up. Beebee stirred beside her, meowing with contempt. Raina shuffled to the war table, where a wad of papyri and her scribal kit lay. Thankfully, a child's finger was no longer there. Her insides had begun to curdle when the guards were discussing it and again when they showed their pharaoh.

Picking up the reed pen, Raina scrawled a simple message at the top of the papyrus sheaf. She lifted it from the others and handed it to Merkhet.

The lingering doubt was small, almost not there at all, but Raina had to be certain. She needed to read it again for herself before informing the pharaoh.

Begrudgingly, he accepted her delay. 'Hurry,' Merkhet said. 'Cancel the Judgments indefinitely. Have every messenger fifteen miles out of Thebes before the sun reaches its peak.'

Raina scrambled her way through the palace and down the dune slope, wishing she would've already heeded the pharaoh's insistence on relocating closer to the palace. Not that a vizier couldn't live among the citizens in the village she grew up in, but it was far from pragmatic. Especially when she left important documents behind in her humble mudbrick home.

Outside the palace gates, Raina had to wince. A gathering of distraught parents, mothers and fathers alike, had amassed during her time in the throne room. They didn't pester her with accusations of incompetence or demand knowledge of what the pharaoh was doing to bring their children home, but their vacant and somber expressions achieved that better than words ever would.

Raina searched for the royal chariot, but it was not there. Some of the guards could be chasing a lead on the children—she clung to that optimism as she walked through the clusters of citizens and around to the stable. She seldom enjoyed riding on horseback but trudging around in her sandals would not serve today.

She flung herself on the black mare in the very first stable, the very same one that Inebni had chosen on their journey to the temple district. Raina knew she had picked a reliable companion, and they set off at a trot.

The stable master began to chastise her. The *sudden and unwelcome invasion*—as he claimed it—was both *remiss* and *bothersome*. Raina just waved the Amulet of Ma'at about in the air behind her and urged the mare to increase her pace.

'Someone of your standing should know better,' the stable master shouted after her. 'A vizier should respect rules and procedures, not flout them.'

She pretended not to hear his sneering condemnation. He had a rather impressive projection on him, perhaps wasted in the stables. The army could make use for him, directing soldiers on the battlefield.

Well away from the stables and its overbearing master, Raina steadied the mare's pace with a gentle tug of the reins, debating the best route to complete her duties. In her mind, she mapped out a near perfect circle, finishing back at the palace.

First, she guided her new companion towards the administration precinct. It was quiet. Since Lufu and his delegates returned to Memphis, few officials were active in the remnants of the once-glorious buildings set around the open square.

Whisking herself off the black mare, Raina entered the building where the royal envoys gathered between journeys. Seated in a ring, many of the two dozen plus men were keeled over in laughter. Holding up her silver feather for them to see, verbal instructions were unnecessary. She handed each of them their individual assignments. Contained within, a separate invitation to a visit the palace upon their return. The promise of access to Pharaoh Merkhet's royal kitchen was enough to snap the envoys out of their morning social.

They all regained their feet, almost in complete unison, bringing a wry smile to Raina's face. People would do just about anything for the privilege of feasting on a fancy banquet. The allure of exotic northern meats and a curated selection of the sweetest, ripest fruits were just too strong for most to ignore.

Raina didn't hang around to farewell the messengers. She was already on her way to complete her next duty—informing the executioner of the pharaoh's decision.

From a busy lane within the markets, Raina thought she could hear the steady flow of the Nile between exchanges of bartering. When she reached the site of the Judgments, it was all she could hear. Raina stood on the cusp of the ellipse, worn into the sand across thousands of trials, by the innumerable spectators that had gathered there. Seemingly ineradicable, not even the wind distorted its curves.

Where would the executioner be if not here?

Raina didn't have the faintest clue. She would have to circle back later or find another way to let him know that the Judgments were suspended. Either way, she swelled with relief. The executioner was a scary man. His bulbous eyes and prominent, curved nose only enforced her fear of him. He lived for the Judgments: executing the will of the pharaoh. Delivering the verdict of their indefinite suspension was something she would rather not do.

The mare swiveled her head, showing a beady eye. 'What is it, girl?' Raina asked.

The horse whinnied this time. 'Need a drink?' Raina gave the beast a reassuring pat along the length of her neck. 'Best give you a name—or do you already have one?'

The mare twisted back around and started forward. Maybe some water was needed. Taking control of the reins again, she said, 'Let's get you to a well in the villages.'

'Excuse me,' a man called out to her.

Raina whirled the horse around to face him. His beard was trimmed and tidy. As he walked closer, she invited him to speak with her hands.

Obliging her, he asked, 'Are you in search of the executioner?'

Answering him with a nod, he continued. 'Between Judgments, spends most his time with the prisoner these days.'

Raina refrained from inquiring about the prisoner he referenced. Besides, when she considered it, she was certain of the identity: Prahmun, the wretched vizier she replaced. In the wake of his Judgment, discussions about Prahmun's crimes were the hottest topic across Thebes.

She bowed before the man, grateful for his time and assistance. In kind, he saluted her.

After he left, she apologized to the mare. 'Sorry, girl, your drink might need to wait,' and guided their course for the detainment pits, just a few hundred feet out of their way.

The executioner was balanced on the lip of the pit. Taunting and bullying, he spat words with venom. 'You putrid jackal. Are you ready for your next dose?' He kicked clumps of sand, showering the prisoner in the coarse grains.

The former vizier was almost unrecognizable. Scars, of varying size and age, were streaked across his body. Some were thin, others chunky and deep. She could not identify the cause of most, but the repeated sunburns were hard to miss. Great red whelps, all oozing pus as they sizzled under the sun.

The executioner was not the first to notice her presence. Prahmun was. A gleeful smile appeared on his gaunt and weathered face, made even creepier by the gaping cavities between missing teeth. 'Well, if it isn't the pharaoh's new puppy. Wearing my amulet, too, I see.'

The executioner twisted around to face Raina and dropped to one knee. 'Excuse my lack of manners, Lady Justice,' he said. 'Got a little … caught up.'

She nodded, pardoning his unintentional disrespect, and hopped off her mount.

'To which god do I owe the pleasure?' he asked.

Keeping one hand on the mare's reins, Raina reached over to him, handing him the scroll she had written at the palace.

The executioner unrolled it, absorbing the directive in a quick glance.

'Indefinitely? How will I preserve my sanity without the Judgments?'

She didn't look at him during his brief remonstration, instead, holding her gaze steady with the man she had replaced. Prahmun adored the attention. He lapped it up, not once breaking eye contact.

'They're all I have,' the executioner went on. 'Them and this horrid excuse for a dung beetle,' he said, pointing with disgust at Prahmun.

The former vizier didn't bite, ignoring the torment altogether. He looked through Raina, or at least that's what it seemed like as he opened his cracked lips to speak to her. 'Is the pharaoh ready to concede yet?'

The discomfort was excruciating. Her silence compounded the agony, but she was not about to talk. Not in the presence of people she did not know, and least of all for the benefit of the vile man in the pit.

'Well?' he insisted, between a row of scattered and rotten teeth. The gums had a tinge of green to them. Raina had never seen anything so repulsive.

'Quiet, you filthy beast. You do not speak unless spoken to,' the executioner said, sweeping an even bigger pile of sand onto Prahmun.

The prisoner couldn't maintain his smirk or arrogant stare this time. He choked on a hefty waft of the fine white particles and bent over, coughing and wheezing. Beside her, the executioner laughed and slapped his thigh, as if it were the funniest thing he had ever witnessed.

While Raina bore no sympathy for the likes of Prahmun, she found no enjoyment in these antics. This was pure savagery, and Egypt was a country that stood above spite and callousness.

The man dismissed as Vizier of Upper Egypt was down on his haunches now. As he choked for water, it gave her much to ponder.

What had transpired between him and the pharaoh? Did Prahmun have knowledge of the Amun Priesthood?

Anything was possible. A severed finger found its way to them. The poor child ...

Raina climbed back onto the mare. She did not farewell either of them, urging the graceful horse to the villages. Confirmation. Clarity. Certainty. She needed to return to the pharaoh with more answers than questions.

Raina surveyed the village from the entrance. Quiet didn't quite match what confronted her. A woeful understatement, in fact. In the absence of the children, the alleys were bare, desolate.

The mare trotted toward a nearby well of her own accord. As the horse started to slurp, Raina hopped off. Her hut was close, and she was happy to walk beside her new friend the rest of the way. Still yet to establish a name for the mare—or more accurately, bother to ask the stable master what it was—she secured the beast just outside her home.

Ever since Raina politely declined Merkhet's insistence of relocation to the palace, guards were always posted at her hut. They paced around the exterior but allowed her to pass by them with little fuss. She was thankful they made no effort to engage in conversation.

Inside, Raina tried to breathe through a mass of regret. Documents and scrolls occupied most of her cramped living quarters. Would she be able to find what she needed among all this mess?

After her parents had begged her to arrange the space better, it would be unacceptable to be undone by her own stubbornness. Raina started rummaging through the tax collection and Nilometer records that dominated the floor, flinging papyri everywhere as she searched for *the* letter. She was certain it would help expose some critical element of what was unfolding—if she could just find the cursed thing.

Her misguided approach to selecting random scrolls yielded no success, and she vented aloud. The guards outside probably heard her, but she didn't care. How could a vizier, whether or not she was worthy of the role, have such inefficient organization methods?

Every papyrus sheaf had the same coloring and texture, and when they were bound up in scrolls, it was difficult to discern the size. Raina started systematically storing each scroll, first unraveling each one to discover its contents and then laying them out flat in the various piles.

She sat an empty pot atop the tax pile, a miniature statue of Thoth on the Nilometer entries. Painstakingly, Raina unfurled scroll after scroll, as she cleared up her hut in search of Taharva's letter. Its stubborn absence was beginning to undermine her assuredness.

Maybe the handwriting wasn't the same. She could not introduce a theory to the pharaoh without evidence—and with each boring administrative scroll she wasted time sorting—her credibility was wavering.

Raina looked around her hut. There were maybe a hundred scrolls still to be allocated a home. She gritted her teeth and kept at it, knowing her fortunes were sure to change. Another three tax records of various grains from farmers north of Karnak. She wedged them beneath the pot. Raina picked up yet another scroll. This one was a little lighter, and when she unrolled it, pure ecstasy overcame her.

Finally, the letter, the one addressed to Taharva. Her eyes scanned the words and handwriting like they had a hundred other times. Her suspicions were confirmed. Raina needed to get back to the pharaoh at once. She ran outside, holding no regard for the lingering mess she was leaving behind.

Back at the mare, a name came to Raina. Would it be remiss for her to assign it to the majestic beast? It likely already had a name. The mare whinnied and that settled the matter. Fortitude—that's what Raina would call her new companion.

When Raina bounded into the throne room, the pharaoh rose to greet her. Straight back and head held high, his pride rested at the fore. Yet beneath his honor lay a vicious weariness, evident in the dark, puffy skin around his eyes.

In her youth, Raina had vowed to never speak again. Her thoughtless words then, borne out of shameful jealousy, had caused great harm to her dear friend Nashwa. Now, if Raina failed to talk—and talk quick— hundreds of children may slip away from any chance of savior.

Raina didn't even contemplate scribing or gesturing her meaning. She just spoke. 'Taharva will not find his family,' she said, handing Merkhet the letter that set the captain's adventure into motion.

Collecting the High Priest's latest demands from the war table, Raina gave that to the pharaoh too. She wanted him to compare the writing style for himself. The shape of the script, the words, the structure.

'I don't believe it,' he said, collapsing back on the throne, a papyrus sheaf in each hand. 'The High Priest orchestrated this. Taharva's family was just a ruse to lure the captain from Thebes—and we were ignorant enough to fall for the ploy.'

'What now?' Raina asked, dread and graveness in her voice.

Merkhet didn't offer anything, not right away. There must have been a thousand different thoughts streaming through his mind. 'We expand our efforts. Search farther and wider than we ever have. If we cannot bring the priesthood to order ...'

He didn't finish, possibly couldn't. Raina put forward another matter of great importance. 'What about Taharva?' she asked.

The pharaoh smiled at her. 'What of him? He will have already figured this out. He reads people and situations better than most.'

Raina forced down a gulp as she agreed with Merkhet. Taharva would have solved this the very moment he sensed something amiss. 'He is already on his way back. I just know it,' she said with more optimism than she felt.

'Exactly. Now, I'm certain we can abandon our scrutiny of Karnak in searching for these vile priests ...' A shade of the milkiest white swept across his face as he trailed off.

'Your Grace, are you—?'

'I worry, Raina. Every day and night. After all the tests and trials we've endured since Father's passing, how much more can the gods bear witness to before they decide Egypt is unworthy?'

'Your heart is yet to be weighed in the Hall of Two Truths, but the gods know your true worth, Merkhet.'

The pharaoh's eyes glazed and welled, on the verge of crying. 'Thank you,' he said. 'In one small statement— spoken aloud, no less—you have confirmed beyond doubt that you deserve the Amulet of Ma'at, Rain.'

She smiled.

Merkhet dabbed his linen across the bridge of his nose, collecting all the moisture. 'Rain,' he repeated. 'Can I call you that?'

Raina nodded. She had no words for him. The guilt of what happened to Nashwa would never leave her, but she would continue to carve her way to atonement with each and every blessing from Ra. Whether Merkhet wanted it or not, she rushed at him. Startled, he dropped the scrolls but managed to wrap his arms around her in a tight embrace.

Not wanting to let go, she squeezed him even harder for a brief moment, then pulled away. Backing away from the throne, Merkhet was already standing up to follow her.

'Which way does the current flow?' he asked.

'The Nile?'

Merkhet gave her an almost harsh piercing look before breaking out into a smirk. 'Yes, the Nile—unless you know of any other majestic rivers that course through our city and lands.'

Raina ignored his jibe, concentrating on redeeming herself with a credible response. 'To the delta,' she said with mustered confidence.

He nodded vigorously, his eyes bright with understanding. She did not know what caused this sudden shift in his demeanor and was thankful when he opened his mouth to elaborate.

'The priests were on a raft, drifting with the currents towards the delta,' the pharaoh said. 'And the children were on a series of galleys right ahead of them. We've been looking at this all wrong.'

'How so?' she asked.

'We were looking for the priests, for the children.'

'What's wrong with that?' Raina's cheeks were flushing hot. Even though she sensed Merkhet wanted somehow to draw out his ideas, resolute stupidity gripped her.

'We find the raft or the galleys and—'

'We find the children,' she finished for him. 'Just follow the currents.'

'Precisely,' Merkhet said, his excitement radiating through her. 'Thank you.'

Confused, she pressed him with a dart of her eyes.

'For making the connection between the letters. We will leave word for Taharva. Horus knows we will need him for what's to come.'

Raina beamed at the possibility of the captain's return. Though they barely knew each other, she missed his calming influence around the palace, on the pharaoh.

Besides, Merkhet had the right of it. If they were to prevail against the priesthood, Taharva would have a role to fulfill.

'Now,' the pharaoh said, standing before the war table, 'let's study this map and see if we can deduce where these insipid priests are hiding the children.'

Merkhet shoved a pendant and toy to the side. Raina joined him, wanting nothing more than to return the missing children to their families and homes. The rebuild of Thebes, of their country, still required energy and attention, and she preferred the physical exhaustion of coordinating those efforts. This emotional torment left her empty, struggling to breathe.

Raina studied the map with an intense scrutiny she had never dedicated to it before. As part of her routine duties, she would sometimes need to estimate the number of solar rebirths for a message to be delivered. On other occasions, it was to learn the location of a place or structure, for which she was not familiar.

But it was never for proposing spots which could hide hundreds of children against their will, and she hoped it never would again.

Merkhet was deep in thought as she watched him. His eyes scanned the length of Nile, lingering around Memphis and the delta, but then he shook his head, and his gaze drifted back to the villages and cities closer to Thebes.

He muttered something, but she didn't catch it. Raina couldn't help from fixating on Merkhet, rather than assisting him. His approach was too fascinating. Settling on a place, he would calculate its rough distance from the Nile and then what the journey to it might be like. At least that's what she assumed from the precise movements of his eyes.

'They can't be too far,' Merkhet said. 'The delta is out.'

Raina didn't need to question him. He was ready to explain.

'The priests must have walked through the desert to avoid detection when they returned for the Opet.'

'How do you know?' she asked.

'Did you receive any reports of a host of priests on galleys or a raft, battling their way south against the currents?' he asked. 'The galleys and the main raft floated downriver for the first time as the festival concluded.'

'Impressive,' Raina said.

Merkhet's response shocked her. 'Don't admire my reasoning. Find flaws in it. We need to find these children before there are grieving parents all over Thebes.'

Raina bent in closer to the map, sharpening her focus. As his vizier, she would not stop until he could rest again at night. He had shown great faith in her, and she would do anything for him, especially as she fought hard for the redemption of her youthful misdeeds.

Chapter 18

It was only once Taharva slipped off his sandals that he could appreciate the spongy jungle undergrowth. It softened his steps, and he sorely needed that after walking so far. The captain was conditioned for movement, action, and the endless days spent on horseback had stiffened his muscles and joints.

Unwilling to dwell on the harrowing events of the tortured children, Taharva urged Tendrence through the dark green canopy. The steed relished the reprieve of carrying Taharva. Free from the burden of weight, he played games with the tripping trunks, leaping excessively clear of them.

At first, the captain welcomed the change in scenery. Even Tendrence had let out a sensational whinny, voicing his approval at the sudden shift in temperature. One thing did catch Taharva by surprise, though. He never imagined that a jungle could be as monotonous or expansive as the desert.

As they were advised by the friendly Nubians, he and his equine companion tried their best to follow the hidden gurgle of moving water. If they were successful in tracking the stream, it would lead them all the way through the jungle to the village among the trees. There, he would find his sister.

Taharva fell to his knees. Head in his hands, he was on the verge of shedding rare tears. Though he could hear the stream, he began to doubt himself. Nothing could guarantee Ebara would be in Nurita, and what if they were just trailing the same patch of jungle, constantly going back on themselves? What if the viceroy's original mark on the map was not an innocent mistake?

He should never have left Egypt. What a pointless journey. He wanted to pound his fist against the bark of the thickest tree for being so foolish. How had he allowed himself to get so carried away by the promise of reuniting with family?

Taharva belonged in Egypt, and had done, for many harvests now. His place was beside the pharaoh, not searching the jungle for a family that he couldn't even be absolutely certain were alive. Such was the sacrifice he had made for their survival.

Tendrence nudged him. His bulbous eyes glowed bright through the dim jungle. The stallion forced himself in close for an embrace.

'Sorry, boy, should never have brought you here.'

There was no sadness in them beacons, just hope, and Tendrence gathered rapid momentum. He had no intention of waiting for Taharva, so the captain was forced to follow at a jog just to keep up.

Then Tendrence skidded to a halt, his hooves leaving a deep track in the loose topsoil. Taharva didn't know why the horse had stopped and pushed himself over his companion's haunch to investigate. The sudden mounting frightened the steed because Tendrence leaned back on his hind legs and tried to buck the captain off.

Clinging onto nothing but mane, Taharva saw the village among the trees. Nurita spread out all above him. Yet as the steed steadied and all four hooves settled in the soil, they were enclosed by a circle of silver spears.

Taharva held up his hands, showing the Nubians bare palms. Hidden away from some of the sun's harsh rays in the jungle, the men were several tinges lighter than the captain's own kin. For the arid settlements in the country's north, there was little shelter from the harsh daylight.

The jungle villagers showed no signs of relenting, their drawn weapons holding steady. The spears were pointed at him and Tendrence. He hadn't expected a warm greeting for an unannounced arrival, but surely, they could sense he meant them no harm. Still, he kept his hands raised as he hoisted a leg over Tendrence's back to dismount the steed.

Taharva shared the horse's unease, as the spears were lowered to contain them. The Nubians were not going to be caught out, no matter how little or much he resembled them.

'I am looking for my family,' Taharva said, unsure whether they would understand his northern dialect. The villagers on the jungle's outskirts had spoken with him but that didn't mean much for the people here. Nurita was as remote as one could get.

The spear-wielding men remained silent, and he had a chance to count them. Eight Nuritans in total, and they all sought clarity from one man.

The man who wore a crown of rich and vibrant

plumage on his head, similar to that of the dead chieftain's at the jungle fringe. The man's overall burliness and uncompromising stare solidified him as Nurita's chieftain.

Could he understand Taharva, and the others were waiting for him to translate? Maybe none of the jungle villagers could understand him. Or all of them could. It was difficult to gauge. They were quiet, unmoving, just waiting for their leader to act, but the chieftain was in no hurry to reveal his intentions.

Taharva recalled the name supplied to him by the viceroy. If the map wasn't accurate, this information had to be. 'Chaka,' he said, bowing before the Nuritan leader, 'I am in search of my family.'

The chieftain responded this time. Same dialect, harsher accent. 'Why would they be here? The northerners prefer huts littered along dust plains,' he said, spitting on a nearby leaf.

'The viceroy told me they were here. Maybe just my sister Ebara. Please, you can lower your weapons. I come only for my family.' Taharva held out the shaft of his bronze spear. The closest man was quick to snatch it.

'We do not associate with any of the pharaoh's subjects, least of all one so dishonorable. Your kin are not here. You're welcome to sup the night, but then you'll be gone.'

Taharva wanted to be wrapped up in the thick foliage as he bowed before the chieftain and his men. What was he doing here, hundreds of miles from Thebes? 'Thank you,' he said. 'Your generosity is appreciated.'

They escorted him into their village, a huge open space between massive leafy trees. A timber set of stairs wound around a trunk and up to the jungle huts. Built around the trees and elevated at the height of the canopy, walkways of timber and rope connected the huts.

The captain's heart was pounding. Skipping beats. Nerves rarely got the better of him, but he couldn't help these. Somehow, he still believed Ebara might be here. He quickly secured Tendrence to a short stump and began the ascent.

The chieftain must have sensed Taharva's desperation because once they had climbed to the summit, he gestured for the captain to begin his search. Not even the spearmen trailed him as he tracked across the many bridges. He poked his head inside every hut, whispering his sister's name. The curious villagers just smiled, not saying anything. Maybe it was just the chieftain who could understand him.

Whatever the case, it didn't matter. Conversation couldn't make his sister appear, and would she have even settled here, so far from their childhood settlement? It was far away from the reach of the Egyptians, but Ebara loved exploring the open plains. Nurita would have suffocated her free spirit much the way this vain endeavor was choking him.

Through the dimness of a hut, a lady resembled what his sister might now look like. But she didn't rush to greet him, and Taharva knew that it couldn't be her.

Disappointment began to swell and set in all around him, but his feet still urged him forward. Why had he been led here? Across another rickety bridge, that swayed under his weight, only one hut remained. At least three times as big as all the others, Chaka's hut was the grandest in the entire village. Its timber had a certain gleam to it, unlike the dried and peeling bark used elsewhere.

Taharva, curious as to the comforts afforded a chieftain in the jungle, walked into the gloom. His muscles became tight and rigid. Bulky elephant tusks and creepy lion heads loomed at him from the shadows. Hung from the walls, their ferocity was captured immemorial.

A shifting, a rustling, drew Taharva deeper into the unknown. His eyes started to adjust, and a woman sat before him, on the edge of her bed. She was not yet aware of him. The length of her hair, her figure—could it be Ebara?

He leaned closer, studying her features. At once, he wished he hadn't. Her nakedness became as apparent as his presence.

The woman shrieked before Taharva could retreat and avert his eyes. 'Sorry,' he said, already shuffling back the way he had come.

Trouble would be on its way to find him. He didn't need a connection with the gods or a gift of foresight to understand that. Could he get back to Tendrence without arousing the ire of the Nuritans? Taharva peered over the edge and muttered a series of curses. The village was set too high in the trees. If he jumped, he would break both legs on impact.

Did he even dare try to outrun them in their own jungle? They would hunt him down within mere moments, then he would have no chance of explaining his innocent mistake, his careless judgment.

What chance did he have of that, anyway? The chieftain would not accept this violation. Whether it was his daughter, wife, or mistress, there would be a swift and fatal consequence for this insult. Already, Taharva could hear the scrabbling of hurried feet on a distant bridge. He was about to be surrounded by the sharpened points of a dozen shiny spears. If the villagers suspected even a hint of wrongdoing, they might gut him before the chieftain arrived.

If Taharva had his own spear, or at least something to wield, he could perhaps take down a couple of men. But an entire village? No chance. The steps were closer now, vibrations rumbling through the timber, and Taharva was not any nearer to removing himself from certain catastrophe.

Clarity struck him hard. The chieftain's hut was isolated. Only one way to get to it. Only one way to get off it. Unless …

Taharva scrambled about the deck, searching for something sharp. Vegetation grew between the planks, and save for the sandals at the entrance, there was not much else. Fur coats were draped outside the hut. Spots of the cheetah, stripes of the zebra—prized assets from victorious hunts.

He patted them down, hoping for a weapon concealed in the coat lining. The captain could have whelped for joy when he cut his hand on a blade. Blood began to trickle from his palm, but he could not delay. The shakes beneath his feet intensified. The spearmen were close now. A bridge away, maybe.

Ripping the coat from its hook, Taharva fumbled to remove the blade from the inner lining. Successful, he held a short hunting knife and rushed to the bridge with it. The first spearman was already part way across.

The captain groaned with regret as he sliced straight through the rope on one side of the bridge. The man was caught between strides and almost tumbled over the side as the bridge lost all its stability. But the spearman survived, steadying himself enough to retreat to safety. So eager to get his feet back on a firm surface, he was almost gutted on the spears of his rushing compatriots.

The Nuritans watched Taharva, assessing the

situation. The captain tucked the blade under an arm pit and held his hands up. He meant them no harm, but the peaceful intent was lost in the screech of the Nubian lady behind him. Now clothed, she was ready to cause him further misery.

Taharva apologized to her again, then stepped onto the bridge. It swayed angrily beneath the burden of his weight. Lying down, he gripped the planks as tight as he could. With his bleeding hand, he severed the rope behind him. Swinging out of the sky, he let the knife drop and clung to the wood with all the strength he possessed.

Through an exhilarating blur, a tree hurried to accost his nose. At the last possible moment, Taharva released his grip and flung himself the last few feet to the ground. Crouched on his knees, he was a tad dazed and disoriented from the sudden fall. His palm, tinged with mild pain, blended into the confusion.

Taharva stood tall in an attempt to gather his wits and bearings. He spotted Tendrence and dashed over to the steed. Once the beast was untied, he jumped up. 'Time to go, boy,' Taharva said, patting the horse.

As he glanced back at the chaos unfolding, agony beset him. One of the Nuritans had his spear—and just like his family—he would surely never be reacquainted with it.

Chapter 19

Merkhet rapped his knuckles on the sleek surface of the wooden war table. Could he find the answer to the priesthood problem on the map in front of him, or would it continue to elude him, as it had done for a full day now?

The merit of each possible location almost became a forgotten concern as Raina began to speak with a relative degree of freedom. What had happened for her to be so guarded? Would she ever confide in him?

'Isis believe me. I forgot to relay,' Raina said.

'What is it?' Merkhet asked her.

'Prahmun has a message for you.'

'When did you—'

'Executioner. Suspending the Judgments,' she said, cutting him off.

Merkhet did not take offense from her abruptness. He could see she was burning to divulge the information. 'Well, what is it?'

'Something smug about you conceding.'

'The hide of the man, after all the chaos he caused. The gods were about ready to descend on us and put an eternal end to our misery.'

'Merk,' Raina said, 'what does he mean by *concede*?'

Merkhet paused, not willing to consider Prahmun as a viable avenue to recover the missing children. Deceit and hurt were at the core of every promise the man ever made. 'If he thinks I will go running to him for help, he is sadly mistaken.'

The vizier went quiet. Perhaps she wasn't willing to stoop to compromises with her wretched predecessor, either.

Upon returning from his exile, Merkhet overruled the maatebes for Prahmun's Judgment. He would need to honor that verdict and himself. He was the living representation of the gods for a reason, and that couldn't involve doubting himself. Too much was at risk for him to be grappling with indecision.

The safety of the children and those he personally cared for. The very foundation of Egyptian society. His legacy and that of his family's—the same burden he'd carried since the Hittites murdered his father.

Merkhet primed himself to declare that the time to act had arrived. If it meant saving the children, he would scour everywhere north of Karnak.

Snefrey appeared in the entryway, a huge grin spread between his ears.

'Really not a good time, Snef.'

'Whatever it is, Your Grace, I'm here to help,' the tomb robber said, taking a knee and composing a serious countenance. 'Told you that already.'

Merkhet looked to his vizier for guidance. Raina had expressed concerns about his boyhood peer in the past, but she did not object now, in facial expression or voice.

The pharaoh wasn't sure who he could involve in matters of such grave importance. Who could he trust? Too many citizens sought personal glory, and it was only getting harder to determine the worth and value of each individual.

As painful as reliving memories of Peronikh were, Merkhet's once brother was a constant reminder of that exact difficulty. A corrupted soul, lost in the eternal chase of power and glory. Had Lufu's soldiers found Peronikh at Aladaglar? Were they on their way back to Thebes with him for a true burial?

After considerable delay, Merkhet said, 'I wish Taharva was here. We could lean on his wisdom.'

Raina murmured her agreement, then he continued. 'We head north, Snef. You may join us if you wish, but it is not expected. You are free to choose.'

Still hunched on the ground, Snefrey met his gaze and shrugged. 'I'll join. North where?'

'Actually,' Merkhet said, 'you might be of great help.' He straightened his back, eager to rid himself of the mounting stress. 'I rescind my offer for you to choose your involvement. You're coming. Now, where would you hide hundreds of children from sight?'

'You know me, Your Grace. Given ample warning, I wouldn't be caught within the Nile's reach of a few hundred children. Even one child is too many. They moan too much. Always hungry, always—'

Merkhet was about to interject, but the tomb robber must have sensed it because he finished with a different thought.

'—What are we waiting for? I'll consider it on the journey.'

'You heard him, Raina. Liaise with Inebni to organize the royal guards. Six will come with us, the rest stay here.'

She bowed before him and left the throne room to set about their imminent departure.

'Let's check the state of the horses. Asim isn't going be happy,' Merkhet said.

Snefrey gave him a quizzical look. 'Who's that?'

'The stable master.'

'Oh, right. When is he ever happy? Chases after me, cursing and yowling, whenever I borrow a horse.'

'And so he should,' the pharaoh said. 'You have no right to use the royal stables.'

'You might be right, but that doesn't change the fact that I have used them long before you first graced the throne,' Snefrey said, a generous dash of joy in his voice.

'Why has the stable master never reported you?'

The tomb robber paused to consider the question. 'Pride, I suppose. Says more about him than it does me.'

Merkhet let out a brief chuckle. Even though he didn't approve or condone the behavior, he had to laugh. Everything in his life of nobility was always so serious, but the stint of captivity in Hattusha had granted him invaluable perspective. The gods would let Merkhet know if he strayed too far from the righteous path—they always did.

'So, when we go there now,' the pharaoh said, 'the stable master won't reveal your devious crimes?'

'Crimes? Those horses need attention and a chance to explore the great expanse. I give them ample of both.'

'What do you think the stable master's role is, then?'

'Scrollworm, you can't trick me into developing a sudden sense of guilt.'

'Answer the question,' the pharaoh said.

'Fine. Is it to complain about how overworked he is? Heard him do a fair bit of that across the seasons.'

'Just how many times have you visited the stables, Snef?'

'You'll be happier not knowing, but if you insist …'

'Forget it, but only because you did consider doing something selfless for once.'

'In the spirit of transparency—and the slim chance that I might one day have my heart weighed by the gods—let me be clear. If we find the children, great. More doing this so we can get back to the work we started and the riches you promised. Remember, the whole reason you enlisted my services in the first place?'

Merkhet led the way through the palace gates, his Khopesh sword sheathed at his side and shield slung over his back. 'Never doubted it.'

They followed the outline of the sand dune all the way around to the stables.

Snefrey groaned aloud, a devious smile never leaving his face. The stable master was absent.

'Find the horses faring best,' Merkhet said.

'How many do we need?'

'Not sure yet. Depends on Raina and Inebni. We'll just take whichever beasts are healthy enough with us. Can you sort that, please? There's a couple of things I must do.'

'As you wish, Your Grace,' the tomb robber said, a mock curtsy to strengthen his sarcasm.

The pharaoh made for the harem village. In the madness of everything, he had neglected one of his most pressing matters. He needed to apologize to Tiaa. Doubting her was wrong of him, and that mistake alone had cost them valuable time.

Maybe embracing her views and impassioned pleas from the outset could have avoided the seizure of the children altogether. He failed to trust her instincts, and now, when it came to culpability, Merkhet was adjacent to the High Priest. He had suppressed the severity that the priesthood problem posed and only one outcome could redeem him now.

Rescue the children and tear apart the Amun Priesthood.

Merkhet wanted to begin that quest with an acknowledgment of Tiaa, but wandering from hovel to hovel, he saw no sign of her or Llora's baby. He did stumble across another woman that was no doubt expecting an apology from him, but the pharaoh averted his gaze and did not address Samena. Peronikh's mother would have to wait for an update. He was not ready to face that conversation yet.

Leaving the village, Merkhet vowed that the best way to truly recognize Tiaa and her tenacious maternal spirit was to find Wuntu. Seeing her son playing games with all the other children would surpass any words he might muster.

The palace was quiet, empty, or so he first thought. For a pleasant change, the veil was not drawn. Haliya was out on the stone terrace.

'How long will you be gone?' she asked.

Words caught in his throat—he had not yet informed her of his impending departure. 'No way to know, but upon my return, I will be glad to talk of our union.'

'I would come with you,' the Hittite queen said, 'to ensure your success, but the sun is nice in this spot.'

Merkhet joined her, trying not to laugh. Her humor was as frosty as the northern lands she hailed from. How could she have such few concerns beyond tanning? He wanted to return to her as fast as he could and catch her carefree outlook.

Chapter 20

Tendrence burst through dense green canopy. A low-lying branch flicked back into place, and unable to dodge it, Taharva accepted the stinging wallop across his nose. The rampaging black stallion somehow managed a gallop, even when the path through the jungle was subtle, hidden. They had little choice but to maintain their haste. Like a government official sent to collect overdue taxes, the rustling of a swift pursuit had harassed them since the outset of their escape.

Taharva attuned himself to the patter of the Nuritans that followed them. A steady rhythm, not near as heavy as Tendrence's hooves churning through the soft topsoil—they were tracking on foot. If he and Tendrence could just reach the desert, the chase might end there. But how long would that take?

The Nuritans possessed intimate knowledge of the terrain, and Taharva was certain that a slender lead would not grant much advantage, if any. He cursed. In the fury of fetching Tendrence, he had not taken notice of the stream, the one thing that could guide their way out of this endless jungle growth. Taharva couldn't even hear the stream's gurgle over the chase of their trackers and the big green leaves whooshing past him.

Perhaps Tendrence could sniff their way to freedom and get them there quick enough to avoid silver being thrust in their backsides. The steed could not sustain such a hurried pace, though. Taharva strained to listen. The chase faded, a little at first, and then altogether.

His breathing steadied. Maybe they could ease up for a little while, but in their frantic desertion of the treetop village, Taharva was unable to retrieve his spear. He had lost his weapon once before, when he accompanied Merkhet during his exile from Egypt. What godly intervention would be required for it to be returned to him again?

Without a weapon, Taharva was reluctant to rest. Though, as they dwindled to a trot, he dismounted Tendrence. Even the stallion had limits. In the tedium of an amble, confronting questions awaited him. Had the viceroy lied to him about his sister? If so, for what cause? Taharva shuddered, unwilling to trace how far that deceit and betrayal might lead, or where it might lead to. He gave a reassuring pat along Tendrence's disheveled mane.

If his family had managed to escape the Egyptian clutches, why would they wait so long to reach out to him?

They wouldn't. The captain sighed, expelling a great torrent of disappointment and anger. His family were gone. Taharva had to accept that now, and if he was intentionally lured this far from Thebes, Merkhet and the rest of his Egyptian family needed him more than ever.

The stream's gurgle started up again, though the jungle was so thick that they couldn't get anywhere near its trickle. With Tendrence trotting by his side, they followed it. There was no way for them to know if they were heading in the right direction, yet resting felt more dangerous, so they continued.

As his hunger ripened, Taharva became adept at spotting slight variances in the foliage. Some of the bugs were crunchy, some outright disgusting. Most induced a gag as they went down, but the moisture pooled on leaves washed away most of the foul taste.

'Don't look at me like that, Ten. What choice do we have?' Taharva picked up an insect by its antennae. Its body resembled that of a snake but had hundreds of the tiniest little legs, all squirming for grip as he held it aloft. The steed snuggled in close to him and slurped up the long, crawly bug.

Snapping twigs and the brushing of leaves. Movement. Somehow, all around them. Taharva dropped to a crouch, dragging Tendrence down with him. The horse obliged with little fuss, and the captain was grateful. Something was near them. Beast or man, it didn't much matter. He was without a weapon and vulnerable.

The rustling came closer, louder. Frenetic movements now, and Taharva was not willing to believe that a predator moved through the jungle with such carelessness. The Nuritan pursuit had caught up with him and Tendrence. But how many men were about to ambush them? Could Taharva spring a surprise on them and gain a weapon?

Appreciative of Tendrence's stillness, the captain kept listening and became even more certain that there were at least two men tracking them.

The sounds the men made started to drift away, and Taharva was able to identify their rough location.

He was tired of running, exhausted from the lack of sleep and slim sustenance. Taharva tied the steed to a thick tree and began to stalk the movements ahead of him. He would need to mount an assault before he crept too far away from Tendrence.

Voices confirmed everything. Two men. Of that he was sure, but Taharva couldn't understand their remote Nubian dialect. The speech patterns were odd, some of the sounds unfamiliar.

With every dangling green leaf the captain shifted, he expected to see the men. But he never did. Had the jungle deceived him, or had he deceived himself? Which way was it back to Tendrence?

As his heart pumped rapidly, the questions stacked atop one another with frightening urgency. Parting from his steed was a terrible decision. When he was ready to curse so loud that the canopy came crashing down, Taharva saw the men.

They were walking ahead of him. Their spears were at their sides, relaxed and not ready for combat.

Could Taharva overpower them, startle them enough to ensure his escape? He didn't want to hurt them if he didn't have to, even though they would not show him the same courtesy. The men kept marching forward, increasing the distance back to Tendrence.

Taharva had to act. Picking up the pace, he leaped through the foliage. He shifted only when the Nuritans did, so their movements muffled his tracks. He was within striking range, and they had not even turned around once.

The men suspected nothing, walking beside each other. Their tone was merry although Taharva understood none of what they said as he lurked behind them.

Ten feet, five feet, then a mere two feet separated them.

The captain sprung through the air and leaned back, putting a foot through each of their spines. Both men tumbled face-first into the undergrowth. Taharva, having landed on his back from a failed flip, flung himself to his feet and dug his knees into their backsides.

Before the Nubians could react, he pulled their spears away from them and prodded the sharp ends at the soft flesh between their shoulders. Taharva applied steady pressure. How was he going to convince them that they should leave him alone? That they should forget all about this chance encounter and scurry home to their treetops?

If he restrained the men, they would likely die. No part of him wanted that. Taharva might not hail from the same village as them, but they were Nubian brethren all the same, and he could not leave them to suffer and starve.

One of them murmured, face buried in the mud and leaves.

'I can't understand you,' Taharva grunted in Egyptian. He spoke the foreign language out of frustration. If he could just communicate with them …

The men cried out in pain. Unintentionally, Taharva had dug the spears in deeper, breaking the skin and drawing blood to the surface. 'Sorry,' he said to them, easing the strangle grip he had on the weapons, which allowed them to get up.

The Nuritan men were hesitant at first, but Taharva didn't stop them from gaining their feet. If they were to live for the next day, they needed to trust him. Equally,

Taharva needed to trust them. They could raise an alarm, and he would never return to Egypt once the chieftain got hold of him.

Resting a spear against each shoulder, Taharva raised his open palms. A gesture of peace—if it translated as such this far south. Neither of the men charged at him, at least respectful of the reprieve they had been granted.

They watched him carefully, though, unsure of what move to make next. Taharva hoped to appear in control of the situation because, really, he was wondering the same thing as them. What next?

Slowly, he shuffled around them. With some encouragements from the spears, the men had swapped positions, and the captain prompted them to walk in the direction of Tendrence. They obliged without complaint. They didn't seem to care if Taharva was captured or not, trudging through the jungle in measured strides. No nervous glances back at him. No anxious chatter between themselves.

As he followed them, Taharva was confident that they weren't conspiring to a reckless and stupid act. If they were, though, he was ready. He had the spears pointed and could harpoon both of them in a swift flourish.

The captain's plan required him to be able to find the steed, though. He began to call for Tendrence. No response, at first, but they kept moving forward, swinging vines and leaves out of their way. The men didn't walk too quick, and Taharva was thankful for it, for pace might entice them into a rash and desperate ploy for freedom.

Tendrence never gave hint of his location, but eventually, the captain did manage to stumble upon the steed. Cautiously maintaining a gap, Taharva gestured for the men to sit. Either they did not understand his hand motion or were reluctant to heed the command. A menacing wave of the spear changed their mind.

Once they were cross-legged, Taharva loosened the bind around Tendrence's neck and set the steed free.

'Don't follow me,' the captain said to the men. He spoke in Nubian and held up the spears to give them the best chance of comprehending his message.

They just stared at him, not offering any form of reply, even though he was certain they knew their survival depended on their cooperation. Taharva signaled for the men to part with one of the water skins they carried. He would have one, and they would keep the other. Hesitant, the bigger of the men handed it over with a toss. The water sack landed at Taharva's feet, and he bent down to pick it up, watching the men with great intent. As he placed it in his pack, the Nuritans didn't even blink.

Taharva was actually going to get out of this forlorn greenery and grace his feet on the familiar dust plains and sands once more. He would never complain about them again. They might be expansive, but they didn't grow around you. Or on you.

'Follow me at your own risk,' he said, holding up the spears for the last time and tugging Tendrence away from them.

When the gap was generous enough, Taharva spun the stallion around to face the men. The captain gripped both spears in one hand as he mounted Tendrence. The men made no attempt to chase or provoke him. The Nubians did not even shift as Taharva guided Tendrence around in a loop and urged the beast forward.

The steed showed an urgency of his own, charging through the canopy and hurtling over any trunks that blocked their way. The fierce desire to return to Thebes was mutual, and only one explanation existed for why they ever left in the first place.

The viceroy wanted Taharva out of Egypt. Why, the captain could not fathom, but he would get his answers and vengeance at the border. Or wherever he had to.

Chapter 21

Sweat amassed along his lower back, though Merkhet tried his best to ignore the discomfort. Returning to Thebes with anything shy of all the missing children would be a catastrophic failure. If they couldn't achieve that, Merkhet shuddered to consider what would become of the pharaohship.

After insisting that he and the rest of the accompaniment scour the lands through every waking moment, he was tentative to change his stance now. So, their procession of hardened stallions and mares tracked the Nile as it wound north, crossing the river at numerous points to explore every village and town.

Even before the temples of Karnak faded into the distance, it became obvious that Raina had reverted to a state of complete silence. She did not engage in any of the conversations between him, Snefrey, and the royal guards. Inebni and the other five guards mostly kept to themselves, too, save for clarifying their directives.

'Am I missing something? Is there a reason you haven't sent for the army?' the tomb robber asked him. 'Could cover a lot more ground.'

Merkhet pursed his lips, deliberating upon his words. Why had he chosen not to involve the army? With the might and magnitude of the soldiers' assistance, they could churn through every hovel and temple before the newly planted crops were even ready to be harvested.

Snefrey looked at him, furrowing. His expression showed that he did not understand the pharaoh's hesitance, and Merkhet wasn't sure he did, either. He was trying to, though. The less involved, the better. More people meant more complications. The pharaoh was certain of that much, but his rationale … less so.

Part of him wanted to have an impact, too. Something from his pharaohship that he could claim. If anything, Taharva was the savior in the Hittite lands, almost single-handedly securing the victory on the frosty slopes of Aladaglar.

'The construction cannot be interrupted. Besides, the priesthood is too volatile. Can't predict how they might react to force.'

'That's your grand response, Scrollworm? We're out here drowning in sweat, and it took you that long to spill that from your lips? For what it's worth, you've completely blundered this whole affair.'

'You want my grand response, Snef? The truth?'

'Please,' the tomb robber said, exasperated. 'At the very least, you owe us that much.'

Snefrey probably had the right of it, but Merkhet was still tempted to unleash a torrent of frustration on his companion. He was tired of carrying around secret knowledge. If it was affecting his judgment, they didn't just deserve to know, they *needed* to know.

The pharaoh exhaled, long and heavy. 'Llora is my sister,' he said.

'Hold my hand up for Horus,' the tomb robber said. 'I was not expecting that. Explains a few things. Onward to vengeance, then? This backside wasn't made for idle sitting.'

'Are you sure about that?' Inebni asked. 'Seems about all you were made for with that narrow frame of yours.'

Merkhet heard the barb but was already withdrawing. Wherever the Amun Priesthood may have settled, he was certain that they were still within a short distance from the Nile. How could they not? Moving tired and hungry children by foot would be too monumental an endeavor. Yet keeping them hushed and still on galleys would have been just as complicated. Citizens would have seen them, and news *should* have reached the palace.

Nothing made sense.

'Abydos and Dendera yielded nothing,' Merkhet said, interrupting the playful exchange between Snefrey and Inebni. 'We keep trailing the course of the river. All the way to Saqqara, Giza, and beyond if we must.'

Snefrey galloped ahead, calling back to them over his shoulder. 'These children better not complain when we find them. Even so much as one ungrateful whelp might spiral me into unabashed tyranny.'

Raina, still not speaking, tensed a little. Merkhet wondered if she might give chase to the tomb robber, just for the satisfaction of slapping away some of his irritating smugness. She didn't, and the silence swelled between them.

How did his father and grandfather maintain Ma'at with such elegance and ease? How did they align the troublesome priesthoods with the values of all Egyptians? He was not even near the shadows of the two pharaohs that preceded him.

For the first time, Merkhet wished his mother wasn't at the northern tip of Egypt, bringing Pharaoh Nekhet's dying vision to life. But of course she was—his poor leadership sent her there.

Was having all his loved ones far away from him an easier ordeal than disappointing them in the flesh, time and time again?

Maybe. He wanted to scream.

As Merkhet roused from a dissatisfying slumber, his weariness refused to be neglected.

He was tired of hassling the fishing villages for information, tired of not having the answers, and exhausted with the complaints of his companions.

Inexplicably, none of the humble villagers had seen the priesthood, the children, or anything unusual in the period either side of the Opet.

Each village was the same. The people were happy to answer their pharaoh's queries, thrilled to break bread and beer with him, but it never went any further.

Merkhet suspected a different truth, the real truth. Everyone was just too afraid to get involved in something they didn't understand. He could accept that. He had to, but Raina and the rest of the accompaniment were becoming more irritable with every failed day.

Unwilling to give in to the dark and grimy grips of

despair, Merkhet had conjured energy and enthusiasm at every breakfast. Yet today, as he and his fellow Thebans were huddled around each other, nibbling on stale bread, his unwavering positivity began to falter.

What would happen if they failed? Would the citizens demand that he surrender to the Amun Priesthood for the sake of the children?

'Scrollworm,' Snefrey said, 'could really use some of your unfounded optimism this morning. Haven't stepped foot in a drinking hovel in ...' He paused, using his fingers to count. When he ran out of fingers, he finished his thought. 'Too long. Far too long.'

'We need a change of fortune. A sign from the gods. Something,' Merkhet said, not hiding the emotion that caught in his throat. 'If we cannot bring the priesthood to order, it could be the end of Egypt. Chaos worse than that of the gods' anger—they would abandon us entirely.'

'Whoa, Merk. Remember that time, just now, when I asked for some words of hope and belief?'

'Sorry,' the pharaoh said, 'but there's no margin for failure. We must succeed.'

Snefrey and Raina rose at once, Inebni and the rest of the royal guards just behind them.

The tomb robber rollicked his hips and twisted his arms, stretching them. 'If I wasn't so gloriously successful at everything I do, would I spend every night getting well acquainted with the hovel's benches and mugs? I don't intend to start losing now. The fresh hops are ours for the taking.'

'The Golden Throne will gift you your very own hovel if you play your part and supply us with some—or all—of your unwarranted confidence.'

Snefrey was already mounted by the time *hovel*

reached his ears, and he darted ahead, leaving the rest of them scrambling to get their horses sorted.

Merkhet peered down at the skin on his legs. Layers upon layers were cracked and peeling. Every stride atop Abacca was starting to make him whelp with pain. If the constant wincing of his accompaniment was anything to go by, the others weren't faring much better themselves.

How much longer could they continue like this? Saqqara, despite its bulging banks of greenery and dense clumps of palm trees, was a long way from the comforts of the royal palace and Thebes.

In some ways he missed the simplicity of their escalation with the Hittites, or even that of the Hyksos when he was a prince. The foreign nations were never shy or secretive in their desires. They came with force, destruction heralding their arrival, and there were no secrets in their misguided quest for ascendancy. Bloodlust and capturing land were the only things that motivated them.

Internal threats, lurking in the shadows, were much harder to handle. Still staring a bleak defeat in the face, the shame of the gods hang heavy upon Merkhet the farther north they went.

They had ridden through the night, and Merkhet was ready for a break. He needed it—a chance to gather himself and his wits. Calling for an immediate halt, a collective cry of relief went out before his companions' feet even landed on the ground. The river was just a stone's throw from where they dismounted.

The banks of the Nile were different this far north. Either side of the river, hundreds of clear bodies of water were scattered about. Despite being drowned, the effectiveness of the dark, rich silt could not be discounted. Waist-high reeds sprouted up and down the banks.

A fisherman approached them along the edge of the vegetation, his net slung over a shoulder. His steps were cautious, a wife and two girls in tow behind him.

'Greetings,' Snefrey shouted.

'I'll handle it from here,' Merkhet whispered just loud enough for the benefit of his accompaniment.

'Why do you get to have all the fun?' the tomb robber asked, lowering his resounding projection.

Merkhet ignored him because the fisherman ambled into earshot.

'Your Grace,' the young man said, stooping into a reverent bow.

'Greetings,' Merkhet said, mimicking Snefrey. 'It is a pleasure to cross paths.'

'Indeed.' The man paused a moment. His smooth skin betrayed him as a young father. Without so much as a single sun wrinkle, he couldn't be much older than Peronikh. His family huddled close behind him, quiet and watchful. 'What pleasure draws you from Thebes?' he asked.

Merkhet bit inside his lip, contemplating how truthful to be. 'No leisure, I'm afraid. Seeking urgent counsel with the Amun Priesthood. Have you seen any priests?'

The fisherman hesitated, swiveling to cast his eyes over his family. The youngest girl broke away from her mother and clung tight to her father's leg.

'What is it?' Merkhet pressed him. 'When did you

see them?'

'Sometime after the Opet?' The man turned to his wife for support, but her face was still, a glaze of fear in her dark pupils.

'And they sailed right on past?' the pharaoh asked.

'Yes,' the fisherman said. 'A fleet of galleys. With all the children aboard, we thought it was a procession of sorts, didn't we?'

His wife nodded, agreeing this time.

The children were alive! Merkhet almost leaped into the air but had to contain himself. The family in front of him were scared, near petrified. The youngest daughter was shaking at her father's side. Did these humble villagers understand the power of the priesthood and the severity of what Egypt now faced?

Their resistance to assist was troubling. Merkhet posed them no threat, no ill will. He was their pharaoh and thankful for their account. It proved that he and his Theban accompaniment were getting closer to the priesthood. They had come this far north, just as the Nile would soon fan out into a hundred different channels.

If the pharaoh and his compatriots had to, they could use galleys or small rafts to cover every single one of them. Yet something told Merkhet that the High Priest had not strayed far from the main flow of the river.

'Did they pass through quick?' he asked the fisherman before removing the Double Crown. He did not want its presence to compound any fear that the girls might be experiencing.

'Not at all. If anything, they were fighting the currents, afraid of being swept away down the wrong channel, or even all the way to sea.'

'You are a great honor to the gods and Egyptians everywhere,' Merkhet said. 'May the Nile continue to provide for you and your family, as it does all of us.'

Abashed, the man bowed. 'Thank you, Your Grace. May Hapi grant us his divine favor.' Upright once again, it looked like the father wanted to say something else. His lips were the slightest bit apart, but he didn't speak.

'Please, if you have something to say, something to ask, you have your pharaoh's blessing.'

'Is-is chaos looming again? Is that why you are here? We have only just rebuilt after the sandstorms. The eternal darkness was …'

'There's not a day that passes,' Merkhet said, 'that we aren't all fighting to stave off the shadows. The gods have provided us this bountiful land, and it is only because of tireless citizens, just like yourself, we will be able to maintain it.'

Appeased, the fisherman bowed again.

Merkhet reciprocated the gesture, satisfied he had given the man an indirect indication of the severity that Egypt confronted without personally burdening him too much.

Chapter 22

Taharva scanned the Egyptian border as he and Tendrence approached it. Not a soul in sight, least of all the viceroy. Yet even as they had fled the jungle and surged northward through the desert sands, Taharva already suspected that.

He hopped off his reliable companion, slamming the bulbous end of both Nuritan spears into the hardened ground. They both rebounded, reverberations pulsing through his arm. Maybe a warning reached the outpost ahead of him. The jungle men could have escaped much quicker than he, but then why would they bother? The Nuritan chieftain was quick to denounce any association with the Egyptian pharaoh and his subjects.

At the nearby cavern where he had slept, Taharva shouted into its vacant, shallow depths until his voice went hoarse. His outcries echoed back at him the entire time; his frustration only mounting.

'Has the desert claimed my sanity?' Taharva asked

Tendrence as they wandered around away from the encampment.

In the shade offered by Pharaoh Turkhet's statue, the steed steeped into a stretch, avoiding Taharva's gaze. The captain didn't take offense, slumping beside Tendrence as he studied the face on the relief. Turkhet's neutral expression somehow captured the benevolence that made him so treasured among the Nubians. Beyond appearances alone, Merkhet resembled his grandfather more than he did his father. Now, as pharaoh, he was striving to be better, to do better—to find ways other than oppression—and Taharva would do whatever he could to support his reign.

Taharva sighed. To do that, he needed to return to Thebes and reunite with Merkhet. The answers he sought would continue to elude him for now.

Before their unfortunate misunderstanding, the chieftain of Nurita was more than accommodating of him. The jungle people had no part in this wasted journey, yet Taharva couldn't shake away all the suspicion. Paranoia was unbecoming, reserved for those treading a lost path. But …

The viceroy wanted him out of the way, maybe even dead. If nothing else held true, the Captain of the Royal Guard was adamant of that.

'Make the most of the break, Ten. We must return with haste. Pray to the gods that tragedy does not beat us there.'

The stallion neighed this time, sadness and acceptance in its elongated tone. Tendrence finished stretching his hind calves, then sunk a little to make it easier for Taharva to climb on his back.

Chapter 23

As Merkhet conversed with the local fisherman and his young family, Raina listened intently. She yearned for something to break the tedium of their journey, and her wish came true.

Finally, the pharaoh's toil was rewarded with some information, some indication of progress. An alleged sighting of the Amun Priesthood was still yet to be verified, though the inclusion of the missing children in the fisherman's account was promising. He had offered that critical detail without any prompt.

Following the departure of the fisherman and his family, the royal guards—excluding Inebni—went to scout the nearby Saqqara necropolis and its surrounding temples. They left not long after sunrise.

Raina and the rest that remained behind enjoyed the reprieve, slipping off their sandals and dipping their feet into the puddles. Ra's journey across the sky was halfway to its peak when the guards returned. Some brisk shakes of the head and glum faces aplenty, the entire party continued north.

The tomb robber was the first to break the silence. 'I've never seen the pyramids,' he said.

'I have once, Snef. Those earlier dynasties were the best builders Egypt has never seen. My efforts as pharaoh are almost sad and worthless in comparison.'

'Your rule is young, Scrollworm, don't be too harsh on yourself. Quite excited to see them in the flesh. How about you, Raina?'

The more the tomb robber's company was forced upon her, the harder she found it to detest his presence. His blatant disregard for order and respect was weirdly amusing. Though, at the conclusion of their quest, she could do without seeing him for an extended period. As Snefrey touched the guard beside him unsuspectingly, perhaps, they all could.

'Never seen them,' she said. 'Will be a real scriber's dream come true.'

Everyone looked at her, mouths agape, and she was not surprised by their immature reaction. Their lone female companion had not said a single word throughout their journey, not even when the pharaoh tried to communicate directly with her. She settled for exchanges of expressions and gestures, writing when those failed.

What did they think of her—strange, troubled? Raina was almost ready to explain to Merkhet the reason she chose not to speak but feared probable rejection. Maybe if they survived this trial, she would be truly ready to own her actions.

Oh, Nashwa. You didn't deserve a fate so cruel. If anything could be reverted in this life …

When Raina did not surprise them further, by continuing to talk, the group dissolved into a stewing silence. Progress was slow. The horses could no longer gallop, as the relentless riding had near broken them. So, they ambled along the western Nile bank. At their current pace, the Giza plateau was at least several days away. Especially as they would need to check any structures or villages along the way.

Immersing herself in the natural wonders helped to pass the time. Raina tried her utmost to just admire the beauty of the northern regions but found that she couldn't punish herself like that, whipping out papyrus to record what she observed. The nearer one ventured to the delta's mouth, the farther inland the Nile's waters reached.

In Thebes, the odd clump of trees might grow by the river, whereas in Lower Egypt, the dense greenery fostered native wildlife. Shaded by the bounty of palm trees, gazelles and ibis gathered around ponds, some of them hundreds of feet from the Nile.

Raina and her companions traced a winding bend in the river. Ahead, on the course of the Nile, lay Memphis—the hub of Ptah and the city of craftsmen. But out to their left, in the distance, a dry dust plateau opened up. She almost dropped her reed pen, gasping, as the three pyramids of Giza dominated the skyline. Enormous, staggering—even from miles away.

The sphinx stared at them, guarding the amazing structures. The Great Pyramid was built on the right of the three, decreasing in size as she scanned to the left. The white limestone reflected the sun sharply, and even though Raina was reduced to a squint, she couldn't tear her eyes away from them.

'Scrollworm,' Snefrey said, 'how have you not built one of these? We could honor your father with a mortuary pyramid and build it so high Horus rests atop the peak.'

'Can we deal with the crazed priesthood first?'

'Skittering scarabs under my skin. Priests ruin everything, don't they?'

Merkhet laughed along with the tomb robber. 'Come on, let's take a closer look. You can't truly appreciate how magnificent they are until you whimper from their base.'

The pharaoh urged Abacca to hasten her pace. Her brown coat gleamed under the sun as she complied. Something was wrong, though. Merkhet began to slap against the mare's flank.

The other horses were more susceptible to gentle nudges on the reins after the pharaoh streaked ahead, but none of them could gain on him.

Raina gulped. What had stirred Merkhet to such sudden action?

Chapter 24

Delay was not an option. The shadowy outline of a small child had darted in front of the Great Sphinx, but Merkhet was too far away for clarity, for certainty. He leaned forward on Abacca, imploring her to break beyond a weary canter. She obliged, though a swift lap around the sphinx and its surrounds yielded nothing. The only shadows were those cast by the magnificent structures themselves.

'What is it, Scrollworm?' Snefrey asked him.

'Nothing. Thought I saw someone.'

The rest of the accompaniment had caught up, and when Merkhet shrugged off his urgent antics, they spread themselves across the plateau. The joy on their faces was visible from wherever they roamed.

Already recording the moment on papyri, Raina cuddled the mane of her horse tight as they inched nearer to the pyramids. Snefrey tapped the side of his horse, urging it to go faster. Under Inebni's direction, the guards broke their rigid formation, admiring the hardened plateau at their respective wills.

In the thrill and rush of exploring, each of them forgot about their mission. The heinous reason that they were drawn so far north, away from their homes and families.

Merkhet would allow them a small reprieve from the pressures of expectation. If anyone deserved it, these devoted people did. He was getting used to bearing the responsibilities of Egypt and could manage a while longer.

Beneath the Great Sphinx, he dismounted Abacca. Pouring some water into his hands, she was not shy in slurping it up. 'You've done great, girl,' he said, rubbing her gleaming brown coat. 'Not much more, promise.' He wasn't lying to her. The northern tip, where the Mediterranean Sea spread out beyond the limitations of sight, was not far away now.

If they could not locate the priesthood and children soon, Merkhet wasn't sure what would happen. Would he recall the military for additional support?

Difficult decisions were part of the pharaohship, but none came more so than when there was a direct threat to two thousand years of tradition.

If Merkhet could not quell the Amun Priesthood, the risk lay not only with the children but to the entire Eighteenth Dynasty. As proud as he was, and as much as he could not contemplate tarnishing his family's legacy, turning his back on Egypt's most innocent and vulnerable was equally incomprehensible.

Despite being warned of the priesthood so many times, he never imagined such disregard and ruthlessness as this. Not from his own people.

Eager to stretch his legs, he hopped off Abacca. He

scratched along her neck, telling her to stay. She was unrestrained but her rigorous royal training would ensure her obedience.

After gulping from the water skin, he left it in the pack straddled to his mare. Shield slung across his back and sword in its sheathe, he wandered to the Great Pyramid, one of the greatest testaments to Egyptian civilization. Would the fortified city, being constructed northwest of Memphis, even come close to rivaling the perfect white sheen before him? If Merkhet wasn't successful in returning the children, would it even be completed?

So much hung in the balance, waiting for the gods to tilt the course of fate.

Raina sat cross-legged before the central pyramid. Her wrist moved in quick strokes, recording everything she saw. Snefrey — and his poor steed — galloped around the structures in massive circles. The guards enjoyed some alone time, examining the pyramids and sphinx at their own leisure.

Beneath the shadow of the Great Pyramid, Merkhet embraced the cool shade. After so many days riding in the unforgiving sun, relief swelled through him. He leaned against the hard white stone, closing his eyes.

A moment of peace was all that he needed. A chance to freshen his perspective.

Even though it was only early in the afternoon, his temples pulsed, calling him to sleep. Merkhet's legs were demanding him to slide to the ground. He didn't have a chance to succumb to the urge because he was falling backwards into darkness …

Chapter 25

Streaking through the palace gates and past the guards on duty, Taharva urged Tendrence up the dune. They had arrived home. As the morning sun crept up behind it, the palace gleamed, awash in a faint orange glow.

Before the tree in the courtyard, Taharva leaped off his companion. Such was the captain's eagerness to announce his return to the pharaoh, he neglected to tie Tendrence up. Bounding through the hallway, Taharva's heart was battering hard against his chest, an army clamoring to burst through a fortress wall.

No guards were posted at the throne room's entrance—a worrying sign. Golden Throne empty. Besides Merkhet's Aten necklace and a toy lion shoved along the back edge, only a single scroll lay on the war table. Braziers unlit, veil to the inner chamber drawn over.

Where was everyone? What had happened in his absence?

'Captain.'

Taharva turned on his heels. 'Guards, guards,' he said. 'Sorry for rushing by you both, but I have urgent tidings for the pharaoh. Do you know where he is? Or Inebni?'

The guards pardoned his rudeness with a brief bow. They exchanged a quick glance, the taller guard speaking. 'We don't know where he is, Captain, but we know his charge.'

'What is it?'

'Retrieve the missing children.'

'And bring the Amun Priesthood to order,' the other guard said.

'What missing children? Who accompanies the pharaoh?'

'Left with Inebni and a handful of guards.'

'Where did they go?' Taharva could sense his impatience rising. Not with the men before him, but the entire situation. Everything since the arrival of that letter from the viceroy …

'Headed north,' one said, turning to his companion.

The other guard grunted an agreement, then added, 'That pompous fellow that's been skirting about the palace went too.'

'What pompous fellow? How long since they —'

'Tomb robber, think he is.' The guards conferred with one another. 'More than a week. Definitely less than three.'

Taharva stared at them, letting the disappointment swallow them. 'Can you be more precise than that? Did Raina go with them?'

'Sorry, Captain,' they said, shaking their heads guiltily. 'Hard to keep track. Each day is the same.'

'What of Raina?' Taharva pressed.

'She might have gone with the pharaoh.'

'Have you seen her?'

'No,' they said together.

'Any other comings or goings here at the palace I should know about?'

'No, Captain. Mostly the cooks. A few servants with supplies.'

The stockier of the guards picked up the scroll from the war table. 'Here,' he said. 'Pharaoh outlined everything for you before he left.'

'Thank you,' Taharva said, taking the scroll with one hand and dismissing them with the other. He couldn't read it. Waving the scroll about in the air, as if that might relay its contents to him, his frustration was rising. He just wanted to speak with Merkhet.

Could Taharva blindly commit to heading north so soon—after just getting back to Thebes—without any knowledge of what awaited him there?

His feet answered for him. He was on the move when a swathe of red caught his eye—the royal guard red, strewn across the dining table. Taharva picked up the uniform, sliding it over his tattered common robe. Far from a perfect fit, the linen threatened to tear about his groin as he walked.

Back in the courtyard, Tendrence must have sensed the conflict within him because he stooped real low, allowing Taharva to almost stroll into a mounted position. The stallion retreated the way they had come, stopping at the gates when the captain tugged on the reins.

His friends might be in danger, but where would he and Tendrence go? Maybe they could check the villages first. Raina lived there somewhere, and it would be helpful to have definite clarity on whether she accompanied the pharaoh.

Taharva led his companion away from the palace. Weariness lashed at every limb and wariness ensnared his mind. Despite the constant strain of chasing shadows since they first departed Thebes, Tendrence still gave it everything as they set course for the nearby villages.

A verbal barrage floated to them on the warm, blustery winds. The screeching came from behind him, somewhere in the direction of the detainment pits. He whirled Tendrence around to investigate, and they closed the gap in a few elegant strides, where Taharva saw the executioner standing beneath a shade covering on the edge of a small pit. He was cursing at the hole before him, spraying thick strands of saliva from his mouth.

The captain peered into the pit. The disgraced former vizier had no cover from the elements—or the executioner—and he was not faring well. Prahmun's skin was lumpy with infections, and where it wasn't, it was red and raw. His smile was a scary sight. Few teeth were whole, even fewer were free of irrevocable rot.

'Captain, how good it is to see you.' Prahmun had aged mercilessly because of his punishment. The sun wrinkles stretched from the edge of his cold gaze to his ears.

Ignoring the depraved monster in the pit, Taharva climbed off Tendrence and turned to the executioner. Much like the High Priest, no one knew the man's name. 'Your Justice,' Taharva said, making up the title and hoping it might grant him some favor during their exchange.

'Captain,' the executioner said, bowing. 'What brings you to my domain?'

'A quest for knowledge.'

The executioner pulled at the sweaty linen sticking to

his chest. 'Aren't we all?' he mused. 'Right. How can I help?'

'Do you have any word of Pharaoh Merkhet or Raina?'

'Knew it!' Prahmun exclaimed. Before either of the men could silence him, the prisoner kept spewing out words. 'He's gone straight into the sanctuary. All he had to do was concede, but no, of course he was too mighty for my help.'

Taharva caught the executioner's arm before he could hurl a loose stone. 'What is Prahmun talking about?'

The executioner shrugged, relaxing and breaking free but not dropping the stone. 'Speaks nothing but lies. Best not give him an audience, after the atrocities he's committed.'

'Well, what of the pharaoh then?'

'Right, sorry. Lady Justice did come by before leaving with the pharaoh. Dropped a tragedy in my lap. The Judgments are canceled indefinitely.'

If Raina was with Merkhet, and if Prahmun knew something …

Taharva dropped to a kneel. 'What do you know?' he asked Prahmun. 'The executioner, here,' Taharva said, pointing to him, 'will be the nicest man you've ever met should you do anything short of what I ask.'

The former vizier paused, considering those words carefully. 'High Priest has built an army and drawn the pharaoh north. The unwitting fool hopes to reclaim the children.'

'North, where? What children do you speak of?'

'I could tell you. Easier to show you, though.'

Taharva had to restrain the executioner again. 'Let me go,' the man panted, his fury still rising. 'Time we ended this deceptive jackal. Egypt will be richer for it.'

'I don't disagree,' the captain said. 'But there may be some use in him yet.'

'Outlived his use by a long while. Let me free and I'll end him right here.'

'I'm sorry, Your Justice,' Taharva said, releasing the executioner. 'I can't allow that.' When he was satisfied that the man would not try to make true on his promise, he turned to Prahmun. 'You won't be showing me anything until I hear about these children.'

Through a mangled mouth of missing teeth, Prahmun said, 'The priesthood is raising an initiate army to challenge the pharaohship.'

'What? Why?'

'Restore order and parity to the lands.'

'Please,' the executioner pleaded with Taharva, 'you must let me kill him. Can't handle these lies anymore. He speaks on behalf of Set, the almighty destroyer.'

'There's too much at stake,' the captain said. 'Here, help me lift this pathetic prisoner out of the pit. He's coming with me.'

The executioner lobbed a stone the way of the Nile, and the fight faded from him. He fetched a rope to haul out Prahmun and tossed it into the pit. Taharva and the executioner hoisted the prisoner up, not an arduous task for the two burly men, but made much easier by the lack of body mass on the former vizier. A withering man, he was lifted to the surface level with two gentle and coordinated tugs.

Prahmun didn't try to run. In such poor condition, would he even be able?

After a silent moment of consideration, Taharva averted his gaze for fearing of being sick. 'Can we get a robe to cover this grotesqueness?'

Adopting absolute compliance and efficiency in the treatment of his prisoner, the executioner tore down the shade cloth to wrap around Prahmun. The former vizier offered no complaint as he was given reprieve from the searing sun.

'That's much better,' Taharva said, no longer able to see the welts, bruises, and burns that marred the prisoner's body. 'Where are we headed, Prahmun? I want to be reunited with my own reed mat for a long and uninterrupted slumber before the grains are harvested.'

'We go north,' Prahmun said, 'but not sure we can travel that quick.' He took tentative steps on muscles that looked likely to give way in a slight gust. His rotten teeth reeked as he spoke—or maybe it was just the stench of a man who lived in a hole through the better part of an entire season.

It filled the air, and a fresh wave of uneasiness seized Taharva. He smothered his mouth and nose with a cupped hand. 'I'll hurl you into the Nile,' he said, his voice muffled. 'If the crocodiles don't take a fancy to you first, then we can ride north.'

Prahmun's lips didn't part this time, but a wicked grin still broke through. It was a face that even the most adoring mother would struggle to love.

'Do whatever you must,' the executioner mumbled. His voice also went strange as he clamped two fingers over his nose. 'Just don't care anymore. Some smells are simply better left undisturbed.'

Taharva couldn't contradict the executioner as they parted ways, and he nudged the prisoner towards the river. Ra's daily procession was well and truly underway now, with the sun shining high above them. 'After you tried to sabotage Pharaoh Nekhet's funerary rites, might be you are owed to the thrashing river beasts. Hapi will decide your fate. He is one of few gods us Nubians can understand.'

Prahmun groaned as he ambled through the palms just off the Nile's banks. 'Must I wash? Water is bound to sting these wounds.'

'You must. Won't be sharing Tendrence with me otherwise.'

'Could always get me another horse from the stable.'

'Not a chance. The pharaoh is already going to murder me for this. Now, get in the water and clean yourself.'

Prahmun stripped, and no sooner had the cloth drifted to the dried river mud, Taharva pushed him into the brown-green drink. The former vizier splashed about near the bank, moaning and wailing until he clambered out. Taharva sniffed the air several times, not caring for subtlety. Prahmun was free of the wretched smell, washed away for the moment.

Once the shade cloth covered the festering pustules and burns again, Taharva lifted the now scrawny man atop Tendrence, and then climbed up himself. The poor steed had little reserve remaining, slumping under the added weight of the prisoner. But what choice did they have?

If Prahmun could be believed, the pharaoh could be in grave peril. Perhaps, the very essence of Egypt was at stake, too. As much as Taharva and Tendrence could benefit from a rest, the risk of inaction was far too great. They had to push on, even if meant suffering in the company of the vile former vizier.

'Where will we find Merkhet?'

'Depends if he has figured out where—'

Taharva cut him off. 'He has.'

'In that case,' the prisoner said. 'Giza.'

'Giza? Just a plateau surrounding the pyramids, isn't it?'

Prahmun spun around. 'Not quite, Captain.' A mocking grin revealed that the swim had done nothing for the rotten teeth, or the repugnant stench wafting from them.

'Face forward, always. Tendrence bears enough of a load without you and your squirming.'

The prisoner huffed as he complied.

'Where could the priesthood hide at Giza?'

'We've got ample time for you to ponder, Captain.' Mockery and torment in his tone this time.

Taharva didn't bother threatening him. The less they had to engage, the better. All the more energy that he could direct to deciphering the breadcrumb clues such as this. Giza, Giza. The pyramids and the sphinx were built on the plateau there. Impervious monuments were hardly places for one to hide. Unless …

They were nothing more than drunken whispers from the hovels—and never confirmed—but Taharva had heard rumor of underground passages beneath the pyramids. Made of solid sandstone, he was certain that the pyramids didn't have a surface entrance, but what if one started burrowing?

Though he was far from an authority on the constructions of past dynasties, the possibility stuck with him as they rode north. Maybe they could be breached. Maybe they did contain passages.

Whatever waited for them at Giza—or elsewhere— Prahmun would not be able to escape Taharva's fury should the prisoner lead him astray.

Chapter 26

Merkhet fumbled for his feet, for understanding.

The limestone block groaned as it shifted back into place. He rushed to squeeze back through the opening, but he was too slow. It was gone, sealed, and the deteriorating light went with it. Darkness sunk in around him.

Tearing at the wall, he found a crack between blocks but couldn't dig his fingers into them. The stones were level. Perfectly in place, all Merkhet could do was trace the huge stones. Tap them. Lean against them. Heave at them with bare palms, but nothing happened when he did any of those things.

Somehow the block had shut on him. Now, he was inside the pyramid—stuck, trapped—and without his brazier. But how had the pyramid even swallowed him up in the first place?

'Think, Merk, think,' he muttered. 'How many scrolls did you read about the pyramids and their mysteries …'

During the years of his royal classes, no papyri in the royal library had been safe from his prying eyes. What could he recall about the Great Pyramid's construction? When was it robbed, and how did the perpetrators gain access?

Snefrey would know the answers. Of course he would. The noble student turned tomb robber may be an arrogant and insufferable young man, but if his own accounts were to be believed, Snefrey was as efficient and as effective as they came.

Before the shadows had set in, Merkhet caught a glimpse of the path ahead. The narrowest of passages, marked from floor to ceiling in hieroglyphs, and he would need to find a way to navigate through it without any light to guide him. Should he wait right where he was—would this be the best place for his friends to find him? Or did the great and eminent Snefrey not even know about this entrance?

Maybe the tomb robber did, maybe he didn't.

Either way, Merkhet didn't relish the idea of remaining idle and not even attempting to surface from the pyramid's confines. With one hand resting on the hilt of his Khopesh sword, he would forge ahead, where the walls of the tight passage could do nothing but guide him forward.

The thought of leading with his sword quickly faded. If he didn't keep his elbows tucked in and arms across his chest, his armlets would chink along the corridor. Even so, his shoulders scraped on both sides of the hieroglyphic walls.

Merkhet tread slowly, testing the ground ahead of him with one loose, dangling foot at a time. He was fearful of tumbling into a mass burial pit, as was the custom for lesser officials. Thankfully, by the time he had kicked a solid wall, he hadn't encountered any. After careful examination of his surrounds, he concluded that the passage spanned in at least two different directions.

He would have to make a choice, somehow. One made more difficult by the realization that he was not even able to sate his rising thirst. The water skin was with Abacca, and if his sudden disappearance gave her a fright, she could be halfway to Memphis by now.

Cool air rushed at him from the passage to his left. Curious, Merkhet went that way. After a dozen or so steps, his shoulders stopped brushing against the stone sides as he walked. He relaxed a little, releasing the tight hug he had been giving himself.

A wider corridor might signify an area of importance, possibly the hallway to the burial chamber of a past pharaoh.

Merkhet kept following it, unsure of where it would lead him. After the grueling and frantic search along the Nile, he could sense something building. Something was about to happen. As the passage started to slope downward, he had never been so sure of anything. All the thankless toil he and his accompaniment had endured since leaving Thebes would finally be rewarded. Even without Ra as his shining guide, it would be so.

The descent was significant. Every step came with a willful effort to prevent himself sliding the rest of the way.

As the floor leveled out, a sharp intake of musty cool air greeted him. Something about that stale draft brought him to his haunches, its iciness spreading through his chest.

Merkhet spluttered, attempting to expel the air that had rattled him. For better or worse, he understood that as he crouched in the depths of the pyramid, the summit of the expedition was near.

Chapter 27

Legs crossed before the central pyramid, Raina absorbed the mystic allure of the plateau and reshaped her experience into words. A state of complete peace imbued her until a great *whoosh* interrupted her.

Somehow, Snefrey's companion still possessed the energy to gallop. However, when she saw the worry etched across the tomb robber's face, she set down her reed pen at once.

Raina stood up, the concern contagious. 'What is it?' she asked. 'Have we had sight of the priesthood? The children?'

'Least of our worries right now,' he said from atop the steed. 'Pharaoh's missing.'

'What do you mean he's—'

'Did a full lap of the pyramids. He's nowhere to be found.'

Raina's shoulders sunk. How could this be happening?

'What do we do?' Snefrey pressed her.

Without hesitation, the plan escaped her lips. 'Put the guards in pairs. Survey the entire plateau, follow the river. Do whatever you must.'

'Consider it done,' he said, setting off at once to alert the guards.

When Snefrey returned, Raina nodded her appreciation. 'What of Abacca?'

'She is over by the sphinx. Merkhet's not with her.'

'Where did you see him last? I got lost in my writing, didn't …' Her voice abandoned her, embarrassment rising.

Snefrey didn't seem to notice. 'Near the Great Pyramid. Let's search together there.'

He offered her an arm, and when she accepted, Raina was hauled atop his horse. She sat in front of him, and he placed an arm by her waist to steady her.

The discomfort of close contact faded quick, for the rush of duty called her. It called loudly, drowning out all else.

As the stallion carried them towards the magnificent structure, they were devoured by the enormous shadow it created. The Great Pyramid was so vast, so impressive, that she had really struggled to find the right words to write about it.

In truth, she was happy for Snefrey's interruption. Well, before she absorbed the stark graveness of his expression and demeanor, then all whims of writing vanished. Gone—and would remain so until they could locate the pharaoh.

Where had he disappeared to? Was he in danger, or causing them needless panic while lost in his own experience of the architectural wonders?

Raina swung around, searching for the royal guards.

She wanted confirmation that everything possible was being done.

A pair of them were in the distance. On the western fringe of the plateau, they were sweeping the area surrounding the smallest of the three pyramids. Also on horseback, they covered ground quickly. Raina saw no signs of the other guards but trusted they were just as busy.

A burst of sudden sunlight jolted her back to the present. Snefrey was guiding them around the pyramid to the northern face. 'Most temples and pyramids have an entrance on this side,' he said. 'He might be inside.'

'Why would he go in alone?'

The tomb robber shrugged. 'Maybe it wasn't willingly. If he were out on the plateau, we'd have sight of him.'

'You're right. Show me the entrance.'

Snefrey eased the steed to a halt, then jumped off. Once again, he offered Raina his hand. She took it, holding her dress in place with her free hand. The impact of the short drop rippled through her feet but did not ache so much with the gracious assistance.

Could she be wrong about the tomb robber? Maybe the arrogance and selfish behavior was a pretense for the man he truly was. Even now, he released her straight away, moving along the sloping triangular face. He gave one open palm to the stone, the arm trailing behind him.

Raina wasn't sure what he was doing, content to watch him go about his work. She didn't have a clue about gaining access to sealed monuments, not like a seasoned tomb robber might. She was amazed at how much he had grown on her. He should be a walking symbol of chaos, but somehow, he defied those reservations with an irritating and undeniable charm.

Snefrey stopped, not even halfway across the face of the pyramid. His hands moved along the blocks, between them, almost as if he were massaging them.

'What is it?' she asked.

He raised one arm, politely silencing her, and continued his task. A man committed—Raina could appreciate that.

'The entrance is here,' he said.

She looked where he was standing but couldn't possibly see how they would be able to get inside. The stones were no different to the ones around them. 'How do you know?'

'Not a matter of seeing.' Snefrey beckoned her over. 'Feel here.'

Raina did as she was invited. At first, she didn't quite understand what he was so adamant about.

The stones were no different in color or shape, a uniform row of white limestone the entire way across. Every single one of them was coarse to the touch, yet none more or less so than their adjacent blocks.

What was she missing? Determined and stubborn, Raina kept searching. The tomb robber's eyes drifted to a particular spot, so she concentrated her efforts there, and even tried her best to imitate his caressing technique.

'You clever little ibis,' she said, running her fingers over a section for the second time.

Snefrey bristled beside her. 'Sorry, was that a compliment?'

Raina shrugged. Imperceptible to the eye, two blocks had the slightest of recessions. Set just back from their surrounding stones, the difference could only be felt by hand—and would only be felt if you knew what you were looking for. 'What now?' she asked.

'We'll round up the guards. Their combined force

can shift these stones.'

A sensible course of action. She couldn't disagree. 'I'll wait h—'

'No,' he said, shaking his head with vigor. 'Splitting up got us into this scramble. Guards may have even found Scrollworm by now, and we can end this fun little side quest altogether.'

The tomb robber could be credited with making many informed decisions under duress. Though shouldn't she, as Vizier of Upper Egypt, be leading the charge? As much as Raina tried to bury the regret and self-loathing deep within her, haunting memories were never far from surfacing. The mere thought of Nashwa and Raina could seize up, unwilling to part her lips. So, if Snefrey could maintain Egypt's interests, then she was also willing to let him be her voice. She could always interject, if required.

On horseback once again, they didn't need to travel far. The royal guards were debriefing outside the temple on the eastern side of the Great Pyramid.

'What news do you have?' the tomb robber put to them.

If the guards were disgruntled or opposed to the chain of command, they did not act it. Maybe when the pharaoh was missing, all manner of courtesy and respect was reduced because Inebni responded at once. 'No sign of Pharaoh,' he said, visibly distressed. 'Plateau and surrounds are clear, but we did spot the fleet of galleys farther along the river.' Sweat poured from his hairline and brows. His breaths were replaced with sighs, and his chest heaved with each of them. 'What do you propose?'

Strangely, Snefrey turned to Raina for consent to keep speaking. Her unblinking eyes granted him his wish. Her wish.

'We last saw him against the Great Pyramid, and given the galleys, the children are surely nearby. We should check the passages and caverns inside.'

The guards grumbled and murmured their assent, and everyone followed the tomb robber back around to the northern face of the grandest pyramid. Raina declined Snefrey's offer to join him on the horse again.

She walked the short distance, her steps slow and methodical. Though the sun was beginning its descent and the pharaoh was still unsighted, she was about to gain access to the interior of the Great Pyramid. Her concern for Merkhet toiled against the emerging excitement, guilt rising as she couldn't quite push away the enthusiasm for the task ahead.

Around the sloped edge, the guards were already grunting and heaving. Upon closer inspection, they had shifted a stone block the better part of a foot and were in no mood for slowing down. Puffing and panting, they committed themselves to the push.

The block continued to groan, no match for the strength of the six royal guards leaning into them. A few more concerted shoves and there was room enough to enter the pyramid on either side of the shifted stone. Light flooded into the now open chamber, but Raina couldn't see much of anything. Yet.

A chorus of cheers went through the party, and they all edged their way to the entrance. The guards drew their spears as Raina and Snefrey fell in between them. Four guards led the way, two protecting the rear. In two uniform lines, they filed into the pyramid on both sides of the stone.

Raina stuck to the left, unable to believe the wide passageway that awaited her inside. The walls were covered in hieroglyphs as far and as high as she could see. She wanted to study their stories, but her excitement won over. Her eyes wandered to the many corridors that streaked away from the main passage, and those were just the ones visible before the darkness reasserted its dominance. She was most surprised to see that some had a steep elevation to them, while others dropped deep below the ground level.

'Which way?' Snefrey asked in a muted whisper.

Raina matched his tone, curious whether the tomb robber may be a little frightened. Or maybe it was just polite to lower one's voice when defiling a sacred monument? 'Why don't we call for Merkhet?'

Snefrey did not enjoy that at all, firmly shaking his head. Once. 'Never raise your voice inside a pyramid or tomb. The gods will judge.'

She didn't flag the hypocrisy, just accepted it. 'Down? Left? Right?'

'Whichever way, we stay together. No one veers from that.'

'You've got it, Snef.'

The tomb robber didn't scold her. He must have appreciated the vote of confidence, even if it was layered with sarcasm. The guards were quiet, cautious. They held their spears at the ready, waiting for a command.

'Do we have a brazier?' Snefrey asked.

'Merkhet had it,' Inebni said. 'Actually, might be with his mare. We could go out and —'

Snefrey held up his hand. 'No, every moment is precious, and chances are we will stumble upon one. Let's press on.' Then he gave a signal to the four guards at the front to begin their shuffle. 'Careful as we go,' he said. 'Could be a hundred or more false pits waiting for a hasty step.'

As they all moved farther inside the pyramid,

Snefrey continued to provide directions. He paused at each crossway, touching the walls and sniffing the air. His actions were beyond the knowledge of Raina, so she was in no position to call him out for the peculiar behavior. That's what it was, though, as the tomb robber basically hugged the wall for answers.

At his discretion, they stayed along the main passageway. It was twice as wide as any of the others they passed and better illuminated from the sun's dwindling rays, though that was marginal. After neglecting several corridors, Snefrey did send them down one on the left.

It had a steep decline and neared complete darkness. A few steps in, Raina had some serious reservations. 'Are you sure, Snef? Does it have to be this one?'

Even though he was right beside her, the visibility was so low now, she could no longer recognize any of his features. 'This is the way,' he said. No waver as he spoke, just utter conviction.

'To what?' she asked him.

Snefrey didn't answer her. Instead, he urged the guards to proceed. They almost all piled on top of each other as the passage narrowed again. Raina was jammed against Snefrey. Grunts, groans, and mild collisions were a lucky thing with all the drawn spears. It took the leading guards a moment to get untangled, but they were able to, then proceeded in single file.

Raina allowed the tomb robber to set the pace ahead of her. He was closer to the guards, closer to the action. She was certain that the passage continued to slope down and had done since they branched off. The darkness was unnerving, though. Snefrey hung out a palm behind him and it covered her face. He didn't remove it—or apologize—so she came to a stop.

She braced herself, not sure whether the royal guard behind her had stowed his weapon. Nothing jutted into her back, and Raina sighed with relief. 'What is it?'

'Quiet,' Snefrey said. 'Listen.'

She did, but straining didn't seem to aid her hearing. Silence permeated the passage.

'I hear something,' one of the guards whispered from the front.

'Me too,' the tomb robber whispered. 'Push forward, slowly now. Use the walls to guide you.'

Raina was happy to be moving again. When they were still, the discomfort of darkness settled around her. They didn't get far, though, before they were halted again. She tried hard to listen.

Nothing. Nothing except for the shallow and labored breathing of the men around her.

'What is it?' she asked them. What was she missing? Around her, she could sense the others leaning forward and holding their breath now. They could hear something.

Snefrey swatted at her, demanding silence. Raina had half a mind to lock his arm behind him and apply firm pressure on his shoulder. With great restraint, she didn't. Then she heard it, too, and that helped her resist hurting him. She just wasn't sure what *it* was yet.

A faint humming of sorts. Maybe even people chanting, which sent a wave of tiny bumps tingling all over her skin.

Within seconds, the balmy temperature inside the pyramid became as frosty as the snow-covered ground in Aladaglar.

Inebni gave voice to her fears. 'What is it?' he asked. 'Maybe we should head back to the surface.'

Raina squeaked her agreement.

'Ceremony,' the tomb robber whispered. 'Ritual, maybe.'

'The priesthood?' she asked, suppressing a gasp.

'Sure sounds like it,' Snefrey said.

'We should send for the soldiers,' Inebni growled.

'What, just retreat? They might have Scrollworm. We can't risk leaving him alone with these unruly vermin.'

Raina didn't like Snefrey's decision one bit, but he was right. If the Amun Priesthood were just ahead—or below—she and the rest of the accompaniment needed to know. They couldn't turn around. Not now. If the priesthood had Merkhet, Raina couldn't leave without him, even to seek help. The pharaoh's safe return was paramount to all else.

'Let's go, then,' she said. 'Time is precious.'

'Easy does it,' Snefrey said, more to the guards than her as they began shuffling forward again.

Every passing moment in that cramped and dark passageway was akin to an entire day, or even a whole season. A terrible thought near crippled her. The pyramids were erected so close to the Nile—what would happen if the floods returned? Would these passages fill with water, drowning them?

The humming, chanting—whatever it was—grew louder and spared Raina from further self-torment. Light started to seep in from somewhere in front of them. Unable to stop herself, Raina shuffled into the back of Snefrey. Not a heavy collision, but enough for him to mutter a curse under his breath.

At a dead end, the walls were vibrating. Except there had to be a way through. Light was creeping in between the stones blocking their passage.

Just as she was about to ask whether they should try shift the blockage, the tomb robber beat her to it.

'Push,' he instructed the guards ahead.

Raina could only make out a dim outline of them as they linked themselves together in a line to heave. It would be much easier on them if they could all get access to the wall, but it didn't seem to matter much.

The stone—or stones—were shifting and more light streamed in through the widening cracks. The humming was not humming, either. It was definitely chanting.

What would be awaiting the Thebans on the other side? The priesthood—or maybe even something more sinister?

Raina held her breath as her nerves reached a crescendo. The gap became large enough for the guards to file into the space beyond, pairing off around each side of the stone. After the second set of guards went through, Raina and Snefrey did the same.

A vast underground cavern revealed itself to her. So vast that it must extend out beyond the surface of the Great Pyramid. Even more incredible, the source of the chanting …

The children. They had found them!

All wearing the same dark robes, their small statures distinguished them from the other Amun initiates. At the far end of the cavern, it looked as if the High Priest was leading the ceremony, but Raina couldn't be sure. She was overwhelmed, and the distance between her and the central figure was staggering.

Now that Raina was in the open cavern, the noise was deafening. The chanting must have drowned out the shifting stone because no attention fell on her or any of the other men accompanying her. She scanned the underground chamber for a sign of Merkhet. She couldn't see him. Where was he? What if he encountered danger back on the surface and his escort were now stuck beneath the pyramid?

'Do we turn back?' she asked her Theban companions.

No one said anything. They were all suffering from shock.

Chapter 28

Raina held steady, unsure of what to do or how to proceed.

The High Priest was the only one facing her, Snefrey, and the guards. Though the children and the initiates all had their backs to them and noses resting between their knees, it would take just one glance from the High Priest to be alerted to their presence in the lit-up cavern. Not wishing for that to happen, Raina tugged on Snefrey, dragging him back behind the safety of the stone. The guards followed.

'What?' the tomb robber begged of her.

'We need a plan.'

Snefrey nodded. 'You're right, sorry. You got one?'

Raina chewed on her lip. Could they overpower the High Priest? Six royal guards had to count for something, but if the priesthood had Merkhet …

'Could we funnel the children out before the High Priest notices?' she asked.

'Doubt it. No way to know how conditioned they are. Not being restrained, and did you see their puny little weapons next to them?'

Inebni agreed with something resembling a bark.

'The children are too much of an unknown,' the tomb robber continued. 'We take out the High Priest.'

Raina squealed before she could repress it. She hoped it was covered by the echo of the chanting. 'Murder him, you mean?'

Snefrey shrugged. 'Why not? The man is rotten. Less morals than me, a raider of tombs.'

'Be serious, Snef. He is the link between Amun and the Egyptians. Not for us to decide his fate.'

He scoffed at that. 'That man has as much connection to Amun as the fungus growth on my stinky big toe.' Snefrey pointed at his feet for emphasis, perhaps unaware that his voice was getting louder with every word.

'Shh,' she said, holding her finger to her lips. 'You'll give away our vantage.'

The guards held steadfast among the bickering, patiently waiting for a plan to form. Raina was about to request their input when some of the guards began to whelp with pain, a pitch reminiscent of a maimed jackal or hyena.

'What is it? Quiet, all of you!' Raina snapped at the guards. But then she was being pulled back inside the cavern.

The force wasn't overwhelming, but she couldn't stop herself from sliding. The tugs were on her waist and legs, and it wasn't until she was back in the cavern and shoved on her backside that she understood.

The children had dragged her. Or were they Amun's initiates now? More than fifty of them encircled the

Theban rescue effort, and their little faces were unresponsive to Raina's pleas. Their eyes were vacant, glazed over. The dim lighting gave an eerie glow to their eyes, and it was beyond creepy.

The royal guards didn't go to ground so easily, but it happened all the same. Snefrey too.

The children had an unsurmountable advantage because none of the guards could even consider raising a weapon against them. Raina and her companions were rendered defenseless as the children cramped all around them, their devoid expressions peering right through them.

Her limbs became heavy. If an opportunity to break free did arise, Raina wasn't sure that she would even make it off the ground. The damning possibilities fell all around her. She, Snefrey, and the guards might never escape this pyramid. Might never see daylight again. She would never scrawl on another scroll again. Never scratch out the shape of a hieroglyph. The High Priest wouldn't just let them leave, not now. That was as certain as the priesthood demanding more land and a grander share of the bounty at harvest collection.

The wait was torment. Would any of her companions be restrained? Was there a worse—more permanent—fate that might befall them? Just how callous and brutal was the High Priest?

The children's luminous eyes swarmed around her, and the helplessness of the situation swelled, expanding in her chest with every strained breath. Snefrey and the guards looked just as uncertain and unwilling to act as she.

Then the High Priest emerged, parting the cluster of children like loose sand in a strong gust. Their small figures scattered from his path but did not leave an escape route open. Were they eager to avoid his ire, or wholly compliant to his cause?

Somehow, the High Priest had lost some of his elderly qualities. The skin around his eyes and cheeks was far more taut, almost sprightly, as if lifelong pain and struggle had just recently departed him. 'So wonderful of you all to join us for this momentous occasion,' he said.

Raina grunted her reply. She hoped it conveyed a succinct summary of the thoughts whirling through her mind—*arrive at your point, you vile old man.*

'Just in time to witness,' the High Priest continued, 'the completion of our training.'

Snefrey fidgeted beside her. 'What training?'

'The Amun Army, of course. Delivered to me for the benefit of Egypt.'

'*Taken* by you,' Snefrey chimed in again, correcting the misguided man.

Raina couldn't resist from joining this time. The High Priest dangled the bait, and she swallowed it whole. The words tumbled out of her mouth so quick, one could be mistaken for thinking that she had ever observed a vow of silence. 'Benefit?' she scoffed. 'Which twisted scrolls do you derive your meanings from? You've done nothing but harm our great country. You're so consumed by zealousness that you are oblivious to the damage you wreak.'

'Ah, you're stronger than Prahmun, I see. Yet your resolve will count for nothing. You are too late.'

'Too late?' Snefrey asked.

The High Priest smirked. 'How could you not be?'

She couldn't bear the unknown much longer. Raina was about to burst in a fit of rage.

He just kept grinning at her, and that was it. She

sprung up at him, latching her hands around his throat. His eyes didn't widen with surprise. They narrowed, accepting the challenge, while his strong hands wrapped around her wrists with all the poise and measure of a cobra.

For a short, sweet moment, Raina thought she might be able to maintain her grip, but the High Priest removed her hands and tossed her back onto the hardened earth.

She lay there, stunned. Collecting herself, Raina uttered a question, and not even the croak in her voice could conceal the venom with which she spoke. 'What have you done with Pharaoh?'

If his face was not gleeful before, it was now. His lips stretched and curled up across his face. 'You've stolen my next question,' he said, laughing deep from the belly. 'You've lost him? How great.'

'They've not lost anyone,' said a voice from behind the circle of priests and children.

As the children parted again, Merkhet stepped into view.

Thirty feet away, he advanced side on, scuttling like a scorpion. Shield raised at his side, the pharaoh's Khopesh sword was drawn high, ready to strike. 'It's time we end this madness.'

Chapter 29

Clinging to the shadows on the peripheries, Merkhet stared into the dim chamber. Afraid his ears and eyes might be misleading him, he eased out into a massive cavern.

Even though he had read every available scroll about the pyramid's construction, nothing contained information about a cavern of this magnitude beneath it. Nor did he know about the strange entrance that led him down here in the first place. The pyramids had many mysteries, some of which may never be uncovered.

Edging farther along the cavern wall, more than half a thousand people were hunched over on their knees, deep in clamorous chanting. All except one, who stood at the front of the congregation. That sole figure had to be the High Priest, and Merkhet's instincts were justified. The summit of the expedition was right before him.

The pharaoh had dreaded this confrontation for too long, since the very moment he read the note left inside the tattered seams of Llora's pocket. Or had the terror set in as early as when his father warned him of the Amun Priesthood threat?

Somehow, the gods had planned it this way. A coming together of wills—a decisive crescendo—between himself and the High Priest.

Even with the confidence and might of the Egyptian Empire behind him, how could he convince the wretched priest that he was acting from immoral foundations? The man was impervious to all such suggestion, as he hid behind the false and wicked guise of Amun.

More mystifying still, the gods did not seem inclined to punish the High Priest. Perhaps even immortal deities could harbor regret for the sweeping devastation that resulted from the recent actions of so few. Why else would they have intervened then, but not now when Amun's name was invoking such colossal injustice?

The gods were giving Merkhet another chance to prove his worthiness as pharaoh, and his sword and shield were raised in readiness. Emerging out of the darkness, he contemplated rushing the High Priest. Could he close the gap and set things right without being noticed?

Maybe he could, but even if the priests and children kept their eyes closed and heads bowed, how would the High Priest respond if Merkhet was not successful?

How could the pharaoh forgive himself if the High Priest lashed out at the children? One poor child was already languishing without a full complement of fingers. The rest of the children were deprived of their families, of the normality of light, laughter, and routine.

The congregation of chanting and ceremony, led by the High Priest, stopped. Like a flock of birds unsettled during an afternoon drink, all the participants took to the back end of the chamber with haste, and Merkhet was saved the agony of deciding a course of action.

Eager to find out what sparked such rapid movement among the congregation, Merkhet trailed the High Priest from a distance.

A stillness permeated the air. There was a degree of uncertainty to it, as if nothing of interest had disturbed their proceedings in the cavern in quite some time. That was soon to change. Merkhet just had to wait for his moment.

He couldn't deny his curiosity, though, keeping pace with the crowd of priests and children. What had garnered their attention in such a frenzy?

It might be Raina or Snefrey. The guards. Whoever was responsible for the stir of activity, the High Priest carved his way through the hundreds of children and initiates. He or his followers never once looked back, so Merkhet was able to keep trailing them. As the nearest wave of tiny legs stopped shuffling, forty or so feet separated him and them.

Voices were active, but Merkhet couldn't quite catch the words or the speaker in the echoes. He walked closer.

When he heard Raina's voice, his world became strained and hazy. He couldn't quite make out what she was saying, but it didn't matter. She was here, in trouble, and the others probably were too.

His minuscule chance of surprising the High Priest was also gone. Merkhet had no chance of parting a crowd of children, unnoticed, to lock his arms around the leopard skin shawl.

Suffocating the High Priest became the pharaoh's sole goal—the only way for Egypt to breathe freely. But how could he make that happen when his friends were at the center of imminent danger?

Merkhet needed to remove them from this deplorable situation. The children, too.

There was only one way he could do that, and it would cost him everything.

But the pharaoh would give the High Priest what he demanded—anything for the safety of his friends and the future of his country.

Raina spoke again, this time loud enough for Merkhet to hear her. 'What have you done with Pharaoh?'

'That was my next question,' the High Priest said, a heinous laugh echoing through the cavern. 'You've lost him? How great.'

'They've not lost anyone,' Merkhet said from behind the masses of children and initiates. The children moved out of the way for him, and he tread slowly, his sword and shield raised. Merkhet spoke calmly as he advanced. 'It's time we end this madness.'

'Thank you, Your Grace. You've exceeded my expectations yet again.'

'Your delusions serve no purpose. All you will ensure is the destruction of the Amun Priesthood.'

'You're here, are you not, Pharaoh Merkhet? I've achieved plenty and played you as the fool all along. Why did I bother raising an army of initiates to overthrow the pharaohship if I could just wait for you to come traipsing on in here? Thank you for securing the fate of Amun.'

A fair distance separated Merkhet from the man he wanted to strangle. Children would get hurt if he tried to rush him now. Of all the possible outcomes, that was the least acceptable.

'I will hear your demands, in person,' the pharaoh said. 'But let my friends return to Thebes, along with the children.'

The High Priest sneered. 'The children are free, as they have always been. The chance to negotiate is over. Surrender yourself now.'

Merkhet lifted his sword and shield higher. 'You lie, and every false utterance delivers you farther from the Fields of Paradise.'

The High Priest found that amusing, a wicked smile slowly curling across his face. 'You are mistaken, Your Grace. Still so much to learn. What a shame you will never get the chance.'

'Don't be so sure,' Merkhet said. 'Justice finds its way, even when we lose faith.'

'Despite his numerous crimes, at least your father was not this ignorant.'

Many were willing and ready to speak ill of his father in his absence. Merkhet never once heard so much as a critical whisper while Pharaoh Nekhet was alive. Egypt was teeming with cowards, none more so apparent than the High Priest.

The citizens shouldn't cower at the feet of their pharaoh, kissing his sandals and relaying false compliments, but they should have the sense to recognize the self-serving individuals among their ranks.

Peronikh, Prahmun, the High Priest. They weren't the first to challenge the pharaohship, nor would they be the last. Was it too much to ask that the unified lands of Egypt actually came together in support and harmony?

'Where does this end?' Merkhet asked. 'The demands never cease. Is it your wish for Amun to be outcast and forgotten, a mere memory buried within your tomb?'

'Always so righteous. Your father and grandfather were no different.'

'I cannot speak for the actions of my ancestors, but nor will I give any credence to aspersions cast by you. It is time we acted for Egypt, not ourselves.'

'I am,' the High Priest snapped.

'Release the children and my friends. Only then, can I meet your demands.'

'You aren't listening. The children are not prisoners. They have made a commitment to Amun, the patron god of Thebes.'

'So why do you hide here in a cavern, hundreds of miles from our beloved capital?'

The High Priest could not be reasoned with. His eyes glinted with the very madness that needed to be eradicated. 'Secure them all!' he screamed. The command reverberated around the cavern as the children and priests reacted to their directive.

A sea of little limbs teemed all around Merkhet. Raina, Snefrey, and the guards suffered the same treatment too. Unless they were willing to strike at the children, the Theban contingent were helpless.

The Amun Priesthood had threatened the Pharaonic order for months, and now, through the actions of their malevolent leader, had every chance of succeeding.

Merkhet didn't want to lower his weapon and shield, though he couldn't strike the children grappling to restrain him, either. The temptation to topple them over with his shield was strong, but he would rather surrender than deliberately harm them.

The High Priest knew it, too. The pharaoh didn't have a means of protecting himself or those he cared for. They were completely at the mercy of the priesthood.

Stubby hands grabbed and groped at Merkhet from all sides. The children blindly followed commands they did not understand, and eventually, he was relieved of his sword and shield.

A great shudder of excitement coursed through the crowd of tiny people. As Merkhet's arms were held behind him, the crown fell from his head. It didn't even reach the ground before a child lay claim to it, scampering well clear of everyone else with the treasured prize held aloft.

These children were not of their right mind. How could they be? They were taught to revere their pharaoh, not remand him and plunder his royal headdress. Their actions made no sense. The worship of Amun didn't need to come at the expense of dedication to country. If only the High Priest could understand that.

Merkhet's hands were bound together with a thin flax rope. Trying his best to free them, he couldn't. Then a path emerged for him between retreating children, and he was prodded towards Raina and Snefrey, who were also tied up.

A short distance away, the royal guards were on their knees. Spears raised, they formed a tight circle. The children and priests were wary, their advance stifled. The tension was rising, some of the initiates coaxing their peers for glory. Yet all that would await them was bloodshed if Merkhet didn't intervene.

'Stand down,' the pharaoh called out to his guards.

They looked at him pleadingly, unwilling to believe the command. When Merkhet nodded, the guards lowered their spears and were soon swarmed.

Once their wrists were bound tight behind their backs, they were jostled over to join him, Raina, and Snefrey. The children slapped and chopped at the guards' legs until they were on the ground too.

The High Priest left the chamber, a victorious grin spanning the breadth of his cheeks. After that, the children were ushered out of the cavern by the senior priests.

A dozen or so of the bigger children remained behind, forming a ring around Merkhet and his accompaniment. Their gleaming, indifferent eyes stirred deep resentment. How could it be that Egypt's most fragile and innocent citizens were so wholly corrupted?

One by one, the braziers were extinguished as the masses departed, until Merkhet was alone—in the dark—with his loyal Thebans and their creepy observers.

No one spoke at first. If his companions were experiencing anything even remotely resembling his own emotions, it all fell on one question: how had it come to this?

An almost joyful exploration of the Giza plateau and the wonders of past dynasties built there. Then this ...

Snefrey was the first to break the silence. 'So, what's the plan?' he asked. 'While my ankles aren't bound, I refuse to believe a false prophet is going to be our downfall.'

'You wish to bumble around in the darkness and gut yourself on one of the children's swords?' Merkhet stared into the blackness, brooding. He wasn't sure the words to inspire them to victory resided in him. The High Priest had them in a bind, in more sense than one. 'Why do the children follow him? What power does he hold over them?'

'He's rinsed their mind of sense,' one of the guards said. 'No child I know, Egyptian or otherwise, would abandon games in the alleys with their friends in exchange for slave labor.'

'Never,' Inebni said, 'has a child dared show a member of the royal guard such disrespect.'

'Are they victims of an enchantment spell?' Snefrey

asked. 'The priesthood must have their own stash of secretive scrolls.'

Merkhet scratched under his chin. 'If we believe that this is sorcery, then we are doomed. Our only hope is to break the hold the High Priest has over the children. We do that, and we stand a chance of alerting Memphis to our plight.'

'That's enough of a plan to me,' the tomb robber said. 'How do we execute it?'

'That part eludes me,' Merkhet said. 'Besides, we have children listening to everything we say.'

A collective sigh went up around him. His companions were looking to him for a solution, and Merkhet wanted more than anything to provide it to them.

Some luck would not go astray, after all the hardship he—and Egypt—had endured in his tenure as pharaoh. What fortuitous moment would arrive for him to turn the odds in their favor, or even offer him and his friends a glimmer of hope.

The gods could not just desert their pharaoh—their living embodiment—without a chance. They just couldn't.

A scuffing noise drew nearer to the captive Thebans. Sandals scraping along the ground, maybe. Merkhet couldn't see anything. Could there be something more sinister than a delusional priest roaming the underground passages?

A terrible thirst gripped him, distracting Merkhet from that unsettling consideration. Vision of an oasis formed in his mind. Murky at first, but then it cleared, and the pool of water sparkled and gleamed. Was this the oasis he encountered in his exile? It could be, but his focus was fading. The yearning to quench his thirst was now his entire existence, and the acute stabbing dryness in his throat somehow spread, limb by agonizing limb. If he and the others were lucky, they would be offered some water. If they weren't, hydration wouldn't be required.

'What better way to squeeze the life out of the pharaohship than to offer you as sacrifices to our great and humble Hidden One.' The High Priest. His voice and infuriating righteousness were unmistakable.

Raina was panting beside him, and Merkhet wanted to reach for her, comfort her, but his hands could not wriggle themselves free. Neither did he have the right words to soothe her, to convince her of a merciful fate.

'Untie me, you vile and sorry man,' Snefrey blurted out. 'You're not worthy of even the gods' mercy if you go through with this. There will be no honor, no redemption.'

'I can scarcely believe it,' the High Priest said, a hint of amusement in his otherwise monotonous croak. 'A petty tomb robber with the morality of a devout priest. Amun will look favorably upon your sacrifice.'

'I'm not petty. How do you know of my profession?'

'Do you really think I wouldn't know about your exploits in my inner sanctum, young man?'

'You do not need to do this,' Merkhet said. 'Release the children. Release my friends. It is me that you want. No one else need suffer.'

'Such a forgetful and sad pharaoh. The moment for compromise and negotiation has passed. You were never fit for such a sacred duty. Thank you, Your Grace, the pity you conjure makes my task even easier.'

Merkhet grazed his teeth together. What awaited them? When would the gods give them a chance to fight? 'What is your grand plan, then?'

'After your screams fade into the flames with your flesh, Amun will become the patron god of all Egypt and beyond.'

'To what purpose?' the pharaoh insisted. Anything to delay from a tragic end.

'Amun has declared it, and so it will be.'

'You mistake your mission, High Priest. You jeopardize everything in your greed and will for power.'

'Do not think to lecture me, young man. You are only pharaoh because I made it so! You have failed where you could never succeed. Say farewell to your sad and helpless friends.'

'What do you mean you made it so?' Merkhet asked, but even as he did so, the answer appeared in his mind. He was watching on at Peronikh's Walking of the Walls ceremony when the High Priest interrupted the proceedings, announcing a vision from Amun.

Merkhet was to inherit the throne, not Peronikh. Had everything up until this moment been orchestrated just out of his reach, devised so that Merkhet would stumble from problem to problem and never seize control?

The High Priest cackled. 'It must be difficult going through life as a servant of your own gullibility. Could a band of Hittites breach our borders and slay a pharaoh in his own capital? Or would they need guidance?'

'Lies!' Merkhet screamed. 'You could never.'

'We'll allow you all to fret over your insignificant existences for a few more days, but fear not, the offerings will begin soon enough.' The High Priest stalked away, and the scuffing of his sandals filled the cavern.

One revelation after another. Merkhet choked back on tears. How could one priest channel so much hatred for his own country?

The High Priest had assisted the Hittites in

murdering Pharaoh Nekhet, and then ensured that Merkhet ascended the Golden Throne.

But why was it so pivotal that he became pharaoh and not Peronikh? Merkhet might never learn the truth because soon he and the rest of the Theban contingent would all be sacrificed to the flame. So much for a merciful departure.

Merkhet could already feel prickles of heat all along his arms and legs, but then the true horror was set upon him. If the fire reduced him to ashes, he could not be mummified. He would not meet his father in the Fields of Paradise.

None of them would.

Chapter 30

Merkhet slumped to the cavern floor, his companions having already succumbed to despair in the pervading darkness. How could they not, when the only thing that could distract them from their rumbling stomachs was the acute thirst that threatened to clamp shut their throats?

Throughout their enduring torture, Merkhet did not share aloud his realization: the precarious prospect of being denied the Afterlife. The collective crushed demeanor of his companions and their sprawling limbs conveyed well enough that they understood the severity of what confronted them. If the High Priest fulfilled his desire to dismantle the pharaohship, the things Merkhet sought would no longer matter. Securing additional land for temples and worship would mean little without the order that governs them. The people would rise against anyone that tried to assert themselves higher than the pharaoh.

Traditions were the foundation of Egyptian society—seemingly the only certainty in a life where nothing else could be taken for granted. Not the floods that sustained them, nor the peace that eluded them. Merkhet couldn't fathom the true extent of the High Priest's immorality, though it was clear that he faced something that challenged even his influence as the pharaoh. Still, he could not just yield to the chaos. Merkhet would not permit such cowardice, after all he had achieved and all that was at stake.

Merkhet lifted his cheek from the cold rock, breaking the silence as he rose. He did not attempt to constrain his voice—they were beyond the point of subtlety. 'We must sway the children. Even just one of them, and we can turn this in our favor.'

'We bribe them,' Snefrey said. 'Bet they haven't had any honey bread since they were stolen away.'

'Or, given their creepy obedience, maybe that is all they have had,' one of the royal guards remarked. 'Besides, where would we pull honey bread from?'

'Have some in my pack. Always do.'

'Great,' Inebni said. 'Whip it out, then.'

The tomb robber waited a moment. 'Can't,' he said. 'Ate the last of it on the plateau.'

The vizier huffed beside Merkhet. Her frustration paled against his own. If they could just ignite a connection among the children ...

'Does anyone know one of the children that were taken?' the pharaoh asked.

No response, just the stifling silence of the dank cavern until Raina spoke. 'What was the girl's name?'

'That's helpful,' Snefrey said.

'Enough,' Merkhet snapped. 'We need to focus. What are you asking, Rain?'

'Can't think … this gloom …' she said. 'You. The palace girl. Peronikh.'

Merkhet shuddered as painful memories surfaced. First of his false childhood brother, then his former lover turned sister. 'Llora, you mean?'

'Yes, her,' the vizier confirmed.

'What about her?'

'Her brother. Your brother?' she asked tentatively.

'Wuntu,' the pharaoh said. 'You're right. Llora was beside herself when he went missing. It was all she could speak of.'

'Must have been an early recruit to the priesthood,' Inebni said. 'Could be our best chance of ridding the corruption from the children's minds.'

'We just need a chance to isolate him,' Merkhet said in agreement. 'Remind him who he really is.'

A brazier flared to life on the far side of the cavern. As more were lit, shadows and figures moved, carrying some of the flames with them. Slowly, the darkness brightened. Around him, Merkhet could see the outlines of his companions and the children tasked with guarding them.

Now that the shadows no longer dominated, Merkhet stood up. His legs and feet were numb from the inactivity. He stretched them out, really leaning into it, as the tingling subsided.

As the unknown figures wandered through the cavern, another brazier flickered into existence. Judging by their height, they were all children. No senior priests among them, least of all the High Priest. Merkhet wanted to cry out in victory. Maybe the gods had delivered them the chance. Optimism coursed through him. The children—if that's who the three people were—headed toward him and the Theban captives. The other children on watch duty shuffled backwards, vacating the direct vicinity.

'I'll talk,' Merkhet said. 'Everyone else stay quiet. Please.'

No complaints sounded around him, and the figures were not far now. Their feet pattered softly on the ground. Light feet. Small people. Definitely children. Merkhet prepared himself to speak. Somehow, he needed to break through to them, inspire them to reclaim their identities and acknowledge their origins. Another opportunity—without the immediate influence of the manipulative High Priest—might not present itself.

Merkhet's task would be easier if the Double Crown were atop his head. A symbol of Egyptian order that the children might respond to, even though it had not induced success earlier. What if one of the approaching three wore it for themselves—how effective would anything he said be?

Aside from the brazier being carried, the lit flames were on the distant side of the cavern. Merkhet could only glimpse the children as the fire danced in front of them.

They were close now. Close enough for him to be sure that they were all young men and that he did not recognize any of them. However, for all he knew, one of them could be Wuntu.

'It is so wonderful for you all to join your pharaoh,' Merkhet said.

The children grunted. How could he get the boys to speak? They were all a similar height and shape—older than eight and younger than twelve.

'Underground caverns are no place to play. Don't you miss the rush of the Nile?'

Still the boys said nothing despite edging closer and

placing a bowl of water just in front of the bound Thebans.

'Thank you,' Merkhet said. 'We are grateful for your kindness.'

'Drink,' they said in unison.

A shiver spread across Merkhet's forearms and down his back. Their voices were strange, hollow and impersonal. 'What are your names?' he asked them.

They did not respond, turning their back on him and his companions. The children set off at a brisk pace back towards the distant light sources.

Desperate now, Merkhet called after them. 'Do you know Wuntu?'

They all stopped walking for the briefest of moments, then started again. The middle child appeared the most reluctant but didn't turn around.

'They know him,' the pharaoh whispered. 'I'm sure of it.'

'Keep going,' Snefrey urged him. 'Don't let them walk away now.'

'Wuntu has a toy lion, and we would like to return it to him.'

The children paused again, and the boy wedged between the others was the first to halt.

Merkhet persisted. 'Llora's waiting to play it with you.'

He regretted the cruel trick instantly, but the central child whirled around. Was that young man Wuntu? It was too difficult in the gloom to identify a hint of resemblance to Llora or Tiaa, or maybe even Nekhet.

The boy didn't attempt to explain his actions as he stepped away from his peers, pulling closer to Merkhet and the others. Was it Wuntu? Could he be restored?

Not knowing with any decisive clarity, the pharaoh

was ready to take a gamble. To do so could be their only hope. 'Your mother misses you, Wuntu. Llora misses you.'

The young man drew nearer still. Tentative steps, but they were steps all the same.

'We can take you to them.'

'We can, we can,' Snefrey said, joining. 'Can escort you home myself.'

The boy, quiet and reserved, was just feet away as his shuffling finished. His two escorts had not shifted from where they stopped. 'I know no home,' he said.

Merkhet studied the boy's face. Something was familiar, but he just couldn't place it. 'What is your name?' Merkhet asked.

'I have no name now,' the boy said.

Merkhet's heart pined. These poor children, stripped of their identity, and for what? He persisted. 'Are you Wuntu?'

'Not anymore. We are nameless in the service of the Hidden One.'

'Amun does not have need of servants, but your mother and sister want you back more than anything else.'

The boy stayed silent, and Merkhet was priming his next words, knowing he could break through to him. If the pharaoh and the rest of his accompaniment could be set free, they would be able to set right this heinous violation.

'I have your lion toy, Wuntu. I can return it to you. Not while we are tied, though. Release us, please.'

One slight step nearer, and a terrible guilt struck Merkhet. The boy—possibly his brother—was missing the top half of a finger.

'Wuntu—' Merkhet tried to apologize and beg for

forgiveness, but then a booming voice echoed throughout the cavern. The pharaoh didn't even need to face the speaker to know who it was. The High Priest.

'Hurry, children,' he had yelled. 'The burning is about to commence.'

Wuntu spun on his heels at once, falling into line with his peers. They raced to join their leader, and Merkhet groaned aloud. He and the rest of his escort were doomed, in this life and the next.

How had it come to this? Why had it come to this? Merkhet didn't know whom to plead to. His father, the gods, or the High Priest? Everything seemed futile now. The part that stung the most: Merkhet would not be the only victim to perish in the flames. If he had acted sooner and given more credence to the obscene demands of the priesthood, maybe this calamity could have been averted.

'Back soon, darlings,' the High Priest said, his cackle reverberating off the chamber's walls. 'Enjoy the cool while you can.'

The braziers were extinguished in rapid succession, and Merkhet and his friends were plunged back into the horrifying darkness.

'Last time I ever help anyone,' Snefrey said.

'You're not wrong about that,' Inebni added.

'Silence,' the pharaoh commanded them. 'Bickering will not serve. We need faith like never before. Wuntu could still do the right thing. He understood what was happening.'

'We have to believe,' Raina said, her voice raspy and quiet. 'It's all we have.'

'That and each other,' Snefrey said.

Merkhet hung his head in shame. His friends were too good to suffer this fate, a fate sealed by his own stubborn incompetence. 'Sorry, everyone. We should not be in this position.'

'Scrollworm,' the tomb robber began saying, as if everything was fine and going according to plan, 'why did you go in the pyramid in the first place?'

'Did you see a child?' Inebni asked.

The pharaoh laughed, surprising even himself. 'I thought I did,' he said. 'Then I just sort of … fell inside.'

Snefrey cheered, a hefty *whoop* bouncing off every wall in the underground chamber 'Secret entrances do exist! Which side was it, Merk? You have to tell me.'

'Settle down, Snef, hardly our most pressing issue,' Merkhet said, straining against his restraints for what must have been the fiftieth time. 'Southern face, think it was.'

'Fascinating. Will be keen to examine it for myself when we—'

Inebni cut in. 'When we what, Snef?'

'When we are rescued by a twelve-year-old boy who doesn't even acknowledge his own name.' Snefrey exhaled after no one responded to him. 'Anyone have eyes on the water? I could really use a drink.'

'Perhaps the gods will grant me night sight after I end you.'

Merkhet didn't need the sun's rays or the flicker of flames to sense Inebni's frustration, but his stomach grumbled, and he withdrew from their argument.

How long had they been inside the pyramid? The pharaoh trembled on the spot as a second and more horrifying question dawned on him: how long did they have left inside the pyramid?

Chapter 31

The High Priest's voice echoed throughout the cavern. 'Lead the sacrifices to the flame.'

A swarm of priesthood children rushed towards Merkhet and his Theban accompaniment, and they were soon being prodded closer to a series of flickering lights.

Shoved into a passage, Merkhet was at the front of the group, Raina right behind him. After some twists and turns, the hallway fed into a ritual chamber of sorts. Inside, they were guided into a cramped corner at the back. Merkhet thudded against the wall, snarling children encroaching the scant space around him. He could not go anywhere.

All over the chamber floor, priests were on their knees. Reverent in conduct, they all faced a flat dais, elevated just enough for everyone to have a clear view of it. At its rear, carved into a stone wall, were the many depictions of Amun. Geese, rams, and snakes surrounded the god in his cobra-headed, crocodile-headed, and ape-headed human forms.

In front of the hieroglyphs, a flame roared at the center of the dais. The thick chunks of wood, arranged in a ring at the fire's base, were already mottled and charred from the heat. Flaming streaks of yellow and orange curled and twirled around each other, fanning wider than the royal guards combined.

The High Priest strode through a gap in the priests, moving more elegantly than ever before, as he climbed the stairs to the dais and the fire upon it.

The beginning of the end. Merkhet sighed, unsure whether he could plead rational sense with the wild and unsound collective of the Amun Priesthood. He needed to try, but his gaze was lost in the strange allure of the fanning flames.

Someone bumped into him. 'What was that for?' he mumbled.

'If you've got a plan, now's the time,' Snefrey said.

Merkhet looked around. The only way out was back the way they had come. How far could they get with their hands bound against an army of priests wielding weapons? Perhaps, the pharaoh and the others could fend off a few children with some well-timed kicks, but as far as he could tell, they would just wind up back in the grand cavern again.

The sheer masses of children would overwhelm them there, and the escape would be foiled before it even really began.

'Open to suggestions,' he whispered so that only Raina and Snefrey could hear him.

'Pretend to join them?' Snefrey offered.

The tomb robber's tone gave away his frivolity, but Merkhet was taken by the idea. It could have some merit. He stared at the High Priest, who was conducting some last-ditch preparations on the dais. Would a man at the pinnacle of priesthood seniority fall for such an obvious ploy? Could he succumb to glaring flattery?

'It's the best we have,' the pharaoh said. 'Go for it, Snef. Don't hold back.'

The tomb robber sidestepped the group of children hemming them in with an expert feign. He pierced the walkway between meditative priests like a barbed arrow. Reaching the altar, Snefrey stooped low to the ground. 'Your Excellency, I must express my admiration. How did you achieve that smoke cloud on the Nile? Sensational. Brilliant. But can the esteemed mind that duped the pharaoh with that wondrous concoction not see that there is another way?'

The High Priest looked down at the tomb robber, contempt on his wrinkled face, which crumpled even more as he searched for the right words to convey the depth of his disgust.

Making use of the delayed response, Snefrey continued. 'Does the priesthood have no use for a man of my particular skills and talents? Why should we part ways now, before I've yet to benefit your cause?'

'Stand tall, you blathering fool, and part with the trifling praise. What is it you want? The sacrifices are set to begin.'

'If we are given to the flames, then we cease to exist, cease to be valuable.'

The High Priest growled, daring for his patience to be tested.

'Spare us, so that we may assist you. Egypt is such a vast land, how will you ever spread the power of Amun, with these small, insufferable children? They have such short legs and—'

'You may join the priesthood—'

Snefrey cut in. 'Fantastic, where do I—'

The High Priest finished talking, as if he were never interrupted. 'If you push the pharaoh into the flames yourself.'

If his own fiery demise meant that Raina, Snefrey, the royal guards, and the children were spared from being scorched alive, Merkhet could accept that, maybe even find some peace in it.

The tomb robber must have shared a similar sentiment because he asked, 'What fate for the rest of them?'

Merkhet's resistance to firm action led them here, to this moment. No one else should suffer because of his mistakes and oversights, though hearing the query aloud hurt, and he couldn't help himself but question Snefrey's loyalty. Why wouldn't a tomb robber secure his own interests first? What difference would their shared history make when the only other choice was death?

The priests rose from their low positions, kneeling tall, in anticipation of the verdict. The High Priest debated internally for what seemed an eternity. 'The pharaoh must be sacrificed. All else may avoid the same demise, should you refrain from annoying me any further. They, too, must prove their worth.'

Snefrey bowed. 'Thank you, Your Excellency. You are most generous.'

'Your duty is not complete yet, young man. The flames are just as much yours until you do as I have bid.'

'Of course, Exalted One. The deed will be done.'

Whether some plan had formed, or an opportunity presented itself to the tomb robber was unclear, but as Snefrey's extravagant flattery continued, the pharaoh just had to trust that it was part of some scheme rather than an act of self-preservation.

'Bring forth the sacrifice,' the High Priest called out.

The children flocked to Merkhet, prodding and shoving him towards the altar. Towards the fire. What had happened to these children for them to be so lost, so damaged? Why could they not understand the severity of their blind actions?

Mere feet away from Snefrey, the pushing stopped. The tomb robber gave him little heed, turning back to the High Priest. He held up his bound hands. 'May I be freed to perform my privileged duty?'

Clad in his leopard shawl, the High Priest deliberated the request. He was searching for any threat or malice in Snefrey but decided against any because he announced for the rope to be cut.

A senior priest rushed forward to carry out the command. Snefrey was liberated from his bind. But was he free, with such an unsavory expectation lingering over him?

'The ceremony is about to commence,' the High Priest declared. He spoke way too loud for the confined chamber, his words reverberating through it as hundreds of children filed in from the passage that led to the grand chamber. They filled whatever voids they could find, joining the priests already on their knees.

Merkhet could sense the perspiration beading all over him, and he wasn't even near the flame yet. Death without the promise of an eternal Afterlife. No reunion with his father. The end of the Eighteenth Dynasty. The end of Egypt's supremacy.

A sacrifice unlike any other.

Merkhet approached the dais. Somehow, it seemed easier to take it upon himself, rather than be forced at spear-point. The bitterness hung all around him, though, pressing down with every smug grin the High Priest flaunted. The man knew he had worn down the pharaohship and his delusions were about to be fulfilled.

Merkhet wouldn't even be able to avenge the deaths of his father and sister. Trudging for the flames, he couldn't bring himself to look back at Raina or the guards. The pharaoh didn't want their pity. They were better off alive than turned into a smoldering heap.

'Amun, hear our chant,' the High Priest roared as Merkhet ascended the altar.

The priests around the chamber began chanting the same two syllables. *A-mun, A-mun, A-mun.*

Staring into the glowing swirl of flames, Merkhet was beyond help now. Horus, his father, Taharva—none of them could reach him now.

A-mun, A-mun, A-mun—the chanting continued.

Merkhet inched nearer to the intense orange glow, not wanting to subject Snefrey to the unenviable role of executioner. Holding his breath, Merkhet held his restrained hands out to the fire.

The end of the Eighteenth Dynasty had arrived.

Chapter 32

Children and priests screamed with raucous intent. Merkhet ignored the uproar behind him as best he could. Yet something about the commotion didn't sound right, not connected to anything he was doing or the anticipation of what was to come.

He whirled around, his heart sinking quicker than a stone cast into the Nile. Prahmun was bounding to the High Priest. How? How could the wretched man be here when …

Then Merkhet saw more of what was unfolding in the rear of the chamber, and it changed everything. Turn-Tide Taharva had arrived, resplendent in his red uniform. Wielding a spear—but not his usual bronze spear—the Nubian looked ready to unleash havoc.

He charged at the gap between the kneeling priests and children, covering tremendous ground. Then a horde of children formed, surrounding him. Taharva faced the same dilemma the rest of the Thebans had.

Could the captain strike a child? He was yet to lower

his weapon, nor try to use it. Taharva was as helpless as Merkhet had been.

In the chaos, Raina, Inebni, and the other guards hurried to assist the Nubian, but their valiant efforts were coming undone before they really began. The Thebans were once again all encircled, and Snefrey might be the only one to escape the pyramid with his life.

The High Priest recovered from the unexpected arrivals, grunting his disapproval. 'So,' he said, 'the viceroy failed, too. Can you believe that there is someone even more incompetent than you, Prahmun?'

Merkhet agreed with the High Priest for once. The vile former vizier was better kept in a pit, and with any luck, he would return there.

What of the viceroy, though? He could not have coordinated with the priesthood to remove Taharva from Thebes, could he?

Yet concocting some sick plot of a family reunion didn't even approach the High Priest's limits when it came to acts of spite and cunning. Did his malice and treachery know no bounds?

The fire's heat spread across Merkhet's back. Somehow, he found the sensation calming. Yet, there was a restlessness within him. So many missed opportunities, so much misfortune.

When Snefrey spoke, though, Merkhet was ready to embrace the warmth. 'Kneel before the sacrificial flames,' the tomb robber commanded.

Merkhet did not move, so torn and gutted at what his efforts had amounted to.

'Kneel!' Snefrey snapped, guiding the pharaoh to compliance. Then he invited the High Priest to advance. 'Come. Witness the end of Pharaonic tyranny. The time of Amun is now.'

Merkhet staring at the glowing embers at the fire's base. Specks of ash landed on his cheeks, but he did not wince. He accepted them as he accepted his sacrifice, anything that might see the children and his friends released.

But he couldn't even be certain of that. What faith could he place in the High Priest, now a greedy predator in the mere moments before taking its prey?

'It doesn't need to be this way,' Merkhet said, his voice reduced to a husk. 'The children deserve to be set free.'

'Hush. The children will receive Amun's blessing. Now, rise,' Snefrey said, forcefully grabbing beneath Merkhet's armpits.

So close to the flames now, the searing heat was all around the pharaoh. Beads of sweat formed and spiraled down his cheeks.

One deep inhale and then it would all be over, but he didn't even manage that. Snefrey shoved him from behind, and Merkhet became one with the roaring flame.

Chapter 33

Merkhet went through the fire at such a rapid pace, that he passed through the flames and slammed into the stone wall behind the dais.

Dazed, he spun around.

Distorted figures, movement everywhere in the chamber.

Snefrey dived into the core of the fire. A seemingly reckless act, vacant of self-preservation, until he flung a clump of ashes into the High Priest's face, who screeched and writhed in pain. Dropping to the ground, his hands immediately rubbed his eyes, smearing the embers.

Taharva burst through a crowd of unsuspecting children. Without a weapon to hinder him, he sent them flying backwards.

Senior priests were taking up arms. Raina and the guards were lost in a flock of flailing bodies, and Snefrey crawled along the dais, clutching at his shoulder.

Their advantage would not last long as spears and

axes began to enter the fray. Merkhet leaped to action. He held his hands over the licking flame, trying to weaken the rope binding them. The searing heat started to soften his resolve, and he was about to pull his hands away when a tiny spark caught on the flax.

Merkhet couldn't breathe, the pain too intense. The rope still had its integrity, though, because he couldn't break it apart yet. The High Priest was recuperating, and if he did, he would be capable of restoring order and control. The pharaoh needed to do whatever he could to prevent that from happening.

The bind was smoking now but so were his hands. Soon, his skin would singe and burn irreparably. Merkhet tested the rope's strength again and this time it near disintegrated under concerted pressure. Breaking free, he dashed across the dais and wrapped his arms around the screaming High Priest, who wriggled and squirmed with the vigor of a man in his prime.

The pharaoh would not let go. Not now, not ever, for the gods had granted them a chance to seize back control.

Snefrey's stellar summation of the situation could not be denied. He had wheedled the High Priest into false comfort with pure audacity and the guile of an alley performer. Through a steadfast and unyielding grip, Merkhet tried purging the guilt of having not trusted the tomb robber.

Clear of the first line of children, Taharva sprinted through a muddle of outstretched spears to climb the altar and reach Prahmun, who was moving to assist the High Priest. The Nubian darted across the former vizier's path and barged him headlong into the flames.

Embers crackled and spit all around Prahmun, catching on the ridiculous broad material wrapped around him. He did not retreat from the fire because he became one with its roar. His horrid shrieks blotted out all other noise, and Merkhet almost abandoned his concentration to watch.

The High Priest was alert to the opportunity and broke the grip of one arm. He managed to tumble the pharaoh over and pin him to the ground. But Merkhet reinstated his firm hold, squeezing the last morsels of air from the crazed priest atop him.

Merkhet couldn't check how the others were faring. Overwhelmed by spear and axe, or thwarting the chaos? His world, for the moment at least, was to deny the High Priest any chance of proceeding with a sacrificial offering. The pharaoh could not fail this task. The strength of Horus, of his father, coursed through his arms now.

Black, empty pits. Those were the High Priest's eyes as he battled against the will of the pharaoh. Merkhet conjured the might and determination of a worthy Egyptian King, but could one moment redeem his periodic lapses of judgment?

The High Priest's grapple was fading. The Thebans might actually escape this struggle beneath the pyramid and set the scrolls straight. Raina might even fulfill that duty herself.

Then Merkhet was lifted off the ground—him and the High Priest both—hoisted high above the raging flames.

Taharva. The conviction of the Nubian was palpable, pounding through his tensed arms.

When the tips of his toes could touch the ground again, Merkhet released the High Priest. He fell away from Taharva, who still held the limp figure. The captain might very well hug the life right out of the High Priest as Prahmun's screeches and wails continued to fill the chamber.

The former vizier—the man responsible for many of Egypt's woes since Pharaoh Nekhet last graced the desert plains—was burning from within. He writhed around, spinning and contorting, but the flames never extinguished.

Merkhet gagged as the stench of singed flesh reached him, a disgusting and bizarre blend of smelted copper and fried pork. The overbearing and unpleasant fumes were the least of his worries. Eight or nine priests circled him and Taharva. They wanted the body of the unconscious High Priest resting in the Nubian's tight embrace. Their raised spears confirmed their corruption was fixed, unmoving. These men and women had lost their sense of morality many moons ago.

Most Egyptians paid homage or attention to a particular god but never so radically, never at the expense of all the other deities. Balance needed to be restored, and it needed to happen here, now. Where the pharaoh hoped that he could reverse the damage done to the children, he was less sure about the priests surrounding him.

'Relinquish your weapons,' Merkhet pleaded with the priests. 'No good can come from this.'

A murderous glint reflected at him from the eyes of a senior priest, and the man spoke with all the venom of an angry asp. 'Would be a shame if children were to get hurt, after all that's happened. Selfish pharaoh responsible for senseless massacre. You should prepare your scribe to record it now.'

Taharva twisted and turned, using the limp High Priest as a shield against the encroaching spears. The Amun Priesthood were beyond help. An amicable and uncomplicated end to the conflict might be impossible.

'Stand down,' Merkhet begged them. 'We can spare

the High Priest,' he said, silencing Taharva's immediate protest with a commanding glance, 'but not if you harm the children. It is time they are taken home.'

The Second Priest of Amun stilled himself, contemplating.

Merkhet gave the man no time to think, flooding him with vivid imagery. 'Your master's lungs could collapse and his eyes burst from his skull with one swift squeeze. Lay down your weapons, and we will preserve him. The choice is yours.'

If the senior priest had ideas of succeeding his unconscious master, Merkhet's entire plan could crumble in a moment. Men with such ambitions didn't care for the consequences of their actions.

Even with the situation swinging in their favor, Merkhet held his breath, almost waiting for everything to unravel in front of him. As if he was drowning, his lungs screamed for air.

Images of his father and mother rushed by him. They were together on the royal terrace, laughing and blissful. They were clambering into the back of the chariot, and Merkhet was wedged between them, reading.

The wholesome visions disappeared as Prahmun's howling ceased. The former vizier was dead, roasted alive, and the sudden hush jarred Merkhet. Looking through a gap of his immediate oppressors, Inebni and two of the royal guards were no longer restrained. They were yet to acquire weapons but were creeping closer to the circle of emboldened priests. Snefrey was armed and deterring some children from joining their leaders.

Raina was not within sight, but she was resourceful. If he could trust nothing else, Merkhet needed to trust that. Then the boy with the missing finger—Wuntu— slipped between two priests and entered the tight ring that contained the pharaoh and captain.

Wuntu approached the Second Priest of Amun, calm and measured. 'Allow me,' he said, gesturing for the priest's spear.

No hesitation, no deliberation, the senior priest yielded his weapon for the young man. Wuntu grabbed it with both hands and faced Merkhet.

'No, you don't have to—' the pharaoh started to croak, but his objection was rendered immaterial.

Wuntu spun around and lanced the Second Priest of Amun right through the throat. The spear stuck in the flesh and blood gurgled around it, running down the weapon's shaft. The royal guards breached the circle in the chaos, disarming the other priests. Some of Amun's followers even dropped to a kneel and placed their weapons down on the ground.

Around the chamber, all the remaining priests lowered their spears and axes, too, placing them on the ground.

The children stilled themselves, blinking. A few looked at the discarded weapons, and then as if they were waking from a deep slumber, the children were hugging each other. Some smiling, some crying. All of them laughing. The fight was over.

Taharva let the High Priest down, laying him near the fire. At least for the moment, the priest was passed out, but Merkhet was certain that the sleeping demon would recover enough to face the gods' judgment for his misguided deeds.

Wuntu sprung at Merkhet from a few feet away. After the initial brace and recoil, the pharaoh wrapped the boy up in a warm hug. When would be the right time to declare their relation to one another? Not now, of that the pharaoh was adamant. 'You are as brave as Horus and Sekhmet combined,' he said, ruffling Wuntu's short hair.

Merkhet released his brother, and Wuntu scurried away to some friends. Taharva was but a step away, and Merkhet dragged him in by the wrist. He didn't care if the Nubian was not fond of affection, Taharva would have little choice but to embrace this one. The captain gripped Merkhet's forearm, and they shared a quiet moment of relief and happiness.

Then the pharaoh helped Snefrey to his feet. The tomb robber's shoulder stuck out at a weird angle, but that didn't stop Merkhet from reeling him in. 'You really had me going there, Snef. I was convinced you were joining the priesthood.'

'Most fun I've had since that Fifth Dynasty tomb I—'

'Don't ruin it now,' Merkhet said, laughing until his chest and ribs couldn't tolerate any more.

The royal guards were ensuring order, rounding up the priests and tending to the children. Merkhet gave each of them an appreciative nod as he searched for Raina.

At the end of the chamber, he found her. Somehow, amid all the chaos, the vizier had located a reed pen and scroll. She was furiously scribbling like she always did. Merkhet cut the gap and swallowed her in the biggest cuddle yet. He didn't care that the reed got caught between them and dug into his stomach.

They had survived. Egypt, the pharaohship, and his family's legacy would endure.

Chapter 34

Merkhet stepped out of the Great Pyramid, on the opposite face to which he entered. Except for the glint of a crescent moon illuminating the plateau around him, nightfall covered the sky.

After unknowingly tumbling inside a secret entrance, Merkhet had spent more than a few days beneath the pyramid. Trading the musty and stale air of the underground passages for the refreshing surface air was when it set in—what he and the Theban contingent had achieved.

Before leaving the chamber, Merkhet had recovered his sword and shield. He brandished them now, slicing through the gentle breeze in a silent triumph. As soon as the Double Crown could be found in the disarray below, he would be closer than ever to restoring his country to prosperity.

Raina, Snefrey, and Taharva stumbled out of the pyramid, joining him. The tomb robber approached, while the captain lingered behind, wrapping Raina under his arm.

'Snef,' the pharaoh said. 'I must head north, past Memphis. Can you stay with Rain and the guards to sort this mess?'

'Of course. Can we revise the original agreement to include the deed to a second drinking hovel?'

Merkhet admired his friend's smirk. The tomb robber could find a way to extract the seriousness from any situation.

'Fine, I'll do it out of the goodness of my ka. What do you need from us?' Snefrey asked.

'Prepare the priests and children for travel. I'll be back soon with the army.'

'As long as I don't have to speak with anyone other than Raina and Inebni.'

'You'll manage that just fine,' Merkhet said. 'You always do.'

Raina and Taharva ambled over, but the pharaoh didn't make a cheeky remark about their closeness. Surprisingly, Snefrey didn't either.

'What now, Scrollworm?' the captain asked.

'You and I will retrieve the army. Will need some assistance to get these priests and children back to Thebes.'

'Great,' Taharva said, dipping his head. More time on horseback.'

'You love Tendrence. Don't deny it.'

The captain made no such effort, leaving to fetch the horses.

'See you in a couple of days, then,' Merkhet said to Raina and Snefrey. 'Thank you both for your unwavering support.'

The pharaoh chased after Taharva, exhaustion not even a mild consideration. He had as much energy now as when he defeated the raging hippopotamus and passed his Pharaonic Trial.

Merkhet pushed Abacca into a fierce gallop. Up ahead was the island, nestled between two minor channels of the Nile, where the new city's construction was taking shape. The base of the outer walls was already erected, a hint of how it would dominate the landscape. From above their walls, the Egyptian army would be able to gaze all the way to Hattusha. When all the work was finished, the fortress would be every bit as formidable as the great Hittite city.

Wooden beams were positioned at various points around the island, bridging the channels and connecting it with the mainland. Merkhet guided Abacca across one of the bridges and between a gap in the wall, dashing for the nearest of many building projects. The foundations of a temple. Beside it, a glorious stable was almost complete. Double the size of its counterpart in Thebes, the magnificent structure would house as many as four hundred horses when it was done. Plenty enough for any military activity. His father's vision was assembling before his very eyes. A city with as much potential as Memphis and Thebes, maybe more.

Merkhet spotted a feminine figure, her black hair gleaming in the sun as she observed the laborers and soldiers. He hopped off Abacca and sprinted to his mother. Taharva didn't follow him, securing the horses.

Startled, Merep squealed when Merkhet wrapped his arms around her. 'What is the—' she started to say, but by then she had spun around and could see him.

'Merkhet, my dear boy. I had no idea you—'

He cupped his hand over her mouth and gripped her tighter. 'We can speak in a moment, Mother.'

She stroked the length of his ponytail, and Merkhet was the most relaxed he had been since before inheriting the Golden Throne.

'What has happened, my son? Something grave has passed.' His mother's voice was gentle, reaffirming, as she whispered into his ear.

Would things settle now? Had he—and Egypt— earned a reprieve from the constant chaos?

Merkhet could not leave anything to chance, not after everything he had faced as pharaoh. He would demand a time of healing. For himself. For everyone.

How could he begin to explain what had happened? He couldn't. Not yet.

'The city is coming together,' Merkhet said, releasing her. 'Have the gods revealed its name yet?'

She stared deep into his eyes, his soul. His mother studied him a moment longer, unsure of whether to allow him to dodge her question so easily. He won in the end because she said, 'They will, given time.'

Her wisdom rivaled her beauty, but they both paled in the shadow of her strength. She, more than anyone, was still mourning the loss of Pharaoh Nekhet.

'What brings you here?' she asked. 'What of the children? Word reached us here not more than seven moons ago.'

News of the children preceded him, even with his and Raina's efforts to shield the north from the tragedy. All the same, Merkhet had no desire to broach any matter that he did not have to right now. 'We must all return to Thebes for a celebration, but first the soldiers are required on the Giza plateau.'

Her eyes pierced through him, similar to how his father's once did. 'The celebration of the return of the children?'

'Well, yes *that* celebration, but also a union of foreign nations,' he said, muttering the last part into his hand.

Merep slapped him playfully in recognition. 'Haliya,' she said, trying her best to stifle a gasp.

He nodded. 'She doesn't know it is going ahead yet, but it was her idea.'

Merep dragged him in for another hug, and when she let him go, she pressed one finger and a thumb against her lips. The whistle that followed could be heard for miles. It left him coiled over in shock, clutching his ears. The soldiers heeded the hint, though. They stopped what they were doing and began gathering for their next instructions.

'I'll head home tomorrow,' she said. 'Let me organize this rabble for you first. Giza, did you say?'

Merkhet rubbed his mother's shoulder. 'Send them direct to the pyramids, and don't fear, we won't get started in Thebes without you.'

'You better not,' she said, her grin lingering.

'Which temple is this, anyway?'

'Did he not tell you, Merk?'

'Who? Tell me what?'

'Your old charioteering friend sent correspondence,' Merep said. 'A late inclusion for the new city.'

'Did he now?'

'He did. You are looking at what will become your father's mortuary temple.'

'I might strangle him,' Merkhet said.

'There won't be a safer place in Egypt once the construction is finished. What better way to honor your father's vision than with his very own mortuary temple.'

Merkhet marveled at the brilliance of the idea. The sheer simplicity of it. 'We're getting closer, aren't we?'

'I don't follow, my son.'

A lump caught in his throat, unsure what he was trying to express. 'To finding some sort of meaning without him.'

A wrinkle of sadness appeared on her face. 'I suppose we are.'

'Is Lufu around, or is he in Memphis?'

'He reported earlier this morning, Merep said. 'He may still be here.' She gestured somewhere beyond the stable and temple, then kissed him twice on each cheek.

'See you soon, Mother,' Merkhet said, a huge smile lingering.

He turned, hastening around the construction of the temple. Taharva followed him, the horses in tow. Merkhet stopped mid-stride when he saw Lufu. Did the vizier have news of Peronikh? An agonizing thought, but one the pharaoh would be spared from dwelling on.

Lufu powered towards him, cradling something in his arms. A bow, the Eye of Horus gleaming under the sun's rays. Horakhty. The pharaoh would not have to suffer any more hunts without his cherished bow, and more importantly, he would not have to wait any longer to learn of the soldiers' efforts in Aladaglar.

'My dear friend,' Merkhet greeted him.

'Your Grace, when was the last time you slept?'

As with his mother, Merkhet did not want to speak about the traumatic saga of the taken children. He diverted the topic. 'How is Memphis treating you?'

'It is good to spend time there,' Lufu said. 'I cannot deny that Raina has given me enough faith to relieve my burdened mind.'

'She is a revelation. What news of Peronikh?'

'None, I'm afraid. After a thorough search, the soldiers returned to me not so long ago. No sighting of his corpse anywhere near the ravine.'

Merkhet groaned. 'I will need to meet with his mother to express my anguish and apologize.'

'Samena can be tricky. Trust your judgment there,' Lufu said, handing over Horakhty. 'Collected it from the craftsman just yesterday. No idea what possessed me to bring it along today.'

The pharaoh ran his fingers along its curved edges and contours. No sign of frayed or splintered wood. His bow was whole again. 'Thank you, Lufu, it is perfect once more, and now we can depart for Thebes.'

'Uh, pardon, Your Grace?'

'A celebration beckons. Would you have me ruin the surprise?'

The vizier frowned. 'I cannot function with unknowns, you know that.'

'Mother will have to fill you in on the way to Thebes, then.'

'Will we at least have a full debrief after the festivities?' Lufu asked.

'Yes,' Merkhet promised. 'See you in Thebes,' he called over his shoulder.

By the time Merkhet departed the construction of the fortress city and tracked the Nile back to Giza, the Double Crown had been located.

In front of the Great Sphinx, Raina handed it to him.

'Thank you,' Merkhet said, covering himself with it right away. Aside from the pride of his thick ponytail, the scalp was usually crisp, clean. Too many nights away from Thebes, hairs were sprouting from everywhere. No strands were the same length, and there wasn't enough for it to grow together yet.

Taharva and Snefrey joined him and the vizier. 'Together, we will ride ahead to Thebes,' the pharaoh said. 'What thought has been given to how we will transport the children and priests?'

On the plateau, the priests were under the watchful eye of Inebni and the royal guards. The children roamed between the pyramids, laughing and playing games.

Snefrey obliged him. 'The guards found the galleys before we were forced to rescue your sorry hide.'

'Well, the currents have started to slow. It will be their quickest way back to Thebes,' Merkhet said, giving voice to his observations. 'Snef, can you let Inebni know that the soldiers will be with him soon to assist? Soon as you do that, we can leave.'

'If we make it three drinking hovels, I'll do anything,' the tomb robber said, already strolling to Inebni.

'Round up the horses, please, Turn-Tide.'

'Anything to sleep in my own reed mat again,' the captain said with a smile.

'I haven't forgotten you, Rain. Can you please fetch Wuntu? It is time I speak with him.'

Merkhet watched on as the vizier strolled to the smallest pyramid, where a group of older children were huddled beneath it.

Would Wuntu hate him for his deceitful actions in the cavern? Or would he just be thrilled at learning of their connection?

Raina was on her way back, Wuntu trailing in her shadow. The vizier encouraged the young boy to approach his pharaoh, and Merkhet waited with bated breath. The fifty feet that separated them may as well have been a thousand, for that's how many thoughts streamed through his head.

Instead of resenting the High Priest, Merkhet was furious with himself. Llora tried to warn him long before hundreds of children were taken. He didn't listen, too busy nursing his wounded pride, and now the true cost of his inaction stood before him. Wuntu, pallid and legs trembling, covered the hand of his missing finger. How long had the boy spent underground? What terrors did he face down there?

'We were so scared,' the young boy blurted out. 'He threatened us and our families. I just wanted Llora and my mother to be safe.'

'You were brave. As courageous as all the Egyptian soldiers that have ever come before you. I'm so sorry that this ever happened to you,' Merkhet said, placing a hand on Wuntu's shoulder. 'Your pharaoh has failed you on more than one account.'

Wuntu bit down on his lip and pulled away.

Merkhet paused, to collect his thoughts. He needed to find a way to do this gently, and he couldn't pretend it wasn't true anymore. Wuntu might not have Tiaa's eyes, but he had Nekhet's nose. The shape and the way it flared as the boy breathed. There could be no doubt.

'I lied to you, and there can be no excuses for it,' Merkhet said.

'Lied?' Wuntu asked.

'Yes,' the pharaoh said, not certain he could manage the rest. 'The High Priest …' He gulped. 'The High Priest took Llora's life.'

'No. No. No!' Wuntu exclaimed, his hands slamming across his ears. He swayed his head back and forth, but Wuntu wouldn't be capable of shaking the truth away.

'I should not have deceived you. It was wrong to do so, but I couldn't see another way. The priesthood had terrified you and the other children into utter subservience.'

Snefrey and Taharva lingered in the background with Raina, having completed their tasks. The horses were all straddled and ready to go.

'Wuntu, there is one more thing I need you to know.'

'If you don't have my lion ...' The boy began to sob.

Merkhet bent at the knees, so that he could look into Wuntu's glistening eyes. 'Your toy lion is at the palace, brother.'

The young boy's face swelled with confusion. 'Br-brother? What do you mean? Is this another trick?'

'No,' Merkhet said. 'Pharaoh Nekhet is—*was*—your father too.'

'I don't believe you.' Wuntu turned on his heels and raced away.

Still on his haunches, Merkhet waited as Taharva, Snefrey, and Raina led the horses over to him.

'That went well,' the tomb robber remarked.

Merkhet ignored him and climbed atop Abacca. It was time he and his companions returned to Thebes.

Chapter 35

Sparse and trite conversation prevailed for most of the journey home. Though Taharva, Raina, and Snefrey were seemingly ready to discuss everything that had unfolded, Merkhet neglected to partake, wanting a chance to process and reflect on his own terms.

As Thebes spread out before him, the crops and grains that trailed the river were flourishing. Some were almost as tall as he was, extending beyond the reach of sight. The harvest would begin soon, but that was not the only surprise.

Initial preparations for an event along the Nile's banks. Approaching the flurry of movement, a deep numbing spiked through his chest. Long black cloaks. Thick flowing beards.

Hittites?! It couldn't be.

He spurred Abacca on, streaking ahead of his companions. This couldn't be happening.

The men were unarmed, but there was no mistaking them. Hittite men. In Thebes.

Taharva pulled in beside the pharaoh, one hand firmly grasping his spear. 'Hittites,' he growled. 'What do you know about this?'

'Nothing,' Merkhet said, shaking his head. 'Must be here to rescue their queen.'

'Doesn't make sense,' the captain said. 'Look, there, the Thebans aren't bothered by their presence at all.'

They were less than three hundred feet from the preparations, and the figures started to come into focus. Merkhet could see Haliya too. She was orchestrating the movement, barking orders and gesturing every which way.

In her royal Hittite regalia, she was as stunning as she was fierce. A black gemstone, poised along her neckline, gleamed as one with her eyes.

'I'm thinking,' Merkhet said, 'that Haliya invited them.' He pointed her out among the crowd of people. Dozens of Theban commoners, a small scattering of royal guards, and the three Hittites.

Taharva grumbled his assent. 'Could be you're right.'

'Thought I was coming home to inform her of our union.'

The captain chuckled. 'Doesn't seem that way to me.'

'There's no sight of rest beneath this crown. Straight back to it.'

'Would you change it, Scrollworm?'

'Guess not. Better go deliver the good news to my gracious Hittite queen.'

'Best of luck, friend,' Taharva said, galloping away on Tendrence.

Merkhet led Abacca at a trot along the final stretch. Raina and Snefrey pulled in beside him. The vizier spoke first.

'I need to go and visit a friend,' she said. 'Nashwa. I'll tell you about her someday.'

'Of course,' Merkhet said. 'We will reconvene again soon. As you can probably see, I'm going to be busy today.'

'Thank you,' Raina said.

Snefrey shrugged next to her. 'Wonder which hovel will pour me a beer this early?'

'Speak to you both later,' Merkhet said, easing ahead of them again.

Haliya noticed him at once but ran in the opposite direction. Bewildered, he hopped off his mount. Not the homecoming he'd expected.

It all made sense when she returned with a young Hittite man. His beard was barely beginning to blossom, but the resemblance was uncanny. The boy—if Merkhet could call anyone that—was much like his father, Silantus.

'You never told me you had a son,' he said to Haliya, changing to their native language.

She shrugged. 'You never asked. Meet him now. This is Manupilis.' The syllables rolled off her tongue with elegance. Hittite was a harsh and guttural speech, but not when Haliya spoke it.

Manupilis held out his hand, which Merkhet took in his own. They locked eyes, assessing one another. The boy's gaze was as fierce as his father's—his mother's, too—but despite his rugged assuredness, he was not a northern winter over fourteen.

'You wish to form a union with my mother?' he asked Merkhet in steady Egyptian. He placed emphasis on some of the wrong sounds, but it was fluent enough.

'I do,' Merkhet said, still holding onto Manupilis' hand.

'Rejoice!' the young man exclaimed. 'The preparations can continue. We can finalize the tribute in at the proper time. What do you say?'

Why was the young Hittite so jovial about the prospect of his mother staying in Egypt as the Great Royal Wife of a rival? Merkhet held his tongue on the matter. He had heard of bartering before a union, but what could Manupilis expect to gain from such an arrangement? More elusive still, why wasn't he brooding and vengeful for the loss of his father?

Merkhet couldn't abate those concerns. He would need to be wary of the youthful Hittite, but thankfully, Manupilis was still scared of his mother. Nor could the pharaoh blame him for that. Haliya was a woman to be reckoned with, a woman Merkhet wanted beside him.

The promise of a successful union gave him a renewed sense of optimism. Finally, he could complete something in honor of his diplomatic grandfather and forge a lasting peace treaty with the Hittites.

'Of course,' the pharaoh said, releasing the young man's hand. 'It will be my pleasure to discuss a bountiful tribute.'

Manupilis stooped into a half bow, then mother and son scurried away, organizing people and decorations along the river front.

Merkhet pressed his linen top against the sweat around his neck and chest, soaking it up. Was he doing this for the right reasons—were lust and diplomacy just cause for a union? The passing seasons would reveal all, including the fate of the High Priest and the rest of the Amun Priesthood. No effort was made to address such matters on the journey home. The pharaoh would need to review the priesthood's movements with Raina and Lufu, maybe even Taharva, so that such wicked plans could be exposed and averted in the future.

First, though, Merkhet had another destination in mind. The villages. He should have realized it before leaving Thebes. Tiaa didn't want to be served and pampered in the harem village. All she wanted was for her family to be whole again, in the comfort of her own home.

Some nearby royal guards were quick to assist him in exchanging horses. They would escort Abacca to the stables on his behalf and provided him with a steed for the journey.

'Your Grace, would you care for the chariot to be retrieved?'

Merkhet refuted their kind offer, though he knew an escort of royal guards was unavoidable. He was content with that arrangement and that of the horse given to him. A deep brown in color, the fur and mane were unkempt. If those characteristics were to be any indication of the stallion's temperament, they turned out to be false. He did not buck or heave as Merkhet clambered on him and was responsive to gentle tugs on the reins.

The short ride to the village was painful. Raw flesh lined the inside of his thighs from all the days spent on horseback. Merkhet didn't know the words he would say, but if he could provide some closure to what could be the most distraught mother in Thebes ...

The village rebuild was almost complete, yet some hovels were faring better than others. No pottery or ornaments sat on the wall outside Llora's family home. The plants were withering in the front garden, obvious signs of an abandoned home or a struggling family.

Merkhet tied the horse's reins to a wooden post and approached the open entryway. 'Hello?' he called out as he rapped on the mudbrick exterior.

Tiaa emerged from within, Llora's daughter in her arms. Upon seeing him, she retreated inside. Merkhet was about to follow her inside and beg for her to hear him out, but after relieving herself of the infant, Tiaa returned.

Crusty remnants of dried tears were streaked all along her cheeks and neck. Still not having the right words, Merkhet dragged her in for a hug. He was just becoming familiar with the healing properties of the act. It carried much power.

'What is it?' she asked, on the verge of fresh tears.

'I'm sorry,' he said, breathing deep to ward off his own sadness. Even with an earnest apology in the open, regret tormented him. So many miscalculations, so much to atone for. The pharaoh needed to become more adept at understanding people and what motivated them.

'For what?'

'Not acting quicker. Llora tried to tell me. You pleaded for me to listen. I was hurting and didn't do anything.'

She pushed him away. Not in anger or disgust but to draw their eyes level. They were a shimmering blue, just like Llora's. 'I forgive you,' Tiaa said.

He tilted his head a touch, grateful for her graciousness. 'There's something you should know. Wuntu will be home soon.'

She shut her eyes, padding the soft protective skin. When Tiaa reopened them, she was weeping. 'Don't,' she said. 'You can't promise me that.'

Merkhet clasped her hands in his. 'Day after next, most likely.'

A pained smile appeared. 'Praise the gods, some fortune at last.'

'He will need time to adjust. He is confused and

scared. I should not have told him we were brothers.'

'Whatever ails him,' Tiaa said. 'We will overcome it.'

'Thank you for understanding,' Merkhet said, smiling at her. 'As soon as the children return, the celebrations will begin.'

'I'll be there,' she said. 'As will Llora.'

Merkhet was about to question what she meant, but then he understood. Tiaa did name the baby girl after her mother, and by doing so, she had managed to honor her daughter.

When preparations could be finalized, he would also honor Llora, with a royal burial.

'Come and visit when Wuntu begins to settle. I have his toy lion,' Merkhet said, then turned on his heels.

Well rested, Merkhet strode into the throne room.

Taharva, Raina, and Snefrey were there, waiting for him. Their discussion faded when he entered.

'Don't suppress your inner thoughts on account of me,' he told them. 'Turn-Tide, can you please fill in some of the gaps? I know you were not able to find your family, and I'm sorry about that. You deserved to be reunited with them.'

Not that Taharva had ever blushed in his life, but he seemed to go close now. Embarrassed, ashamed? What was it?

'I respect your decision,' Merkhet said to the captain, 'to not sour the victory of locating the children and thwarting the priesthood. That applies for all of you, actually. Thank you for patience. It was important that we did not rush into rash assessments on the journey home, but it is best we learn from them now.'

'The High Priest lured me away with false information and the viceroy maintained the pretense,' Taharva said. 'In my absence, you were all needlessly vulnerable.'

'How did they know about your family?' Snefrey asked.

'Might not have. My public liberation at Merkhet's Heb-Sed could have given the priesthood ideas, and at the border, my eagerness may have revealed vital clues, too.'

'Matters not,' Merkhet said. 'What's done is done. The High Priest is all mine, but you will get your chance to confront the viceroy.'

Taharva nodded. 'Thank you, Scrollworm.'

'Raina, what are we proposing to remove the priesthood's disproportionate power? I want real thought given to this before Lufu arrives.'

She delivered an anxious glance Merkhet's way, eye contact fleeting. He had not considered that, mortal danger aside, the vizier might revert to her vow of silence.

However, Raina did speak. 'Monitor them closely. Redistribute their tax allowance and the entirety of their resources evenly among the other temples.'

The pharaoh smiled, satisfied with her succinct summation. 'Good. Oh, and make sure you organize the feast we promised the envoys. Not convinced they're worthy of the reward, after we visited every village between here and Giza ourselves, but I digress.'

Raina met his gaze, accepting her charge.

What of the mortuary preparations, Snef?'

'I've got the perfect location sorted. You will never believe how long and arduous the search was to... What? Why are you grinning at me like that for?'

'No reason.'

'You already know, don't you?' Snefrey asked. 'Of course you do. Gee, thanks, Merep! Is it too much to ask to deliver a surprise yourself these days?'

'Appears that way,' the pharaoh said, chuckling.

'After your big day and night, I'll head north to oversee the construction myself.'

'Being built inside the fortress city, it is less important than when I first enlisted your service, but please do take care with whomever you involve.'

'Of course, Your Grace,' the tomb robber said with a serious tone and expression. Then he smirked and spoke again, ruining it. 'Does the High Priest steal children during the Opet?'

'Speaking of the embodiment of chaos ... How soon can we re-establish the Judgments?'

'Tomorrow, if you desire?' Raina asked him.

Taharva laughed before he even spoke. 'Executioner might just give birth to a litter of kittens when you inform him.'

'No,' Merkhet said. 'Not that soon. Let's celebrate first. When we do call upon the maatebes, they will not fail us. The High Priest will come to know the true meaning of Ma'at's justice.' He brushed past his friends, climbing onto the throne. 'Rest some more, everyone. Please.'

They heeded his dismissal with a curt bow, performed in succession, and then left.

Not a moment later, the royal physician entered.

'Sahra,' Merkhet said. 'How are you? I was just about to send for you.'

'I'm well. Suspect I'll be busy tending the children when they arrive.'

Merkhet nodded. 'Maybe even some of the priests too. Any word from the embalmers?'

'Yes,' she said, 'I bear news. My reason for disturbing you.'

'Never a disturbance. Please,' the pharaoh said, gesturing with an open palm, 'tell.'

'The preparations are almost complete and should coincide with the traditional seventy days between death and burial. The embalmers have completed the mummification and the sarcophagus is ready.'

'Excellent. Have the embalmers sorted a tomb?'

'They have, but I've not seen it myself.'

'Thank you, Sahra. Your treatments and organization are invaluable to my pharaohship. One last thing, though, before the children return?'

The physician smiled. 'Of course.'

'Can you visit the High Priestess of Isis?' Merkhet asked, placing his Eye of Horus seal in her hand.

'What shall I ask of her?'

'That she learn the necessary prayers and spells to lead Llora's burial.'

'And how long does she have?' the physician asked.

'Day after the High Priest's Judgment. If she can prevail, the rest of the funerary preparations will be complete by then.'

'I'll make it so.' Sahra said. She didn't bow, but she did crouch before him to stroke Beebee.

A servant with a sharp blade lingered in the hallway outside the throne room. 'Your Grace, is now a good time?' the young man called in cheerily.

'As good as any,' Merkhet said, lifting the Double Crown off his head and placing it in his lap. 'Ra's blessings to you, Sahra.'

The physician departed, but Beebee's purring stayed. Ambling to the throne, the servant wet the pharaoh's head with a dripping cloth.

As water trickled down Merkhet's back, he closed his eyes and tried not to squirm because the blade was already gliding across his scalp.

Merkhet awoke to a steady drumming, coming from the throne room. He grumbled some sort of permission to enter.

His vision was blurry, but the pleasant squeak of Raina's voice was unmistakable.

The children were almost home.

The vizier departed as he rose and rubbed the corners of his eyes. It was early, but the sun pierced the slight gap beneath the terrace veil. Haliya continued to sleep.

Her imminent second union didn't seem to cause the widow any grief. Merkhet wished he could say the same for himself. His stomach churned, but not just in relation to having his own Great Royal Wife. He was anxious about many matters.

The High Priest's Judgment, most of all. Would things ever be simple? Could he ever have moments of true rest, much the way his Hittite queen did?

She was so peaceful, so captivating. The servants would wake her soon, though.

Dressing into his white ceremonial robe, he left

Haliya to her slumber. Merkhet walked through the palace to rouse his mother. She had arrived back in Thebes the night before and was residing in the same quarters he did as a young prince.

Her intuition was as formidable as ever. 'Merk, is that you?' she asked as his footsteps approached.

'The union will be today,' he said, holding his ground outside the room. 'The children have almost reached Thebes.'

'I'll put on my dress right away. Hold on, won't be long.'

Merkhet smiled because he could hear the happiness in her voice. 'No rush, Mother. I'll see you there. Take the chariot with Haliya and her son once it returns to the palace.'

Her response was lost in the rustling of something, maybe her dress.

'See you soon,' he called.

The golden chariot waited for him at the palace gates. Merkhet didn't recognize either of the horses that were tethered to it. Abacca, Tendrence, and all the others were recuperating at the stables.

Taharva commanded the reins. 'Ready, Scrollworm?'

'No,' the pharaoh said, laughing nervously. 'Won't stop me, though.'

The captain urged the horses into a trot, guiding them through the administration precinct. Not many people were active yet, but with the children on their way home, the city would soon be a flurry of movement, tears, and celebration. After long last, families would be reunited.

On the fringe of a cluster of palm trees, Taharva brought the chariot to a halt. The benches for the guests were arranged in the clearing between the river and the towering trees, so that each had a clear view of the Nile. The tables for the food and drink were set behind the final row of benches.

'Good luck, Scrollworm,' Taharva said, winking. 'Must be such misery waking next to her.'

Merkhet grinned as he hopped out of the chariot. The captain was right—it was downright awful.

Passing through the benches, he headed for the river. So much had changed yet much was the same. He could watch the currents flow by endlessly.

As the joyous news of the children's expected return spread, citizens gathered along the banks. Even though the sun would peak soon, the midday heat did not deter them. Merkhet suspected nothing would today. Mothers, fathers, and siblings had not known peace across the planting season. They would know it well this afternoon, though.

Servants from the royal kitchen began to arrive with food for the celebration. The smell of cooked meat and spices tormented the pharaoh. Such delicacies were rarely tasted outside the comfort of the palace.

The benches started to fill, and Merkhet regretted arriving so early. A full dose of sun had hit him flush across the face. When Raina and Snefrey appeared, occupying the bench closest to where the ceremony would take place, Merkhet understood that Haliya would be with him soon. So, too, would the children.

Merkhet tried to abate some of the nervous energy settling in his toes and fingers by scanning the faces around him. He didn't get far, though, before whoops of delight stole his attention. A fleet of galleys, dozens in total, could be seen upriver.

Families cheered and danced on the banks. Even the few citizens that were not awaiting children of their own clapped and whistled. Merkhet reveled in the cheerful atmosphere, easily as rewarding as when he defeated the hippopotamus along this very same riverbank.

As the galleys wedged in mud and silt, the children bounded onto land in their droves. The royal guards accompanied them. The soldiers escorting the Amun initiates would come later.

The frantic outstretched arms of parents swallowed their children whole as the golden chariot emerged in Merkhet's peripherals. The timing couldn't be more perfect. He didn't want the attention of the entire city. The special people in his life—and Hailya's—were more than enough to celebrate this occasion.

Taharva eased the chariot to a halt. Merep and Lufu were the first to disembark, then Manupilis. Lastly, Haliya. A ravishing black dress, of the Hittite custom, flowed with her curves as she was helped down by her son and Merep. She wore the same black jewel pendant around her neck as when Merkhet first met her.

Manupilis led his mother through the palms and guests, heading straight for him. She weaved her way through the obstacles with grace and confidence.

Merkhet gulped. Did he deserve such an elegant and commanding woman?

Had Egypt deserved to be thrown into the throes of chaos? Had he deserved to be exiled and become a Hittite captive? Had the children deserved to be taken from their families?

Merkhet wasn't quite sure he understood it, but somehow, this life wasn't about what you deserved. The gods were mysterious in their workings, and you just had to trust in yourself to see it all through. The good, the bad, and everything in between.

Families began to flock around the benches as Haliya

and Manupilis stood beside him. The young Hittite broke away from his mother, handing a scroll to Merkhet. 'Peace,' he said.

'Peace,' Merkhet agreed, loud enough for those gathered to hear.

The crowd roared with delight as Manupilis faded into the palms, and they began to chant as one. 'Pharaoh Merkhet, our Horus on Earth. Horus on Earth. Horus on Earth.'

Hearing the appreciation of his citizens made all the trials worthwhile, and the overwhelming joy stole his focus away.

Merkhet might have seen an Apis bull being led along the Nile's banks. He might have seen Taharva and Raina holding hands. If he gazed skyward, he might have seen the approval of his father, too, cast among the cloud formations.

But he only had eyes for Haliya. She held out a hand for him, which fit into his own, as harpists plucked a magical melody. They danced between palms and river, not a care in the world. Egypt was whole again, and Merkhet was bursting with life and love.

Snefrey joined the dance, performing exaggerated movements as he shuffled ever closer. 'I haven't forgotten,' he whispered into the pharaoh's ear. 'When can I expect my very own drinking hovel?'

Merkhet shoved him away, beaming the entire time, and returned his attention to his Great Royal Wife. She studied him, smiling.

'What?' he pleaded with her.

'The future of the dynasty grows within me.'

'Great Horus! Are you sure it's a boy?' Merkhet asked as he dragged her in.

'Careful,' she said, reprimanding him with a scowl.

'Women can be pharaoh.'

'Yes, sorry. Course they can.'

'Fret not, my Egyptian honey, for I'm as sure as I was with Manupilis.'

'Our very own son?'

They were still swaying to the rhythm of the harpists. Nobles and citizens alike had joined them in dance.

'Our very own son,' she said.

With Haliya by his side, the future of the Eighteenth Dynasty would be secure, and no threat could harm them from within.

With a great northern fortress, no threat from beyond their borders could ravage them.

Prosperity beckoned and Merkhet could not contain his delight. 'Praise the gods!' he bellowed above the celebration.

'Praise our pharaoh!' the people roared back.

More Stories

Congratulations on finishing another book. You're quite the reader. Why would you stop now?

The good news is that you don't have to. I've got more Egyptian stories (among others) that are just waiting to be read.

Join my casual, non-invasive mailing list and you can discover all my stories today.

About Cameron Brett

Cameron is a writer of stuff. He loves hedgehogs and philanthropy.

Isn't it weird how these are all written in the third person?

The impersonal route is not for me. I'm making a stand, and I'm making it now (if that wasn't immediately obvious). So that maybe, just maybe, we could make this a little less … bland.

Go on. Head over to www.thecameronbrett.com and find something to read. There is an actual about me there. It's quirky as all heck. Promise.